VILLAINS TRIUMPHANT—

They're the characters you love to hate, the men and women who've made evil deeds a way of life. And when bad people make bad choices they invariably get caught, suffer resounding defeats—or at least annoying setbacks—in other words, they lose and they pay the price. But not every villain is a bumbler, and some of them have got to be winning at least some of the time. Here, then, are stories of those treacherous thieves, murderers, tyrants, and traitors who've found the way to make villainy pay:

"The Specter of Tullyfane Abbey"—Even Sherlock Holmes can occasionally fail to hold his own—when the foe he faces is Moriarity. . . .

"Doubting Thomas"—He'd learned the truth about Santa when he was a little kid, but getting the rest of the world to realize Santa was naughty not nice was another matter entirely. . . .

"Horror Show"—A washed-up actor, his glory days had been when he played that diabolical creature, the Shrike. Now the Shrike's reign of terror was over for good—or was it . . . ?

VILLAINS VICTORIOUS

VILLAINS VICTORIOUS

Edited by

Martin H. Greenberg
amd John Helfers

DAW BOOKS, INC.
DONALD A. WOLLHEIM, FOUNDER
375 Hudson Street, New York, NY 10014

ELIZABETH R. WOLLHEIM
SHEILA E. GILBERT
PUBLISHERS
www.dawbooks.com

ACKNOWLEDGMENTS

Introduction © 2001 by John Helfers.
All Things Being Relative © 2001 by Tanya Huff.
The Mould of Form © 2001 by Rosemary Edghill.
The Specter of Tullyfane Abbey © 2001 by Peter Tremayne.
Doubling Thomas © 2001 by Kristine Kathryn Rusch.
The Whiteviper Scrolls © 2001 by David Bischoff.
A New Man © 2001 by Ed Gorman.
Souls to Take © 2001 by Gary A. Braunbeck and Lucy Snyder.
Nina © 2001 by Pauline E. Dungate.
Horror Show © 2001 by Tim Waggoner.
Death Mage © 2001 by Fiona Patton.
King of Thorns © 2001 by R. Davis.
The Usurper Memos © 2001 by Josepha Sherman.
To Speak With Angels © 2001 by Michelle West.
Hereos and Villains © 2001 by Peter Crowther.

CONTENTS

INTRODUCTION

by John Helfers

Simply put, this book is about evil.

Because, let's face it, evil is a necessary force in our everyday life. As had been so often postulated, without evil, good cannot exist. Two halves that form a whole. Two sides of the same coin. Light and darkness. Yin and yang.

History has been full of villains, men and women against which a man, a country, even the world have fought. The list is long, and features those whose acts against goodness have made their names notorious decades, even centuries later. Nero, Marie Antoinette, Hitler, Pol Pot, Hussein. Despots, tyrants, dictators— all have, in the end, gotten what they deserved.

It is true in fiction as well that every hero must have a truly worthy villain. For it is against this formidable opponent that the hero measures himself, that he stands for everything his enemy opposes. Beowulf and Grendel. Cinderella and her stepmother. King Arthur and Mordred. Robin Hood and the Sheriff of Nottingham. Tom Sawyer and Injun Joe. Sherlock Holmes and Professor Moriarty.

It is the villains who actually make the heroes what they are, forcing them to reach deep down inside themselves and become more than ordinary men and women. Without someone to fight against, heroes would not exist.

And so it is high time that the villains got their day in the sun, as it were. Often just existing to have their plans foiled, their lives ruined, their secret hideouts destroyed, it was about time for evil to have its day. What happens when the bad guys win? How do they go about implementing their nefarious plans? Are they really all that bad?

With that in mind, we assembled the finest fantasy authors writing today, and gave them a simple idea: write a story where the bad guys win. And the book you are holding today is the result. From Rosemary Edghill's prequel featuring one of the most famous villains of literature of all time to Peter Crowther's poignant story about why evil must be evil, villains of all shapes, ideologies, and wickedness are finally given their due in these fourteen stories about the people we love to hate. So turn the page and explore the other side of good and light. Join us and read about *Villains Victorious*.

ALL THINGS BEING RELATIVE

by Tanya Huff

Tanya Huff lives and writes in rural Ontario with her partner, four cats, and an unintentional Chihuahua. After sixteen fantasies, she's written her first space opera, *Valor's Choice* (DAW, April 2000) and is currently working on a sequel. Her newest book is a sequel to *Summon The Keeper* called *The Second Summoning* (DAW, March 2001). In her spare time she gardens and complains about the weather.

"Majesty, this is Cornelius Dickcissel, the scribe." Dropping to his knees, the short, plump man tried to remember everything he'd been told as the queen turned her head toward him.

Never look her in the eye. Keep your hands out where she can see them. Don't speak until she gives you leave. Don't wear black, she doesn't find imitation flattering. And whatever you do, don't remind her of her age.

"You are Cornelius Dickcissel?"

"Yes, Majesty." Her voice saying his name made all the hair on his body stand on end. He tried, unsuccessfully, not to sweat. His own voice quavered a bit. As he couldn't hope she hadn't noticed, he could only hope she wouldn't mind.

"You are the author of *Sir Harold, His Brave Battle With the Great Pernicious Worm and His Subsequent Death and Devourment?*"

"Yes, Majesty."

"Good book; I was impressed that you took the time to consider the dragon's point of view. Title needs work, though."

"It was my editor's title, Majesty."

"Baxter!"

"Majesty?"

"Have his editor killed."

"Yes, Majesty."

"Cornelius Dickcissel, look at me."

Over one hundred and seventy years old, the queen had left behind the edged, ethereal beauty of her youth but not without one heck of a fight. Only a blind fool could fail to notice the magical enhancements. Only a suicidal fool would give any indication. Her eyes *were* amber as the songs insisted although the tiny flecks of darkness in the golden depths were probably not the trapped souls of the men who'd loved her and lost.

Probably not.

Don't look her in the eye.

He hurriedly dropped his gaze and raised it again considerably faster; the tight black bodice being rather remarkably low cut.

"Do you know why you're here, Cornelius?"

He'd been making a conscious effort not to think about that. For lack of a better answer, he fell back on the catechism of his school days. "I serve at the pleasure of Her Majesty."

"Yes, you do and, right at this moment, it pleases me to have you write the story of my life."

"Me, Majesty?"

"Do you see another Cornelius Dickcissel in the room?"

"No, Majesty."

He would write the story of the queen.

Him.

Cornelius Dickcissel.

He'd lived his whole life as far from the center of the empire as it was possible to get and still be in the empire, scratching out a literary career by rewriting local legends. And now this. This would . . . He swallowed, hard, as he realized. This would make his fortune!

The Dark Queen: My Story as told to Cornelius Dickcissel. He could see it now: a tasteful woodcut of the queen on a plain white cover. Every bookseller in the empire would move hundreds of them. And not just the booksellers—the mercers, the drapers, even the apothecaries!—everyone would be falling over themselves to buy a copy. There'd be sales of subrights to the players and possibly foreign sales as well—although there wasn't anything very foreign very close, not anymore.

Pity I spent that money having my will made up. Still, he couldn't have known, and it was the traditional response to a personal summons from the queen.

"Baxter will find you rooms in the palace and provide you with the necessary supplies. We'll start tomorrow in my solar. I'd like to start today, but one of the royal accountants has made a total mess of the tax rolls and I have to torture him to death."

"I was an only child; my sisters were jealous of my talent and beauty."

"Majesty?" Cornelius wet lips gone suddenly dry as the queen stopped pacing and turned a basilisk stare on him. Her solar was the top room in the palace's tallest tower. From it, she could see her kingdom spread out all around her, the verdant forests, the well-tended fields, the prosperous villages, the line of dark smoke where a rogue proletarian was being burned at the stake. "You told me to interrupt if I didn't understand. Don't you mean you were a *lonely* child? An only child can't have sisters."

The queen smiled. "My point exactly . . ."

I was five when I realized something would have to be done. Bella, who was twelve and as full of herself as only a twelve-year-old can be, was under the mistaken impression she would grow up to be the most powerful mage in the kingdom. And at nine, Celeste was the acknowledged beauty of the family. Bella would taunt me because I could only do baby magic and Celeste had a nasty habit of calling me Carrots.

Early one morning in the nursery, Bella used a broadly theatrical and totally unnecessary gesture to light a candle on the other side of the room.

"Even I can do that," I told her, and lit the candle beside it. The implication that she, too, could do only baby magic made her very angry and, instead of attempting something simple, she jumped right to the most difficult magic she knew—transformation, becoming in quick succession a lion and then a bear.

I convincingly cowered in fear and, when she was herself again, I clapped my dimpled hands and cried, "Do more."

"What shall I become?" she asked me breathing heavily from the exertion but so very pleased I was impressed by her.

"Can you be a mouse?"

"Just watch me!"

And she was.

Which was, of course, when I let the cat in.

Our nurse had been excessively fond of "Puss in Boots"—although I can't remember her ever telling the story again.

Later that day, as Celeste was staring at her reflection in the smooth, dark water of an old abandoned well, the boards, solid enough to hold a five-year-old, gave way and she plummeted into the depths. Fortunately, she'd never learned to swim. Well, not fortunately for her, perhaps.

It was at about this time I discovered I looked magnificent in black.

So suddenly bereft of two of their three children, my parents doted on me until their untimely deaths just before my eighteenth birthday.

"Untimely, Majesty?"

"Untimely," the queen repeated a little sadly. "The poison worked quicker than it was supposed to, and I actually had to have a legal guardian for the remaining months of my minority."

Cornelius searched for something to say and settled at last on, "I'm sorry."

"It wasn't pleasant, but I was young. I survived."

As he dipped his pen, Cornelius decided not to ask the obvious.

"Alone at last, I used my family's money to travel and learn—merchants, mages, assassins, politicians, I left no stone unturned in my search for knowledge. In fact, that's where I found a number of the politicians . . ."

It wasn't until he heard the soft phut, phut of her foot tapping against the carpet that Cornelius realized the queen was waiting for a response. He looked up from his notes to find her staring at him. "Majesty?"

"Stone unturned . . . politicians . . ."

He checked his notes. "Yes, Majesty, I got that."

She sighed. "Never mind. My teachers taught me that knowledge is power but only a fool would deny that power is also power. . . ."

The prince, heir to a small kingdom, was handsome and charming but, honestly, not too bright. For that matter, neither were his parents. Royal marriages should be considered state contracts and given as much attention as declarations of war and the resultant peace treaties. Which they often were. But when this particular prince couldn't decide on a bride, what did his parents do? They threw a grand ball at the palace to which they invited every young woman in the kingdom and told the prince to choose.

I wore gold, the exact same shade as my eyes. My hair cascaded down my back like falling flames. The prince couldn't take his eyes off me.

Until *she* arrived.

The perfect princess: blonde hair, blue eyes, her dress a frothy sweet concoction of white and blue, and on her feet the most ridiculous pair of glass slippers.

"Glass slippers, Majesty? Wouldn't they be . . . I don't know, breakable?"

"Yes."

She stank of magic. And destiny.

I, personally, have always felt you make your own destiny.

Too charming to leave the woman he was currently partnered with, the prince was making a fool of himself trying to keep this vision of loveliness in sight.

To give credit where credit is due, she was aware of her effect on him and, smiling sweetly, went out into the garden so that he could finish his dance.

When the prince and I were married, some weeks later, we decided to hold the reception in that same garden. The summer flowers were beautiful and it seemed such a shame for our guests to have to stay inside.

Cleaning up behind the dwarf euonymus shrubs, the gardeners found the body of an urchin girl wearing the remains of ragged clothing covered in cinders and ash. Most of her blonde hair had been taken by small animals to make nests, and it was no longer possible to tell what color her eyes had been. No one connected her to the mysterious princess who'd made such a brief appearance at the ball although, had they bothered to check, they might have found shards of glass in the ruins of her throat.

The king and queen died that fall. She had a little trouble with an undergarment—it quite took her breath away—and as he was running to her aid, he choked on a bit of apple. After a lavish double funeral, my husband and I took the throne.

"As it happens, I took it considerably farther than he did, but that is a story for another day. From the looks of your notes . . ." The queen nodded toward the piles of ink-blotted paper lying like drifts of leaves on the table—her life from childhood to throne. ". . . you'll have quite enough to do for a while. I have given you the bare bones of a story, Cornelius Dickcissel. It is up to you to clothe it in the extras that people seem to require. Adjectives. Adverbs. Semicolons. Tomorrow morning, I shall read what you have done to my words."

"Tomorrow morning, Majesty?" He would have been appalled at the way his voice emerged as a terrified squeak had he not been so terrified at the appalling fate he'd meet in the morning. Even had his right hand not been cramping painfully, there was no possible way he could turn two jars of scribbled ink into the first section of a book by morning.

"Is there a problem with that?"

"Majesty, the proper writing of a book takes more time than the telling of it. There are, as you say, adjectives, adverbs . . . ?

"Semicolons?"

"Yes, Majesty. Semicolons. And other punctuation."

"*Other* punctuation?" She raised a hand to forestall an answer and frowned thoughtfully. "I did quite like what you did with the dragon."

"Thank you, Majesty."

"Tomorrow morning bring me as many pages as you have completed and, if I approve of your *punctuations*, we will continue."

"And if not, Majesty."

"Then you won't continue."

"The book?"

The queen smiled. "Also the book. What is it, Baxter?"

"I beg your indulgence for the interruption, Majesty." The queen's personal assistant bowed deeply. "The dwarves have arrived."

"Yes, thank you, Baxter. You wouldn't think it to look at them," the queen told Cornelius as she stood and shook out her skirts, "but dwarves make the most amazing coffins. I've done quite a bit of business with them over the years."

Cornelius slid off the stool to his knees as she swept by him, skirts whispering suggestions for mayhem against the carpeting.

"This is good. You've definitely captured the way I had to work to gain power, how nothing was handed to me. *What most amazes, gentle reader, is that such a delicate beauty could have the persistence and strength necessary to climb over eight bodies of those dear to her in order to reach the place at the pinnacle her destiny demanded she fill. . . .* This is the sort of writing that made the story of Sir Harold so enthralling."

"Thank you, Majesty."

"But there were nine."

"Nine, Majesty?"

"Bodies."

"My apologies, Majesty." Taking a deep breath, Cornelius very nearly squared his shoulders. "Majesty, there are places where more detail . . ."

"Would slow things down."

"Yes, Majesty."

"Are you ready to continue?"

"Yes, Majesty." While any other answer would have come with a low survival rate, he found he was more than ready—he was fascinated.

It was the tradition in my husband's kingdom for the queen to have her own small guard, their function mostly ceremonial. By the end of my first year as queen, I had provided employment for a number of young men who had previously been considered unemployable and added to our manufacturing base. Metalwork mostly. The man with the rivet concession made a small fortune.

After my husband . . . died, his council wasn't entirely certain that my slender shoulders were up to the weight of government.

"Majesty, how did your husband die?"

She turned from the window. "It was a tragic accident during an inspection of the kitchens." Crossing the room, the queen pulled an ornate wooden box off the high curved shelf that circled the solar. "He was leaning over too far and fell into one of the ovens." When opened, the box played a sweet, melancholy tune. "Baked instantly." She held the box toward Cornelius. "Gingerbread?"

"No, thank you, Majesty."

"Just as well, there's not much left."

I dealt with the council in the traditional way, replaced the carpets, and set about consolidating power. By the time I finished, the entire system had been admirably streamlined. I gave the orders, and my knights saw that they were carried out. With no more hereditary nobility, the common people were closer to the throne than they'd ever been and were able to rise in position based on merit rather than birth. With the understanding that ultimately the land was mine, I divided the grand estates amongst the people who worked them and, after the quiet midnight executions of a few malcontents, the country prospered.

My largest problem turned out to be my knights. Granted, a certain amount of burning and pillaging was necessary in the beginning, but they were getting out of hand. Some men are just like that. Give them an inch and they'll want to be the ruler. . . .

* * *

"Oh, very clever, Majesty!"

The queen sighed. "A polite chuckle would have been more believable and wouldn't have spilled the ink."

"Sorry, Majesty."

"I'm not retelling that bit. You can write it up tonight from memory."

I was prepared for the coup attempt. Large men in black plate mail with red cloaks and plumes don't sneak worth a damn. They clanked into the throne room one afternoon, absolutely destroying the parquet flooring with their spurs. I was extremely annoyed; the old chancellor had been washing that floor with his tongue since the change in power, and it looked wonderful.

The captain could see I was upset. He pulled off his helm, and his cruel mouth twisted up in a rather attractive smile. Somehow, he'd managed to keep all his teeth. "A pity to kill one so beautiful," he said, pulling his sword, "but I'm not so stupid that I'd let you stay around. I'd be dead before . . ."

He was dead before he hit the floor, and the others were only half a heartbeat behind. The impact of all that steel was deafening.

Do you remember my parents?

Cornelius looked up from his notes, more than a little confused by the non sequitur. "Your parents, Majesty?

"Yes. This time, I got the dosage right. From the moment I discovered what my less than faithful knights were planning, I started poisoning them.

After that, it was all in the timing. I haven't had a moment's trouble from them since."

A drop of ink fell from his quill and splashed back into the inkwell, sending dark ripples over a dark surface. "Majesty, are you saying that the knights, the knights who ride today, are the same knights who were with you back a hun . . . ?"

And whatever you do, don't remind her of her age.

Outside the solar, gray-green clouds rolled over the sun.

". . . back when you first came to power?"

"Of course." Russet brows drew in. "You didn't know?"

"No, Majesty."

"Do your friends and neighbors know?"

"I don't think so, Majesty."

Visibly upset, the queen took up her favorite position at the window. "This is *exactly* why I need my story told. Some of my greatest work, forgotten in my own lifetime. With dark necromancies, I create a cadre of dead men to enforce my will and provide continuous policing at a cost other governments only dream of, and barely six generations later what have they become? Literal shadows of their former selves. It's too depressing. I can't go on today. Write up what I have told you. And Cornelius . . ." She paused at the door, delicate features stamped with sorrow. ". . . make it terrifying."

"That won't be difficult, Majesty."

The queen had cheered up by the next morning. "I have sent word to the knights that they're to lift their visors when dealing with individuals—it's not necessary for mass slaughter, of course, but there's absolutely no point in having created a tool and then

never using it. Thank you, Cornelius. Without you,
who knows how long this sorry state of affairs would
have continued."

"I live to serve, Majesty."

"Yes . . ."

He really, really didn't like the speculative expression on her face—now that he knew living wasn't an
actual requirement for serving.

Once I got my own small kingdom in order, I did
what any conscientious ruler would do: I looked
about for economic opportunities. The kingdom to
the north was in a shocking state of anarchy when I
arrived, the people without direction for almost a
hundred years while their royal family was trapped,
sound asleep in their palace, behind a barricade of
thorns.

I'd never seen such a mess. Brambles grew over,
under, and around each other, twisting, tangling, and
trapping approximately sixteen young men on their
eight-inch spikes. Princes all, you'd think one of them
would have had the brains to bring an ax instead of
a sword.

In almost one hundred years the barrier had grown
to be three times the height of a tall man. It had
clearly never been pruned. Have you any idea how
much dead wood a hedge accumulates in only *one*
year?

When I was five, I could light a candle.

I backed my army a safe distance away.

"Smells like pork," someone said after a while.

"The fire has reached the palace," I told him.

The new map, drawn in the ashes, doubled my
borders.

My new subjects had gotten out of the habit of

paying taxes, but once they were convinced of the benefits a centralized government could provide— maintained roads, standardized schooling, access to foreign markets, enough manpower to wipe out the entire family of any opposition up to and including second cousins, in-laws, and pets—they came around fairly quickly.

With my northern border secure, I led my army widdershins around the perimeter.

The surrounding royals had interbred past the point of stupidity. And chins.

To the west, the ruling prince was looking for a bride by sticking a pea under a pile of mattresses. The result: a list of minor injuries and broken bones as, one after another, the young women rose in the night to use the commode. He'd have been significantly better off putting more money in defense and less in bedding.

To the south, the king had stuck his only daughter up on a glass hill and promised her hand and the kingdom to whoever could reach her. If you'll remember, we previously discussed how glass . . . breaks.

To the east, three princes had been sent out on quests by an ailing king unable to choose which should be his heir. Maybe he honestly didn't know which one had been born first, I didn't stop to ask. I set up roadblocks, and when the princes returned, they were given state funerals. I still use the telescope, but the apple rotted and the flying carpet was a cheap knockoff for the tourist trade.

"Majesty, did no one ever oppose you?"

"Not in the early days. People who put their daughters on glass hills in order to give away their kingdom to the first idiot with a sledge hammer aren't exactly masters of strategy and tactics. And the less said about that moron with the pea the better."

"But later . . . ?"

"Later, there were heroes." To Cornelius' surprise, the corners of her full mouth curved up into an abstracted smile. "We'll talk of them tomorrow."

The thing I loved best about heroes is that they were larger than life. In the beginning, they were almost indistinguishable—big, honorable men in plate mail on big white horses. As long as they behaved themselves en route, the knights had orders to let them reach me. I had a great deal of work to do in those early years, but nothing broke up the monotony of governing like dealing with one of those silly paladins.

They usually arrived with three misconceptions.

That my army of thugs and cutthroats had been afraid to face them.

That I was an evil queen because I had conquered the surrounding countries and slaughtered the nobility.

That because their cause was just, they would prevail.

My army was extremely well disciplined and would face anything I told them to. Military victories made me an effective general, not an evil queen, and no one seemed to miss the dead nobility except the live nobility outside my borders. And they never did prevail. . . .

"Seven paladins died, right down there in that courtyard believing until the end that their righteousness made them invincible although two through seven also wore powerful charms that kept me from using my magic against them."

Did she want him to look? Before Cornelius could decide, the queen turned from the window.

"Did you know they actually used to issue challenges? Well, there's no reason why you should, I suppose. They died long before your grandfather was born." Seven closed helms sat on the shelf next to the wooden box of gingerbread. Reaching up, she tapped a scarlet nail against the first.

"I, Sir Gerald de Faunae, do challenge the champion of the Dark Queen to single combat. When he is defeated, she will surrender herself to . . . Ribbit!"

The croaking continued as the next helm, then the next, offered its challenge, identical to the first except for name and final exclamation—two arghs, three gurgles, a shriek, and a whimper. Cornelius couldn't help thinking that two through seven would have been better off without the charms.

As the final ribbit faded, the queen fought to bring her laughter under control. "Oh, mercy," she sighed, wiping her eyes. "I'd forgotten how funny they were. Anyway . . ." She dropped back into her chair. ". . . after this lot, the paladins stopped coming. Maybe they ran out of big, honorable men. Maybe they ran out of white horses. I never knew."

"Is that when they started calling you the Dark Queen, Majesty?"

The queen smiled. "No." After a moment, she continued, as though Cornelius had never interrupted. "Further expansion was as much political as military and the heroes became . . . What is it, Baxter?"

"It's getting late, Majesty, and before you can prepare for tonight's reception for the Gambanize ambassador, you have to meet the winner of the school essay contest."

"School essay contest?"

"Yes, Majesty. Five hundred words or less explaining why you allow the Beltains to live in peace to the north."

"Because they make an admirable buffer against the frost giants."

"And that *was* the winning essay, Majesty."

"Excellent. Cornelius."

Cornelius, who'd been trying to rub feeling back into his right hand, jumped.

"I want you to attend the reception tonight."

"Majesty, I don't . . ."

Her eyes narrowed as she stood. Baxter visibly braced himself.

". . . know how to behave at such a function. I don't want to embarrass you."

"You won't." It wasn't so much reassurance as command. "You'll be able to observe me interacting with foreign dignitaries and add it to the book. Besides, there'll be free food and alcohol—I hear writers like that sort of thing."

Cornelius smiled weakly. "Doesn't everyone, Majesty?"

"Not around here. Baxter will find you suitable clothing."

"If this is the small throne room," Cornelius breathed, staring wide-eyed at the nine gigantic chandeliers hanging from the mirrored ceiling, "what must the large throne room look like?"

"Actually, it's fairly utilitarian," Baxter told him. "This one is used to impress. The other is for business, which means everything has to be washable. A word of advice—if you're having seafood, stick to the white wine."

"Why?"

"The queen dislikes it when people drink the wrong wine."

"Oh." Then he got it. "Oh! Doesn't that whittle away at the guest list?"

"Not anymore."

The queen and the Gambanize ambassador entered together. The queen looked magnificent. The ambassador, nervous.

With the exception of the ambassador's party, all the guests were self-made men and women who'd been able to take advantage of the queen's policies and rise to the top. In the Empire, everyone was equal under the queen and no one had red wine with the crab cakes. Cornelius, a mid-list scribe from the outer provinces, had never dreamed of finding himself in such company—or at least, he'd never dreamed of finding himself in such company and surviving it.

He sidled close to the queen in time to hear her say, "Actually, it's been years since much of my GNP went to the military. I find it much more efficient to put the money into teachers."

The ambassador shook his head, the beads woven into his beard swaying gently. "I do not understand."

"Every child in the Empire, regardless of wealth or social standing receives the same excellent education until they're ten. I control that education."

"It cannot be so simple."

"Really?" The queen graciously accepted an offered canapé. "How many kingdoms has Gambania conquered . . . ?"

"Three!"

"And held?"

As the ambassador shrugged sheepishly, the queen smiled.

Which was when it happened.

One of the guests ripped open the wide orange leg of his trousers, yanked out a small crossbow that had been strapped to his thigh, and pulled the trigger screaming, "Death to the Dark Queen!"

Aiming first might have been an idea.

Cornelius' world constricted to the point of the crossbow quarrel speeding toward his throat. Impossibly slowly, he saw the queen push the ambassador in front of him with her left hand while she drew a throwing dagger from a cleavage sheath with her right. The would-be assassin would have hit the floor a heartbeat after the ambassador had either heart still been beating.

Then the world sped up again, and Cornelius tried to remember how to breathe.

In a silence complete but for the sound of bladders emptying, the queen crossed the room.

"You call that a hero?" She poked the cooling corpse with the pointed toe of one black leather boot. "I wouldn't call him a hero if you made him into a sandwich." She gave the silence a generous count of three, then swept the room with an edged gaze. "Sandwich . . . hero sandwich . . . oh, never mind," she muttered, as appreciative laughter finally swept the crowd. "Not one of you got it first time around, so there's no point pretending." Bending, she retrieved her throwing dagger, stepped over the body, and swept out the nearest door.

Unfortunately, it was the servants' entrance.

Heart pounding, Cornelius followed, pushing past

the trio of panicked sheep in the suddenly far too tight red-and-black livery. He caught up when the queen allowed it, in the solar.

She was standing at her favorite window overlooking the courtyard, leaning on the windowsill, desultorily feeding bits of raw meat to a raven.

"Majesty!" Dropping dramatically to his knees, he threw open his arms. "You saved my life!"

"Yes, I did. I'd say that made your life mine, but it always was." She sighed deeply. "I'm feeling old, Cornelius Dickcissel. Where was the rush? Where was the excitement?"

"Here!"

The sound of his fist sinking into the layer of fat on his chest brought a questioning gaze around toward him.

"Majesty, up until tonight your story has been just that to me, a story. But now!" He heaved himself up onto his feet. "Now, tonight, it has been brought to life." With adrenaline courage, he stepped to her side. "Allow me to bring it to life for others. Majesty, you are beautiful, and dangerous—deadly even. You are an archetype, Majesty, and an archetype deserves more than one mere book!"

"What are you talking about?" Queen and raven watched him with much the same expression.

He wet his lips and leaned toward her. "I'm talking trilogy, Majesty! A big fat trilogy!"

"A trilogy?"

"Yes!"

The queen smiled.

"MajesTEEEEEEEEEEEEEEEEEEEEEE . . ."

She shook her head and dropped down onto the window seat. Dark necromancies and dead heroes were one thing but a trilogy? What could possibly have possessed Cornelius Dickcissel to suggest such a thing?

He should have known it wouldn't fly.

The body hit the flagstones with a wet melon kind of splat.

At least not more than sixty feet.

"Baxter."

"Majesty?"

"I'll be needing a new scribe. . . ."

THE MOULD OF FORM
by Rosemary Edghill

Rosemary Edghill lives in the beautiful Hudson Valley with various books, computers, and other animals, and is a frequent contributor to DAW anthologies, as well as the author of twenty-something novels, including the Bast mysteries and the Twelve Treasures series. Her latest book is *Beyond World's End*, with Mercedes Lackey.

> Art thou aught else but place, degree and form
> Creating awe and fear in other men?
> —William Shakespeare, *Henry V*

I grow as tired as any man of hearing it said that one cannot know what those years were like unless one lived them, for such words make mock of that learning which is the mark of civilization and the adornment of an English gentleman, but even I must admit that in this case it is true, for only those who lived through those years of madness, hope, and possibility can understand how we thought in those days, as if all the world had been washed new and there had been no Adam's Fall to mar us. It has been said that since the Restoration, there is no sin save bad form, and I think perhaps that is true as well. When the appearance of virtue is all that one retains, then appearance matters.

I was born James Cruikshank—I have another name now, of a more suitable aspect—in London-town in 16–, when the Old King was a prisoner of his subjects and all men were architects of possibility. Our rulers were men no better than ourselves, and in that we saw the refashioning of the world. That they were as greedy and venal as the nobility we had cast down was something no one saw, for in those days, men lived on dreams.

The Protector had molded England's destiny since before I was born. My father had opposed him, King Charles' man first and last, and labored to the destruction of his entire fortune in hope of a deliverance that could only be years in some distant future, for the King was executed at St. James Palace in '49, and his heir was but a child. The Sealed Knot unraveled, like all such things of moonshine and phantasie, and my father died in poverty, fled to France to escape the condign punishment of the victors. Meanwhile my mother and I lived upon the charity of a distant cousin, in a cramped unloving house within the Great Smoke itself, and so upon the streets of London-town I supped full at the banquet of futures and possibilities, though circumstance had barred me from my place at the table.

Yet even in exile and death my father still had his friends, and it was through the sponsorship of one of them that I was given a chance to rise again in the world, for, by what influence I know not, this distant friend secured me a place at Eton.

In those days, Eton had become a resort of gentle-men, and the children of the New Men mingled here with the oldest blood of England. Friendships made here would lead to preferment later, for good form had made its first triumph over blood when the Old

King died, and in the world men had made, the appearance of virtue was more important than its expression.

The school fees were large, as befit an institution founded by Great Harry, that profligate and luxurious monarch, and my mother was reduced to desperate stratagems to raise them. Her cousins, who grudged us both food and roof, wanted me put to a trade. The London of that day held more work than hands, and I might have found a ready place as a clerk, for I had already my letters and some Latin, but this my mother would not permit, seeing in it the long slow slide into obscurity and extinction. Our name, our blood, was all the world to her now that my father was dead, and in me she saw the opportunity to make his dead bones live again. And so she would see me established at Eton, and then Oxford, upon a path to *gentilesse* and advancement. Within her plans, I wove plans of my own: to become a partisan and supporter of that great Commonwealth that ushered my father so neatly out of position and life, to join with my peers in that freemasonry of ability that held all English in its giddy thrall.

In the end, I threw away all her hopes and my own for no more than childish pride.

The compass of my brief years had introduced me to hardship, to poverty and fear, but never had I imagined the existence that awaited me at school. It was as if I were cast into hell, there in the Long Chamber at the close of day. The strong preyed upon the weak, subjecting them to unimaginable tortures while the masters of the school pretended to see nothing. Though I represented my condition as strongly as I could in my few letters home, my mother likewise refused to hear. Schooling was the hallmark of a gentleman, and schooling I must have, though it cost me my soul.

It is from those hellish days, I think, that my whole hatred of boys stems. For though I was fallen among that company of the bestial and cruel, there were those I hated more: the careless golden souls who walked through chamber and hall as if untouched by their surroundings. Prefects and tutors vied for their regard, and cruelties and punishments alike fell lightly upon their oblivious shoulders. Their futures were assured— futures of rank and privilege among men of learning and dignity. In light of such future satisfaction, the present was a dim and trivial shadow.

There was one of them, a boy named Peter, whom I hated with a particular rancor, for from the moment I met him, four years into Purgatorial exile, he treated me as his equal, showing me all consideration despite the difference in our estate. With careless ease, he drew me into his charmed circle, the world of barely remembered surety and privilege that I had known in dimmest infancy, and treated me as if I belonged there.

It was my downfall.

It did not seem so at first. Peter was just my age, but while I had a Puritan's face, with a long jaw and heavy coat of black beard which I had begun to shave in my twelfth year, Peter was all golden boyhood, the downy peach fuzz of his skin barely beginning to ripen into coarse manhood. His family had bent supplely with the prevailing political winds, but while many suspected them of Royalist sympathies, they were seen to be ardent supporters of the Commonwealth, and so had weathered the storms of the 'forties and 'fifties with their lands and consequence intact.

The difference between his family's fortunes and

my own did not escape me, and I hated Peter all the more for it. But once he was seen to take an interest in me, the worst of my torments stopped, so simple self-preservation entailed smiling prudence, to follow Peter and his golden lads wherever Fortune led me.

You will find it odd, perhaps, that under his influence I became even more zealously Puritan than I had been before, for Peter was the living opposite of that vengeful, joyless philosophy. But my envious hatred, all the more ardent for its secrecy, was vexed to madness by his careless innocence, though at the time, it seemed to me only that I thought more clearly than ever before. The Old King and his favorites, those golden children of decadence and privilege, all had been swept away by the cruel modern winds of change that brought with them fierce possibility and clear-eyed rationalism. Just as there would be no more of ghosts and mummery at the Lord's Table, so our lives would not be guided by the dead hand of ancient kings, nor our destinies by blood and birthright. I saw explicitly what I had only dimly sensed before: that this new world, bright and hard and ruthless as steel, held a place for me that the old one never had.

But to claim it, I still must climb the ladder out of this hell, a ladder made out of favors and friendships, and of smiling, always smiling, when my heart turned to a crucible of vitriol within my bosom.

I have said that my family was impoverished, my mother little better than a pauper. Despite this she managed to send me small gifts of money from time to time; small money and pawnable trinkets. With these I maintained a foothold upon the society of Peter's set, though I was hard-pressed to repay even so simple a courtesy as a round of drinks at the corner alehouse. As for the young gentleman's other vices—whoring, gambling, hunting—they were as far beyond my reach as the mountains of the moon.

Peter affected to see none of this. At this remove, it is hard for me to say whether that indifference came from malice or a genuine greatness of heart, but I will tell you this: the damage they invoke is all one, and so I despised him all the more for flaunting what I did not and could not have as if I might ever attain it. To withstand such blandishments forever would tax the fortitude of a sinless angel, and I was not made of such celestial stuff.

As I said, my mother did what she could for me financially, but in my fifth year at Eton, she died at last. Of grief, of melancholy—or of starvation and pneumonia at the delectable fountainhead of her cousin's charity, there is no man living who can say. But in her dying, a small legacy came to me, and in that moment of unexpected largesse I was at last able to seem what I truly wished to be—an independent gentleman of rank, a full member of that gilded company surrounding my insensible patron. With funds beyond the bare necessity at last at my disposal, I entered fully into the pleasures of the idle scholar. Gaming was forbidden by the rules of the school, but then, so were most of our diversions. The need for secrecy, for misdirection and confusion, gave our pleasures an added spice.

At first, it truly seemed that God had favored my commission. I wagered and won, increasing my wealth. I had a strong head for drink, and a cool head for cards. The combination was felicitous, and I won handily. What I should have seen as a warning, I saw instead as an opportunity, and in seizing it, doomed myself entirely.

Perhaps the sun of Peter's countenance began to shine less brightly on me then. I began to have to work for that regard which I had heretofore unthinkingly accepted as a beggar's alms, to compete for my place where once I was assured it as of right. But to return once more to the outer darkness of an unsponsored life was unthinkable: those incubi who had withheld their blows when I entered this charmed circle of fellowship awaited me avidly should I be thrust from it, and I feared them with the sincerity with which I feared death and the pains of hell. Triumph and fear and a new coat of green velvet trimmed with modest gold lace made me reckless; I plotted my victories without regard for my standing among these charitable peers, badgering them into wagers that were heartless in their rapaciousness.

And when at last my luck began to fail, I saw what armor my temporary wealth had granted me, making tender a skin which had once been armored against the harshest blows of Fate. Having once been raised to the heights, I could not bear to acknowledge my poverty and return to my former place.

And so I began to cheat at cards.

This was a far graver offense than the trespasses against the law of the land which I had heretofore blithely committed. This was a transgression against Good Form itself, that hallowed and unspoken code by which a gentleman of England lived. Even poverty might be carried off with a certain elan, debt and lawlessness managed with insouciant grace, so long as one feigned obliviousness to one's humble estate—so long as one demanded with each unspoken word to be accorded the rights and privileges of a gentleman.

But I was no gentleman, if only in my heart, and so I cheated at cards.

At first I hoped only to halt the slow exsanguination of my assets, to blunt the worst of my luck. But in the months since I had come into my mother's legacy, some intangible line of credit had run dry, and what I had once received as a gift, I now must pay for. But I was without coin of any sort—not the Commonwealth's gold angels, not wit and style, and not the forbearance of Peter's friends. I had outstayed my welcome, and I was made to feel it. But still I could not bear to return to what I once was. I became more predatory in my gamesmanship, more reckless in my cardsharping.

And at last I was discovered.

It was a night like any other. We gamed, defiant of curfew, in a corner of the public rooms of a High Street tavern. I had added luck to the mechanic's skill, and I was emboldened to feel pleased with my success, until Peter's hand fell lightly upon my wrist and I stared into his merciless eyes. In that moment, I felt—not shame, but a vast groveling betrayal of self, the yearning to accept any punishment, any disparagement, if only this moment could never have come. Gladly would I embrace my tormentors, renounce my place, vanish into the vast unwashed obscurity of the proletariat, meekly accept all I had raged against, all I had hoped for, if I could unmake the journey that had led to this moment. It was weakness, cowardice, and I, who had been a coward a thousand times over in my life, despised myself most of all for the despairing love I felt in the instant of its forfeiture.

"Bad form, Cruikshank," Peter said coolly, regarding the cards that spilled from my sleeve.

If demons had slain me in that moment, if the earth had opened beneath my feet and I had toppled into the fiery Pit, I would have been no more dead to him than I became in that moment. He withdrew his hand, the secreted cards dropped from my sleeve to the table, and my life was over. In moments I sat alone at an empty table, nearly swooning, and all around the tavern I could hear the venomous whispers growing: *Cheat . . . cheater . . . bad form . . . bad form. . . .*

When I came to my senses once more, I found myself walking through the fields outside of town, long after the locking of the school gates. I wondered if, by any faint merciful forbearance, I would be able to brazen out the scandal, knowing in my heart that it was impossible. When I returned to my lodgings in the morning, there were bailiffs outside my door to prevent my entry, my possessions forfeit to those I had preyed upon. Though technically I was still enrolled, Eton, like every public school, has a morals clause in its charter. I had forfeited my right to be called a man of good Christian character, and my remaining tenure within these hallowed precincts could be compassed in hours.

I left my lodging and began to walk vaguely in the direction of my cousins' house. Why, I do not know; there was no possibility that they would take me in once more, and in truth, I had become so much a Puritan in my sojourn at school that the thought of accepting their charity was repugnant to me for more than ordinary reasons. Still, I walked, drinking nothing on my way but Adam's ale, and as I did my spirits began to revive. In the new world that men had made of the conceit of kings, surely there would

be a place for me. I would go to the City. I had yet
a few coins in my pockets, and by the deployment
of those wicked skills that Peter had so disparaged I
could gain myself a stake to go on with. I might yet
win through, now beholden to no man's favor.

But as I walked, a distant roaring came to my ears,
as of a thousand voices raised in cheering, and I
began to see curious sights along the road. The closer
I came to London, the more people I encountered,
and every man seemed privy to some great secret
that had eluded me, for most of them were roaring
drunk. Though after watching a few of them ride by
me insensibly, I did attempt to attract the attention
of the travelers so as to gain their news, I had no luck
until at last I encountered a solitary man wheeling a
barrow, upon which were piled what seemed to be
all his worldly possessions.

"What news, man?" I asked him.

"News! Why the best news there ever was! Have
you not heard?"

"Heard what?" I asked, bewildered. I had been
seduced into oblivion by my vices for so long that I
no longer followed the daily doings of the Young
Protector, Cromwell's son.

"The King has come again! The King has come
again!"

It was not to Christ that this pagan reveler referred,
but to Charles: the son of the Old King had returned
from his French exile to lord it anew over his father's
subjects. And every man who had seen the Old King
out with such delight now cheered with equal delight
for the return of the son, or so it seemed that morning. The doughty old yeoman I had hailed was jour-
neying to London to see the king, having sold up his
holding to do it. He urged me to drink a toast to the

king's health, and I knew that to be less than eager would earn me a sound thrashing. And so I drank the health of that chiefest member of the band of gilded youth that was my nemesis in strong English ale, and went numbly on my way, as he did upon his. I did not need to see this new royal court to know that it had in it no place for me.

So I walked once more without destination, this time against the throng, heading to what circumstance I knew not. As the road filled with more and more Englishmen converging antlike upon London, the journey began to take on (for them) a carnival air, and (for me) the dress of nightmare. I did not lack for food—bread and even meat were pressed by the pilgrims upon their fellows—and surely I did not lack for drink, for the king's heath was drunk in wine, in gin, in ale, and in brandy with every passing mile. The same spirit of hectic jubilation seemed to possess my fellows as had possessed me in certain nights at the tables, a sense of soaring above the surface of the Earth, unfettered by its limits. But on this day I was as cast down as they were exalted, for the people's joy at the king's return seemed to me to be the final betrayal of the certainties of my brief existence. My head reeling with emotion and strong drink, I staggered at dusk from the road into the new-plowed fields to find what shelter I could in the night. It was spring, but I did not fear the night dews nor the other misfortunes that could befall one who slept far from bedstead and rooftree. Neither moon-madness nor the malice of the faeries had power over one whose heart had been burned away to ash.

So I thought then, and so I do still think, for I have never yet taken harm of the faeries, and indeed I account many of them to be my great friends. It is only mortal boys who yet have the power to wound me, and I hold all that race my implacable enemy. So I lay down that night with a bleak and carefree heart and slept, cushioned on a bounteous tide of drink. And as I slept, all the world changed.

I awoke in the depths of night, with the full moon just stepping down from midheaven, and got slowly to my feet, wondering what had summoned me from my only refuge. All around me was stillness and the sleeping English countryside, but there was no darkness while Diana, that witches' goddess, bleached the sky to paleness with her silver mirror. I felt alert and clearheaded, as lively as though someone had called my name, and in fact something had. In the distance a steeple clock rolled the hour, and went on tolling, madly, through two dozen strokes, then three. For a moment fury filled me, for I thought it must be tolling for the king, and waited hopefully for the angry verger to flog the sexton from his untimely celebration. But the bell tolled on, until I was certain that all within its sound must be deaf, or dead, or slumbering too deeply for it to waken them.

And then I saw that from which I would have run shrieking only days before, whether as staunch Puritan or hopeful scholar. But both scholar and divine have a stake in the world as it is, and to fling aside the laws of God and Nature for uncertain gain would seem to be very madness. But both God and Man had rejected me—for the king's return must surely be such a sign of Divine partisanship as to form a dire omen—and so I stood as still as if I had been elf-shot, watching the ship come on with a distant sense of wonder.

For ship it was, sailing grandly above the tilled springtime fields as serenely as any vessel ever sailed

upon the sea. She was a full-rigged galleon, her hull
bleached to moonlight silver and her lanterns burning with the red fire of hell itself. Only the faint creak
of rigging and sails could be heard over the monoto-
nous tolling of that distant bell, and I saw no sailors
upon her deck or aloft. Whatever force sailed this
ship, it sailed her as silently and as mysteriously as
a cloud upon the wind. Her sails were black, a darker
shadow against the sky, and I remember thinking at
the time that this was the most profligate wonder of
all, to spend such costly adornment upon that part
of the ship which so often was carried to the bottom
of the ocean by a storm. Though if a storm came here
to trouble this vessel, and strip her of her gauds,
would not the parts be cast merely to the ground,
and lie there simple of recovery?

I have said that the White Ship was in every way
like a ship of water, and so she was, save in one.
When the ship reached me, she stopped as neatly as
a carriage might stop at the coachman's command,
and hovered above me in the sky. I had stood my
ground all the time she had glided toward me in that
unearthly silence, thinking, in so much as I thought
at all, that the White Ship would pass me by and sail
undisturbed upon her secret errand, leaving no proof
of her presence behind.

But then she stopped, hanging perfectly motionless
in the air above me, rocking as gently as a ship at
anchor in calm harbor. I had thought her entirely a
craft of moonlight and shadows, but now that she
was upon me I could see her mermaid figurehead
thickly crusted in silver leaf, and the letters that
burned like fire along her carven bow. "Revenge"
was what they spelled, and in that entranced, daz-
zled moment I realized I longed for her above all

things: revenge, sweet revenge, to slake the guilt-filled burnings of my wounded heart. The land was closed to me—I would go to sea, turn pirate, drench the world in blood and sorrow until I had washed away all record of weakness and folly and the laughing faces of golden boys.

"Ahoy to the land below!" a voice called from above me. I looked up, and beheld, leaning over the edge of the railing, the most extraordinary personage I had ever seen, a tall man in a long gray velvet coat and smalls of silver satin that were no more bright than the silvery peruke upon his head. Around him stood his crew—small dark men the size of children, wearing nothing that I could see save paint and gold collars. I knew then that I had fallen among the Midnight Folk who sail upon the Sea of Dreams, and that the tolling of that bell which I had marked was but the striking of the hour of midnight, impossibly extended. When it had struck its full measure of twelve times twelve the ship would be gone, to sail other seas than this.

"Ahoy the ship!" I called in return. "Take you passengers?"

From my place upon the ground I saw the captain smile. "Nay, sirrah! We are no fat merchantman to cosset the frail bellies of landlubbers. We are honest workingmen, pirates all!" He smiled at me, with teeth as long and white as a wolf's, and in that moment any sane man would have turned away, would have run until he reached the nearest church and there thanked God on bended knee for his deliverance.

I did not.

"Then take me for a pirate!" I cried, in that moment making my decision. A scrap of schoolboy

Latin came back to me. *Alea iacta est:* the die is cast. "Take me with you, and if it please you, I'll have no more of the land!"

The captain turned to shout an order, and to my horror and despair, the *Revenge* began to move slowly away. But at the same time, a ladder was flung down to me, dangling down far below the keel, though yet a yard above my head. I ran after the White Ship, leaping up recklessly and grabbing for the sanctuary she offered. The rough hemp burned my hands where I clutched it, and it seemed to me that the ship was moving faster now, for I could feel a cold wind on my face. *It is not too late to jump*, I told myself, but I had no real desire to fling myself back into the world of men that had so betrayed me and itself. And so I climbed, into an unknown world that was yet friendlier to me than the one I was leaving.

The rope ladder swung and twisted, a pendulum with me its hapless weight, suspended between earth and air. At last I gained the relative stability of the ship's hull, and my ascent became swifter. I did not look down, but with some distant part of my mind I registered that the infernal tolling of the church bell had ceased. The only sound now was the creaking of the ropes, the wind whipping past my face.

At last I gained the rail, where there were hands waiting to pull me up, and after a seeming eternity, I had solidity beneath my feet once more. At last I could confront my rescuer face-to-face.

The captain was a tall man, as unearthly fair as starlight. I could see now what I had not seen before, that his eyes glowed with the lambent beastfire of one who has no soul. Such is the mark that God Himself has placed upon the brute creation, that it might be distinguished from the sons of Adam, and if I had not known before the nature of those into whose hands I had commended myself, I must in all justice know it now.

"Welcome to *Revenge*," the faerie captain said, and held out his hand to me. "Captain Goodfellow bids you greeting."

I took his hand right willingly, and a shock of cold at that touch thrilled through me to my very bones. It was, paradoxically, a warming thing to one numbed beyond sensation by the myriad blows of Fate, and in that spirit I welcomed it. I, who had set my foot upon so many paths to fortune, had found the last road I was to tread.

"Come, come," he said. "You will be weary from your journey, and there is much for us to discuss."

He turned, leading the way to the master's cabin, and it was as if in looking away from me he at last freed my attention to inspect my surroundings. The crew were busy at their tasks as I had not seen them before—trimming the black sails, retrieving the ladder that had borne me aloft, performing the thousand tasks that must be enacted in every moment of a ship's life. Above me the stars were unwinking, the moon a bright coin burning as refulgently as the sun in this eternal midnight. Beyond the ship's rail, all that could be seen was cloud, blotting out the land below as we sailed to a destination outside my philosophies.

The painted men of the crew watched me with avid glowing eyes, but I felt no fear of them. Mortal man had dealt me all the sharpest blows of my life, and I did not fear those who were otherwise. At last, having gazed my fill upon this eldritch vessel, I followed my new master below.

I had never before been aboard a ship of any sort, so I knew not what to expect. But the captain's cabin was oddly familiar, bearing a more than passing kinship to the closets of the wealthy and powerful men whom I had visited in my life. There was a fine Turkey carpet laid upon the deck, and linen-fold paneling upon the walls, and the room itself was brave with candles. Their honest yellow light did much to reassure me, though had they been the blue and sulferous lamps of hell I would not have been deterred from the course I had set myself to follow, for all beneath my eye was in the first style of excess, and excess was like cool water to my fevered spirit. There was a wealth of bright silver plate upon the sideboard, and with his own hands Captain Goodfellow poured me a rich measure of a fine oporto, thick and red as blood. I drank it off at a gulp and felt its warmth race through my veins, steadying my nerves. Without a word from me, he poured another, and I drank that as well, at last feeling the cold of his handclasp fade from my bones.

"Well, now, Master Scholar. What think you of our company?" he asked.

"It matters not what I think, if you will have me," I blurted out with clumsy truthfulness. "For there is no place left on Earth for me."

"Bravely spoken," he answered. "And in truth, we welcome few as we have welcomed you. But as I have said, *Revenge* takes no passengers. Are you willing to become fully one of us, to enter into all our sport and amusement? For we sail the Sea of Dreams, and voyage to lands that few of the mortalkind have known. Before you I spread a table of riches and hardship, privation and glory."

He gestured, and I saw a table laid out in the center of the cabin. I had not seen it when I entered, and I would have been willing to swear, should any such oath have been asked of me, that it had not been there a moment before. It was dressed all in white damask, in the fashion of the table at the Lord's Supper, and upon its surface there were two tall silver candlesticks with tall white tapers aflame, an inkwell, and a book laying open before them.

"All who sail with us must sign articles," Captain Goodfellow said. "Loyalty to your fellows, confusion to your enemies, obedience to me, and no regret for what you have left behind."

"I can promise all these things," I said, and he clapped me jovially upon the shoulder.

I stepped up to the table then and gazed down upon my fortune. The Great Book was before me, its pages thick with signatures, but all the names indighted there were blurred, and I could not read them. When I touched the page, it was as cold beneath my fingers as black iron on Christmas Day, and there was a space at the bottom ready for my name.

Captain Goodfellow held the silver pen out to me. "Put down your name, Master Scholar, and you shall be one of us."

I clasped the pen between my fingers and dipped it into the captain's silver inkwell. I wrote my first name—James—in bold flowing letters, but then I hesitated. Not for weakness' sake, but for a notion that had come into my head. This was my birth into a new life, and I vowed that in it I would be the foolish and villainous Cruikshank no loner. Among this gallant company I would take a new name.

Something stronger.

Something sharper.

And so I signed "James Hook" in a bold sweeping style, and sealed my destiny among the Midnight Folk.

The form is all that matters.

THE SPECTER OF
TULLYFANE ABBEY

by Peter Tremayne

Peter Tremayne is the pseudonym of Peter Berresford Ellis, a Celtic scholar who lives in London, England. He conceived the idea for Sister Fidelma, a seventh-century Celtic lawyer, to demonstrate for his students that women could be legal advocates under the Irish system of law. Sister Fidelma has since appeared in eight novels, the most recent being *The Monk Who Vanished*, and many short stories which have been collected in the anthology *Hemlock at Vespers and Other Sister Fidelma Mysteries*. He has also written, under his own name, more than twenty-five books on history, biography, and Irish and Celtic mythology, including *Celtic Women: Women in Celtic Society and Literature* and *Celt and Greek: Celts in the Hellenic World*.

"Somewhere in the vaults of the bank of Cox and Co., at Charing Cross, there is a travel-worn and battered tin dispatch box with my name, John H. Watson MD, Late Indian Army, painted on the lid. It is filled with papers, nearly all of which are records of cases to illustrate the curious problems which Mr. Sherlock Holmes had at various times to examine."

— *"The Problem of Thor Bridge"*

This is one of those papers.

I must confess that there are few occasions on which I have seen my estimable friend, Sherlock Holmes, the famous consulting detective, in a state of some agitation. He is usually so detached that the word calm seems unfit to describe his general demeanor. Yet I had called upon him one evening to learn his opinion of a manuscript draft account I had made of one of his cases which I had entitled *The Problem of Thor Bridge*.

To my surprise, I found him seated in an attitude of tension in his armchair, his pipe unlit, his long pale fingers clutching my handwritten pages and his brows drawn together in disapproval.

"Confound it, Watson," he greeted me sharply as I came through the door. "Must you show me up to public ridicule in this fashion?"

I was, admittedly, somewhat taken aback at his uncharacteristic greeting.

"I rather thought you came well out of the story," I replied defensively. "After all, you helped a remarkable woman, as you yourself observed, while, as for Mr. Gibson, I believe that he did learn an object lesson : . ."

He cut me short. "Tush! I do not mean the case of Grace Dunbar, which, since you refer to it, was not as glamorous as your imaginative pen elaborates on. No, Watson, no! It is here," he waved the papers at me, "here in your cumbersome preamble. You speak of some of my unsolved cases as if they were failures. I only mentioned them to you in passing, and now you tell me, and the readers of the *Strand Magazine*, that you have noted them down and deposited the record in that odious little tin dispatch box placed in Cox's Bank."

"I did not think that you would have reason to object, Holmes," I replied with some vexation.

He waved a hand as if dismissing my feelings. "I object to the manner in which you reveal these cases! I read here, and I quote . . ." He peered shortsightedly at my manuscript. " 'Some, and not the least interesting, were complete failures, and as such will hardly bear narrating, since no final explanation is forthcoming. A problem without a solution may interest the student, but can hardly fail to annoy the casual reader. Among these unfinished tales is that of Mr. James Phillimore, who, stepping back into his own house to get his umbrella, was never more seen in this world.' There!" he glanced up angrily.

"But, Holmes, dear fellow, that is precisely the matter as you told it to me. Where am I in error?"

"The error is making the statement itself. It is incomplete. It is not set into context. The case of James Phillimore, whose title was Colonel, incidentally, occurred when I was a young man. I had just completed my second term at Oxford. It was the first time I crossed foils, so to speak, with the man who was to cause me such grief later in my career . . . Professor Moriarty."

I started at this intelligence for Holmes was always unduly reticent about his clashes with James Moriarty, that sinister figure whom Holmes seemed to hold in both contempt as a criminal and regard as an intellect.

"I did not know that, Holmes."

"Neither would you have learned further of the matter, but I find that you have squirreled away a reference to this singular event in which Moriarty achieved the better of me."

"You were bested by Moriarty?" I was now really intrigued.

"Don't sound so surprised, Watson," he admonished. "Even villains can be victorious once in a while." Then Holmes paused and added quietly, "especially when such a villain as Moriarty enlisted the power of darkness in his nefarious design."

I began to laugh, knowing that Holmes abhorred the supernatural. I remember his outburst when we received the letter from Morrison, Morrison, and Dodd which led us into "The Adventure of the Sussex Vampire." Yet my laughter died on my lips as I caught sight of the ghastly look that crossed Holmes' features. He stared into the dancing flames of the fire as if remembering the occasion.

"I am not in jest, Watson. In this instance, Moriarty employed the forces of darkness to accomplish his evil end. Of that there can be no shadow of doubt. It is the only time that I have failed, utterly and miserably failed, to prevent a terrible tragedy whose memory will curse me to the grave."

Holmes sighed deeply and then appeared to have observed for the first time that his pipe was unlit and reached for the matches.

"Pour two glasses from that decanter of fine Hennessy on the table and sit yourself down. Having come thus far in my confession, I might as well finish the story in case that imagination of yours decides to embellish the little you do know."

"I say, Holmes . . ." I began to protest, but he went on, ignoring my words.

"I pray you, promise never to reveal this story until my clay has mingled with the earth from which I am sprung."

If there is a preamble to this story, it is one that I

was already knowledgeable of and which I have already given some account of in the memoir I entitled "The Affray at the Kildare Street Club." Holmes was one of the Galway Holmes. Like his brother, Mycroft, he had attended Trinity College, Dublin, where he had, in the same year as his friend Oscar Wilde, won a demyship to continue his studies at Oxford. I believe the name Sherlock came from his maternal side, his mother being of another well established Anglo-Irish family. Holmes was always reticent about this background although the clues to his Irish origins were obvious to most discerning people. One of his frequent disguises was to assume the name of Altamont as he pretended to be an Irish-American. Altamont was his family seat near Ballysherlock.

Armed with this background knowledge, I settled back with a glass of Holmes' cognac to listened as he recounted a most singular and terrifying tale. I append it exactly as he narrated it to me.

"Having completed my first term at Oxford, I returned to Dublin to stay with my brother Mycroft at his house in Merrion Square. Yet I found myself somewhat at a loose end. There was some panic in the fiscal office of the Chief Secretary where Mycroft worked. This caused him to be unable to spare the time we had set aside for a fishing expedition. I was therefore persuaded to accompany Abraham Stoker, who had been at Trinity the same year as Mycroft, to the Royal to see some theatrical entertainment. Abraham, or Bram as he preferred to be called, was also a close friend of Sir William and Lady Wilde, who lived just across the square and with whose younger son, Oscar, I was then at Oxford with.

"Bram was an ambitious man who not only

worked with Mycroft at Dublin Castle but wrote theatrical criticism in his spare time and by night edited the *Dublin Halfpenny Press*, a journal which he had only just launched. He was trying to persuade me to write on famous Dublin murders for it, but as he offered no remuneration at all, I gracefully declined.

"We were in the foyer of the Royal when Bram, an amiable, booming giant with red hair, hailed someone over the heads of the throng. A thin, white-faced young man emerged to be clasped warmly by the hand. It was a youth of my own age and well known to me; Jack Phillimore was his name. He had been a fellow student at Trinity College. My heart leaped in expectation, and I searched the throng for a familiar female face which was, I will confess it, most dear to me. But Phillimore was alone. His sister Agnes, was not with him at the theater.

"In the presence of Bram, we fell to exchanging pleasantries about our alma mater. I noticed that Phillimore's heart was not in exchanging such bonhomie nor, to be honest, was mine. I was impatient for the opportunity to inquire after Phillimore's sister. Ah, let the truth be known, Watson, but only after I am not in this world.

"Love, my dear Watson. Love! I believe that you have observed that all emotions, and that one in particular, are abhorrent to my mind. This is true, and since I have become mature enough to understand, I have come to regard it as opposite to that true cold reason which I place above all things. I have never married lest I bias my judgment. Yet it was not always my intention, and this very fact is what led to my downfall, causing the tragedy which I am about to relate. Alas, Watson, if . . . but with an if we might place Paris in a bottle.

"As a youth I was deeply in love with Agnes Phillimore who was but a year older than I. When Jack Phillimore and I were in our first year at Trinity, I used to spend time at their town house by Stephen's Green. I confess, it was not the company of Phillimore that I sought then but that of Agnes.

"In my maturity I could come to admire *the* woman, as you insist I call Irene Adler, but admiration is not akin to the deep, destructive emotional power that we call love.

"It was when Bram spotted someone across the foyer that he needed to speak to that Phillimore seized the opportunity to ask abruptly what I was doing for recreation. Hearing that I was at a loose end, he suggested that I accompany him to his father's estate in Kerry for a few days. Colonel James Phillimore owned a large house and estate in that remote county. Phillimore said he was going down because it was his father's fiftieth birthday. I thought at the time that he placed a singular emphasis on that fact.

"It was then that I managed to casually ask if his sister Agnes was in Dublin or in Kerry. Phillimore, of course, like most brothers, was ignorant that his sister held any attraction for the male sex, least of all one of his friends. He was nonchalant. 'To be sure she is at Tullyfane, Holmes. Preparing for her marriage next month.'

"His glance was distracted by a man jostling through the foyer, and so he missed the effect that this intelligence had on me.

" 'Married?' I gasped. 'To whom?'

" 'Some professor, no less. A cove by the name of Moriarty.'

" 'Moriarty?' I asked, for the name meant little to

me in that context. I knew it only as a common County Kerry name. It was an Anglicizing of the Irish name Ó Muircheartaigh, meaning 'expert navigator.'

" 'He is our neighbor, he is quite besotted with my sister, and it seems that it is arranged that they will marry next month. A rum cove, is the professor. Good education and holds a chair of mathematics at Queen's University in Belfast.'

" 'Professor James Moriarty,' I muttered savagely. Phillimore's news of Agnes' intentions had shattered all my illusions.

" 'Do you know him?' Phillimore asked, observing my displeasure. 'He's all right, isn't he? I mean . . . he's not a bounder, eh?'

" 'I have seen him once only and that from a distance in the Kildare Street Club,' I confessed. I had nothing against Moriarty at that time. 'My brother Mycroft pointed him out to me. I did not meet him. Yet I have heard of his reputation. His *Dynamics of an Asteroid* ascended to such rarefied heights of pure mathematics that no man in the scientific press was capable of criticizing it.'

"Phillimore chuckled.

" 'That is beyond me. Thank God I am merely a student of theology. But it sounds as though you are an admirer.'

" 'I admire intellect, Phillimore,' I replied simply. Moriarty, as I recalled, must have been all of ten years older than Agnes. What is ten years at our age? But to me, a callow youth, I felt the age difference that existed between Agnes and James Moriarty was obscene. I explain this simply because my attitude has a bearing on my future disposition.

" 'So come down with me to Tullyfane Abbey,'

pressed Phillimore, oblivious to the emotional turmoil that he had created in me.

"I was about to coldly decline the invitation when Phillimore, observing my negative expression, was suddenly very serious. He leaned closed to me and said softly: 'You see, Holmes, old fellow, we are having increasing problems with the family ghost and, as I recall, you have a canny way of solving bizarre problems.'

"I knew enough of his character to realize that jesting was beyond his capacity.

" 'The family ghost?'

" 'A damned infernal specter that is driving my father quite out of his wits. Not to mention Agnes . . .'

" 'Your father and sister are afraid of a specter?'

" 'Agnes is scared at the deterioration in my father's demeanor. Seriously, Holmes, I really don't know what to do. My sister's letters speak of such a bizarre set of circumstances that I am inclined to think that she is hallucinating or that my father has been driven mad already.'

"My inclination was to avoid opening old wounds now by meeting Agnes again. I could spend the rest of my vacation in Marsh's Library, where they have an excellent collection of medieval cryptogram manuscripts. I hesitated—hesitated and was lost. I had to admit that I was intrigued to hear more of the matter in spite of my emotional distress, for any mystery sends the adrenaline coursing in my body.

"The very next morning I accompanied Jack Phillimore to Kingsbridge Railway Station and boarded the train to Killarney. En route he explained some of the problems.

"Tullyfane Abbey was supposed to be cursed. It was situated on the extremity of the Iveragh Peninsula in a wild and deserted spot. Tullyfane Abbey was, of course, never an abbey. It was a dignified Georgian country house. The Anglo-Irish gentry in the eighteenth century had a taste for the grandiose and called their houses 'abbeys' or 'castles' even when they were unassuming dwellings inhabited only by families of modest fortune.

"Phillimore told me that the firstborn of every generation of the lords of Tullyfane were to meet with terrible deaths on the attainment of their fiftieth birthdays even down to the seventh generation. It seems that first lord of Tullyfane had hanged a young boy for sheep stealing. The boy turned out to be innocent, and his mother, a widow who had doted on the lad as insurance for comfort in her old age, had duly uttered the curse. Whereupon, each lord of Tullyfane, for the last six generations, had met an untimely end.

"Phillimore assured me that the first lord of Tullyfane had not even been a direct ancestor of his, but that his great-grandfather had purchased Tullyfane Abbey when the owner, concerned at the imminent prospect of departing this life on his fiftieth birthday, decided to sell and depart for healthier climes in England. This sleight of hand of ownership had not prevented Jack's great-grandfather, General Phillimore, from falling off his horse and breaking his neck on his fiftieth birthday. Jack's grandfather, a redoubtable judge, was shot on his fiftieth birthday. The local inspector of the Royal Irish Constabulary had assumed that his untimely demise could be ascribed more to his profession than to the paranormal. Judges and policemen often experienced sudden terminations to their careers in a country where they were considered part of the colonial occupation by ordinary folk.

" 'I presume your father, Colonel James Phillimore, is now approaching his fiftieth birthday and hence his alarm?' I asked Phillimore as the train rolled through the Tipperary countryside toward the Kerry border.

"Phillimore nodded slowly.

" 'My sister has, in her letters, written that she has heard the specter crying at night. She reports that my father has even witnessed the apparition, the form of a young boy, crying on the turret of the abbey.'

"I raised my eyebrows unintentionally.

" 'Seen as well as heard?' I demanded. 'And by two witnesses? Well, I can assure you that there is nothing in this world that exists unless it is due to some scientifically explainable reason.'

" 'Nothing in this world,' muttered Phillimore. 'But what of the next?'

" 'If your family believes in this curse, why remain at Tullyfane?' I demanded. 'Would it not be better to quit the house and estate if you are so sure that the curse is potent?'

" 'My father is stubborn, Holmes. He will not quit the place for he has sunk every penny he has into it apart from our town house in Dublin. If it were me, I would sell it to Moriarty and leave the accursed spot.'

" 'Sell it to Moriarty? Why him, particularly?'

" 'He offered to buy Father out in order to help resolve the situation.'

" 'Rather magnanimous of him,' I observed. 'Presumably he has no fear of the curse?'

" 'He reckons that the curse would only be directed at Anglo-Irish families like us, while he, being a pure Milesian, a Gael of the Gaels, so to speak, would be immune to the curse.'

"Colonel Phillimore had sent a calèche to Killarney Station to bring Phillimore and me to Tullyfane Abbey. The old Colonel was clearly not in the best of spirits when he greeted us in the library. I noticed his hand shook a little as he raised it to greet me.

" 'Friend of Jack's eh? Yes, I remember you. One of the Galway Holmes. Mycroft Holmes is your brother? Works for Lord Hartington, eh? Chief Secretary, eh?'

"He had an irritating manner of putting 'eh' after each telegraphic phrase as a punctuation.

"It was then that Agnes Phillimore came in to welcome us. God, Watson, I was young and ardent in those days. Even now, as I look back with a more critical eye and colder blood, I acknowledge that she was rare and wonderful in her beauty. She held out her hand to me with a smile, but I saw at once that it lacked the warmth and friendship that I thought it had once held for me alone. Her speech was reserved, and she greeted me as a distant friend. Perhaps she had grown into a woman while I held to her image with boyish passion? It was impossible for me to acknowledge this at that time, but the passion was all on my side. Ah, immature youth, what else is there to say?

"We dined in somber mode that evening. Somber for me because I was wrestling with life's cruel realities; somber for the Phillimores because of the curse that hung over the house. We were just finishing the dessert when Agnes suddenly froze, her fork halfway to her mouth. Then Colonel Phillimore dropped his spoon with a crash on his plate and gave a piteous moan.

"In the silence that followed I heard it plainly. It was the sound of a sobbing child. It seemed to echo all around the room. Even Jack Phillimore looked distracted.

"I pushed back my chair and stood up, trying to pinpoint the direction from which the sounds came.

" 'What lies directly beneath this dining room?' I demanded of the Colonel. He was white in the face, too far gone with shock to answer me.

"I turned to Jack Phillimore. He replied with some nervousness.

" 'The cellars, Holmes.'

" 'Come, then,' I cried, grabbing a candelabra from the table and striding swiftly to the door.

"As I reached the door, Agnes stamped her foot twice on the floor as if agitated.

" 'Really, Mister Holmes,' she cried, 'you cannot do battle with an ethereal being!'

"I paused in the doorway to smile briefly at her.

" 'I doubt that I shall find an ethereal being, Miss Phillimore.'

"Jack Phillimore led the way to the cellar, and we searched it thoroughly, finding nothing.

" 'What did you expect to find?' demanded Phillimore, seeing my disappointment as we returned to the dining room.

" 'A small boy, corporeal in form and not a spirit,' I replied firmly.

" 'Would that it were so,' Agnes greeted our return without disguising her look of satisfaction that I could produce no physical entity in explanation. 'Do you not think that I have caused this house to be searched time and time again? My father is on the verge of madness. I do believe that he has come to the end of his composure. I fear for what he might do to himself.'

" 'And the day after tomorrow is his fiftieth birthday,' added Phillimore soberly.

"We were standing in the entrance to the dining room when Malone, the aging butler, answered a summons to the front door by the jangle of the bell.

" 'It's a Professor Moriarty,' he intoned.

"Moriarty was tall and thin, with a forehead domed in a white curve and deeply set eyes. His face protruded forward and had a curious habit of slowly oscillating from side to side in what, in the harsh judgment of my youth, I felt to be a curiously reptilian fashion. I suppose, looking back, he was handsome in a way and somewhat distinguished. He had been young for his professorship and there was no doubting the sharpness of his mind and intellect.

"Agnes greeted him with warmth while Phillimore was indifferent. As for myself, I felt I had to suppress my ill humor. He had come to join us for coffee and brandy and made sympathetic overtures to the Colonel over his apparent state of ill health.

" 'My offer still stands, dear sir,' he said. 'Best be rid of the abbey and the curse in one fell swoop. Not, of course, that you would lose it entirely, for when Agnes and I are married, you will always be a welcome guest here. . . .'

"Colonel Phillimore actually growled. A soft rumbling sound in the back of his throat, like an animal at bay and goaded into response.

" 'I intend to see this through. I refuse to be chased out of my home by a specter when Akbar Khan and his screaming Afghans could not budge me from the fort at Peiwar Pass. No, sir. Here I intend to stay and see my fiftieth birthday through.''

" 'I think you should at least consider James' offer, Father,' Agnes rebuked him. 'This whole business is affecting your nerves. Better get rid of the place and move to Dublin.'

" 'Nonsense!' snapped her father. 'I shall see it through. I will hear no more.'

"We went to bed early that night and, I confess, I spent some time analyzing my feelings for Agnes before dropping into a dozing slumber.

"The crying woke me. I hauled on a dressing gown and hastened to the window through which a full white moon sent its soft light. The cry was like a banshee's wail. It seemed to be coming from above me. I hastened from the room and in the corridor outside I came across Jack Phillimore, similarly attired in a dressing gown. His face looked ghastly.

" 'Tell me that I am not dreaming, Holmes,' he cried.

" 'Not unless we share a dream,' I replied tersely. " 'Do you have a revolver?'

"He looked startled.

" 'What do you hope to achieve with a revolver?' he demanded.

" 'I think it might be efficacious in dealing with ghosts, ghouls, and apparitions,' I smiled thinly.

"Phillimore shook his head.

" 'The guns are locked below in the gun room. My father has the key.'

" 'Ah well,' I replied in resignation, 'we can probably proceed without them. This crying is emanating from above. What's up there?'

" 'The turret room. That's where Father said he saw the apparition before.'

" 'Lead me to the turret room, then.'

"Spurred on by the urgency of my tone, Phillimore

turned to lead the way. We flew up the stairs of a circular tower and emerged onto a flat roof. At the far end of the building rose a similar, though larger tower or, more accurately, a round turret. Encircling it, ten feet above the roof level there ran a small balcony.

" 'My God!' cried Phillimore, halting so abruptly that I cannoned in to him.

"It took me a moment to recover before I saw what had caused his distress. On this balcony there stood the figure of a small boy. He was clearly lit in the bright moonlight and yet, yet I will tell you no lie, Watson, his entire body and clothes glowed with a strange luminescence. The boy it was who was letting out the eerie, wailing sounds.

" 'Do you see it, Holmes?' cried Phillimore.

" 'I see the young rascal, whoever he is!' I yelled, running toward the tower over the flat roof.

"Then the apparition was gone. How or where, I did not observe.

"I reached the base of the tower and looked for a way to scramble up to the balcony. There was only one way of egress from the roof. A small door in the tower which seemed clearly barred on the inside.

" 'Come, Phillimore, the child is escaping!' I cried in frustration.

" 'Escaping, eh?' It was the Colonel who emerged out of the darkness behind us. His face was ashen. He was clad only in his pajamas. 'Specters don't need to escape, eh! No, sir! Now that you have seen it, too, I can say I am not mad. At least, not mad, eh?'

" 'How do I get into the turret?' I demanded, ignoring the Colonel's ranting.

" 'Boarded up for years, Holmes,' Phillimore explained, moving to support his frail father for fear

the old man might topple over. 'There's no way anyone could have entered or left it.'

" 'Someone did,' I affirmed. 'That was no specter.
I think this has been arranged. I think you should
call in the police.'

"The Colonel refused to speak further of the matter
and retired to bed. I spent most of the night checking
the approaches to the turret room and was forced to
admit that all means of entrance and exit seemed
perfectly secured. But I was sure that when I started
to run across the roof toward the tower, the boy had
bobbed away with such a startled expression that no
self-respecting ghost in the middle of haunting would
have assumed.

"The next morning, over breakfast, I was forceful
in my exhortations to the Colonel that he should put
the matter forthwith in the hands of the local police.
I told him that I had no doubts that some bizarre
game was afoot. The Colonel had recovered some of
his equilibrium and listened attentively to my argu-
ments.

"Surprisingly, the opposition came from Agnes.
She was still in favor of her father departing the
house and putting an end to the curse.

"We were just finishing breakfast when Malone announced the arrival of Professor Moriarty.

"Agnes went to join him in the library while we
three finished our meal, by the end of which, Colonel
Phillimore had made up his mind to follow my advice. It was decided that we accompany Colonel Phillimore directly after breakfast to discuss the matter
with the local Inspector of the Royal Irish Constabulary. Agnes and Moriarty joined us and, having
heard the story from Agnes, Moriarty actually said
that it was the best course of action, although Agnes

still had her doubts. In fact, Moriarty offered to accompany us. Agnes excused herself a little ungraciously, I thought, because she had arranged to make an inventory of the wines in the cellar.

"So the Colonel, Phillimore, Moriarty, and I agreed to walk the two miles into the town. It must be observed that a few miles' walk was nothing for those who lived in the country in those days. Now, in London, everyone is forever hailing hansom carriages even if they merely desire to journey to the end of the street.

"We left the house and began to stroll down the path. We had barely gone twenty yards when the Colonel, casting at eye at the sky, excused himself and said he needed his umbrella and would be but a moment. He turned, hurried back to his front door, and entered. That was when he disappeared from this world forever.

"The three of us waited patiently for a few moments. Moriarty then said that if we continued to stroll at an easy pace, the Colonel would catch us up. Yet when we reached the gates of the estate, I began to grow concerned that there was still no sign of the Colonel. I caused our party to wait at the gates. Ten minutes passed, and then I felt I should return to find out what had delayed the Colonel.

"The umbrella was still in the hall stand. There was no sign of the Colonel. I rang the bell for old Malone and he swore that as far as he was aware the Colonel had left with us and had not returned. There was no budging him on that point. Grumbling more than a little, he set off to the Colonel's room; I went to the study. Soon the entire house was being searched as Jack Phillimore and Moriarty arrived back to discover the cause of the delay.

"It was then that Agnes emerged from the cellars, looking a little disheveled, an inventory in her hand. When she heard that her father had simply vanished, she grew distraught and Malone had to fetch the brandy.

"In the wine cellar, she told me, she had heard and seen nothing. Moriarty volunteered to search the cellar just to make the examination of the house complete. I told Phillimore to look after his sister and accompanied Moriarty. While I disliked the man, there was no doubt that Moriarty could hardly have engineered the Colonel's disappearance as he had left the house with us and remained with us outside the house. Naturally, our search of the cellars proved futile. They were large and one could probably have hidden a whole army in them if one so desired. But the entrance from the hall led to the area used for wine storage, and no one could have descended into the cellar without passing this area and thus being seen by Agnes. No answer to Colonel James Phillimore's disappearance presented itself to me.

"I spent a week at Tullyfane attempting to form some conclusion. The local RIC eventually gave up the search. I had to return to Oxford, and it became obvious to me that neither Agnes nor Moriarty required my company further. After that, I had but one letter from Jack Phillimore and this several months later and postmarked at Marseille.

"Apparently, at the end of two weeks a suicide note was found in the Colonel's desk stating that he could not stand the strange hauntings in Tullyfane Abbey. Rather than await the terrible death on his fiftieth birthday, he proposed to put an end to it himself. There was attached a new will, giving the estate to Agnes in acknowledgment of her forthcoming marriage and the house in Stephen's Green to Jack. Phillimore wrote that although the will was bizarre, and there was no proof of his father's death, he nevertheless had refused to contest it. I heard later that this was against the advice of Phillimore's solicitor. But it seemed that Jack Phillimore wanted no part of the curse or the estate. He wished his sister joy of it and then took himself to Africa as a missionary where, two years later, I heard that he had been killed in some native uprising in British East Africa. It was not even on his fiftieth birthday. So much for curses.

"And Agnes Phillimore? She married James Moriarty and the property passed to him. She was dead within six months. She drowned in a boating accident when Moriarty was taking her to Beginish, just off the Kerry coast, to show her the columnar basaltic formations similar to those of the Giant's Causeway. Moriarty was the only survivor of the tragedy.

"He sold Tullyfane Abbey and its estate to an American and moved to London to become a gentleman of leisure, although his money was soon squandered due to his dissipated lifestyle. He resorted to more overt illegal activities to replenish his wealth. I have not called him the 'Napoleon of crime' without cause.

"As for Tullyfane, the American tried to run the estate, but fell foul of the Land Wars of a few years ago when the Land Leaguers forced radical changes in the way the great estates in Ireland were run. That was when a new word was added to the language—boycott—when the Land Leaguers ostracized Charles Boycott, the estate agent of Lord Erne at Lough Mask. The American pulled out of Tullyfane Abbey, which fell into ruin and became derelict.

"Without being able to find out what happened when James Phillimore stepped back beyond his front door to retrieve his umbrella, I was unable to bring the blame to where, I believed with every fiber in my body, it lay; namely, to James Moriarty. I believe that it was Moriarty who planned the whole dastardly scheme of obtaining the estate which he presumed would set him up for life. He was not in love with poor Agnes. He saw her as the quick means of becoming rich and not content to wait for her marriage portion, I believe he forged the suicide note and will and then found an ingenious way to dispatch the Colonel, having failed to drive him insane by playing on the curse. Once he had secured the estate, poor Agnes became dispensable.

"How he worked the curse, I was not sure until a singular event was reported to me some years later.

"It was in London, only a few years ago that I happened to encounter Bram Stoker's younger brother, George. Like most of the Stoker brothers, with the exception of Bram, George had gone into medicine and was a Licentiate of the Royal College of Surgeons in Dublin. George had just married a lady from County Kerry, actually the sister of The McGillycuddy of the Reeks, one of the old Gaelic nobility.

"It was George who supplied me with an important piece of the jigsaw. He was actually informed of the occurrence by none other than his brother-in-law, Dennis McGillycuddy, who had been a witness to the event.

"About a year after the occurrences at Tullyfane Abbey, the body of a young boy was found in an old mine working in the Reeks. I should explain that the Reeks are the mountains on the Iveragh Peninsula which are the highest peaks in Ireland and, of course, Tullyfane stands in their shadows. The boy's body had not badly decomposed because it had lain in the ice-cold temperatures of the small lochs one gets in the area. It so happened that a well-known Dublin medical man, Dr. John MacDonnell, the first person to perform an operation under anesthetic in Ireland, was staying in Killarney. He agreed to perform the autopsy because the local coroner had noticed a peculiar aspect to the body; he observed that in the dark the corpse of the boy was glowing.

"MacDonnell found that the entire body of the boy had been coated in a waxy yellow substance; indeed, it was the cause of death for it had so clogged the pores of his skin that the unfortunate child had simply been asphyxiated. Upon analysis, it was discerned that the substance was a form of natural phosphorus, found in the caves in the area. I immediately realized the significance of this.

"The child, so I presumed, was one of the hapless and miserable wretches doomed to wander the byways of Ireland, perhaps orphaned during the failure of the potato crops in 1871, which had spread starvation and typhus among the peasants. Moriarty had forced or persuaded him to act the part of the wailing child whom we had observed. This child was our specter, appearing now and then at Moriarty's command to scream and cry in certain places. The phosphorus would have emitted the ethereal glow.

"Having served his purpose, Moriarty, knowing well the properties of the waxy substance with which he had coated the child's body, left the child to suffocate and dumped the body in the mountains.

I waited for some time after Holmes had finished the story and then I ventured to ask the question to which he had, so far, provided no answer. As I did so, I made the following preamble.

"Accepting that Moriarty had accomplished a fiendish scheme to enrich himself and that it was only in retrospect you realized how he managed to use the child to impersonate a specter . . ."

Holmes breathed out sharply as he interrupted.

"It is a failure of my deductive capabilities that I have no wish to advertise, Watson."

"Yet there is one thing—just how did Moriarty manage to spirit away the body of James Phillimore after he stepped back inside the door of the house to retrieve his umbrella? By our own statement, Moriarty, Jack Phillimore, and yourself were all together, waiting for the Colonel, outside his house. The family retainer, old Malone, swore the Colonel did not reenter the house. How was it done? Was Malone in the pay of Moriarty?"

"It was a thought that crossed my mind. The RIC likewise questioned old Malone very closely and came to the conclusion that he was part of no plot. In fact, Malone could not say one way or another if the Colonel had returned as he was in the kitchen with two housemaids as witnesses at the time."

"And Agnes . . . ?"

"Agnes was in the cellar. She saw nothing. When all is said and done, there is no logical answer. James Phillimore vanished the moment he stepped back over the threshold. I have thought about every conceivable explanation for the last twenty years and have come to no suitable explanation except one . . ."

"Which is?"

"The powers of darkness were exalted that day, and Moriarty had made a pact with the devil, selling his soul for his ambition."

I stared at Holmes for a moment. I had never seen him admit to any explanation of events that was not in keeping with scientific logic. Was he correct that the answer lay with the supernatural, or was he merely covering up for the fact of his own lack of knowledge or, even, more horrific, to my susceptibilities, did the truth lie in some part of my old friend's mind which he refused to admit even to himself?

Pinned to John H. Watson's manuscript was a small yellowing cutting from the *Kerry Evening News;* alas the date had not been noted.

"During the recent building of an RIC Barracks on the ruins of Tullyfane Abbey, a well-preserved male skeleton was discovered. Sub-Inspector Dalton told our reporter that it could not be estimated how long the skeleton had lain there. The precise location was in a bricked-up area of the former cellars of the abbey.

"Doctor Simms-Taafe said that he adduced, from the condition of the skeleton, that it had belonged to a man in mid life who had met his demise within the last twenty or thirty yeas. The back of the skull had been smashed in due to a severe blow, which might account for the death.

"Sub-Inspector Dalton opined that the death might well be linked with the disappearance of Colonel Phillimore, then the owner of Tullyfane Abbey, some thirty years ago. As the next owner, Professor James Moriarty was reported to have met his death in Switzerland, the last owner having been an American who returned to his homeland, and the Phillimores being no longer domiciled in the country, the RIC are placing the matter in their file of unsolved, suspicious deaths."

A few lines were scrawled on the cutting in Dr. Watson's hand which ran: "I think it was obvious that Colonel Phillimore was murdered as soon as he reentered the house. I have come to believe that the truth did lie in a dark recess of my old friend's mind which he refused to admit was the grotesque and terrible truth of the affair. Patricide, even at the instigation of a lover with whom one is besotted, is the most hideous crime of all. Could it be that Holmes had come to regard the young woman herself as representing the powers of darkness?" The last sentence was heavily underscored.

DOUBTING THOMAS

By Kristine Kathryn Rusch

Kristine Kathryn Rusch is an award-winning fiction writer. Her novella, *The Gallery of His Dreams,* won the Locus Award for best short fiction. Her body of fiction work won her the John W. Campbell Award, given in 1991 in Europe. She has been nominated for several dozen fiction awards, and her short work has been reprinted in six *Year's Best* collections. She has published twenty novels under her own name. She has sold forty-one in total, including pseudonymous books. Her novels have been published in seven languages, and have spent several weeks on the *USA Today* Bestseller list and *The Wall Street Journal* Bestseller list. She has written a number of *Star Trek* novels with her husband, Dean Wesley Smith, including a book in last summer's crossover series called *New Earth.* She is the former editor of the prestigious *Magazine of Fantasy and Science Fiction*, for which she won a Hugo. Before that, she and Dean Wesley Smith started and ran Pulphouse Publishing, a science fiction and mystery press in Eugene. She lives and works on the Oregon coast.

Tommy Ulrick discovered the scam when he was six. He remembered everything about the night clearly: the winter dampness in the air, the smell of woodsmoke mixed with ocean, waking on his flannel sheets with an urgency that seemed only to happen

in childhood. He slipped out of bed and hurried to
the bathroom—one of those herky-jerky emergencies
where he jiggled all the way, holding himself, and
praying he'd arrive on time.

Which he did, just barely. He remembered the relief, and as the relief grew, so did his chill. Someone
had left the large bathroom window open, letting the
December cold inside, allowing people on the street
below to see his most private moment.

He glanced out—still too compromised to pull the
window closed—to see if anyone was watching. The
neighborhood Christmas lights were off, the house
lights were off, even the few porch lights that stayed
on late were off. Only the streetlight broke the darkness, casting pools of pale light through the thin fog.

He was safe. No one could see him. He shook himself off, tucked himself back inside his flannel pajamas, reached to close the window—and froze.

There was movement on the roof of the house
across the street.

Well, not a house, actually. It was too big to be a
house. It was the Sutter place, which his mother used
to call, "the only bona fide mansion on the Central
Oregon Coast." Later when he learned the history of
it, when he was older and into such things, he discovered that his mother had been wrong—there had
been other mansions, just none as visible, none quite
as centrally located as the one on the street below
their little two-bedroom ranch.

Still he struggled, trying to get the window closed,
the wind blowing against him, plastering the ice-cold
snap buttons against his bare chest. Somehow the
battle became him against the window, and he was
losing.

Then he saw the movement again. And what had

looked like shadows became three men dressed as Santa Claus, dark sacks against their backs, struggling with the dormer on the side of the house.

He watched, horrified, as they tugged it open. Then they disappeared inside, one by one, none of them looking up at him, none of them noticing.

Then, from inside, white-gloved hands pulled the dormer closed.

Oh, Tommy did all the right things. He woke his parents, who called the police. His dad stared out the bathroom window a long time, as if he could see something different. Tommy stared too, pointed out the sleigh on the front lawn, saying it hadn't been there when he saw the men, but his dad just ignored him.

So did the police after they arrived. They walked around the Sutter place, saw no evidence of false entry, saw nothing out of the ordinary, and said so. They came up to Tommy's house, listened to his story, and told his parents not to let him watch so much television.

Then they left.

Tommy's mom made him use the bathroom one more time before he went to bed. No one had closed the window and as he looked out on the mansion below, he saw that the sleigh was gone.

Only this time, he didn't tell anyone. He sneaked back to bed, pulled the covers to his chin, and shivered for the rest of the night.

Christmas was never the same after that. Tommy made sure there were no Santa Claus decorations in the house. He wouldn't sit on the Santa man's lap at the mall, and he wouldn't watch any Santa shows on television. He told his parents that he didn't believe, and they seemed saddened by it, but they thought it understandable.

After all, the Sutter place had been robbed that night. Apparently the police had arrived to late to do anything about it. Tommy had seen something. Turned out the dormer window was askew. There was even a bit of extra ash in the fireplace that next morning, and men's shoe prints tracking all over the house.

One of the police officers came by to apologize and to take Tommy's statement again. The theory was that the men had used the Santa Claus outfits as a ruse to get into the house, figuring they could pose on the roof like Christmas decorations if a car went by.

Brilliant, the police called it.

Humbug, Tommy would have said to himself if he had known the word then. Complete and total humbug.

He had seen the dark side of Santa, and was never ever going to be the same again.

Childhood lost, cynicism found. Outwardly, Tommy Ulrick was the same as all the other little boys of his age, unless someone mentioned Santa Claus. It got so bad that his parents used to warn people not to use the name. At Christmas, he became sullen and fearful, and there didn't seem to be anything anyone could do about it.

His parents thought he would grow out of it. It was a phase, they said, brought on by a traumatic childhood event, and, as Tommy got older and realized that his attitude toward the Jolly Old Elf was socially unacceptable, he stopped talking about it.

Instead, he turned inward. He studied. He learned everything he could about the enemy, and what he saw he didn't like.

It was, he came to understand, the biggest fraud ever perpetrated on the public. A round-cheeked old man masquerading as a saint who gave toys to children, all the while using those children to hide his own greed. In fact, the old man used his scam to teach greed.

In Tommy—now Thomas—Ulrick's life, Christmas ceased to be about love and peace and goodwill toward all men. Instead, it turned into a holiday about stuff. Who bought the most, who spent the most, who got the most. Even people who belonged to other religions gave into the Christmas frenzy. They treated it as a secular holiday, so their kids wouldn't be left out of the stuff-getting.

It was, Tomas realized, a shameful thing.

And when he turned thirty, he'd finally had enough.

Later, he figured, everything culminated that year. His parents had died in a car accident the year before. He'd taken a leave of absence from his big city reporter's position—a forced leave of absence: reporters are supposed to do everything they can to get a story, but apparently "everything" did *not* include breaking a few minor privacy laws. His third fiancée left him just like all the others had when she realized that he hated Christmas. Apparently his fiancées could tolerate different religions, different attitudes toward money, but not a bah-humbugish attitude toward Christmas.

It was, he discovered, the ultimate deal-breaker.

So on Christmas Eve of that year, he sat down at

his kitchen table, in his comfortable two-bedroom ranch style house in the Portland suburb of Beaverton, and, like he used to do when he was starting an article, made a list.

1. Adults all acknowledge there is no Santa Claus.
2. Children are encouraged to believe in Santa Claus.
3. Santa doesn't give gifts. Parents do, thus perpetuating the myth.
4. From Halloween on, people see Santa Claus on the streets, and think nothing of it.
5. People decorate their homes with Santa Claus iconography, making it easy for fake Santas to hide.
6. The only thing that people do when they see a Santa is give him something. (Does the Salvation Army really still exist? Do they sanction those little red change boxes? Is this a direct part of the scam or is this something else encouraged by the Evil Santa Brigade?)
7. Was the lump of coal more than a metaphor? Perhaps, in the early years, the Santa thieves left only a lump of coal when they cleaned out a house.
8. Naughty or nice. Who's to determine? Based on what criteria?
9. Robberies increase supposedly because houses are more vulnerable. People in the holiday spirit aren't as vigilant.
10. Fires increase. Arson to cover up robberies?
11. More people commit suicide during the holidays than at any other time of the year. Real suicides? Or more coverups—killed when they

discover someone who isn't supposed to be in the house?

12. Was Clement Moore in on this?

13. How long has this been going on?

Thomas stopped, chilled to the bone. One man against a centuries-old tradition of duplicity and thievery.

He had to stop this. But how?

It came to him as he woke up the next morning. There had to be a grain of truth to everything in the myth.

He sat up, his frayed cotton sheets pooled around his waist. He was willing to believe that the original Santa thieves went down chimneys, just like the stories. A roof was a great access point for a robber, and a hundred years ago, children used to climb into chimneys to clean them. Skinny children, but children nonetheless. He didn't believe that fat old men slid down chimneys—but that was the impossibility that made the idea seem so ludicrous. Better to go back to the truth.

And he would wager that a lot of Santa's Helpers went through the front doors, too.

He rubbed his hands together. He felt like he was finally onto something.

He got out of bed, and grabbed his robe, sliding it on as he made his way to the kitchen. He didn't believe that Santa operated from the North Pole—too cold, too remote, too impractical—but he would wager that there was a hideout. It didn't have to be very big—not like the factory portrayed in all those stupid Christmas movies. After all, Santa wasn't making toys. He was stealing stuff.

The hideout had to be a place to run to, a place to hide, a place to split up the wealth, like the Hole-in-the-Wall of Western Outlaw lore.

And if he found the Hole in the Wall, the hideout, he found the bad guys.

He had the power to stop this scam once and for all.

It was easier than he thought. It just took time.

After all, he had data from thirty years of collecting. His newspaper training made him an excellent sleuth. He searched for robberies, fires, and suicides, throwing in a few surprise deaths from heart failure and a couple of thwarted attempts.

He made a cybermap and marked out all the hits in the United States for the last fifty years, searching for a pattern—and what he found terrified him. If his assumptions were true, and he had no reason to think they weren't—then he was dealing with something so large that he could barely contemplate it.

Every state got hit, every county, every town—and in the right statistical proportions. In fact, that's what gave the plot away. The statistics were too perfect. No cluster of suicides in Denver in any one year, for example, or no extra fires in San Jose. Apparently the statisticians hadn't noticed that every city had just about the same number of robberies, deaths, and fires in the weeks before Christmas. The ever-so-slight variations came from what he would consider to be unconnected events—gang killings, insurance fraud arson, and the robberies caused by non-affiliated thieves (whom, he noted, usually got caught).

He expanded his search to include Britain and western Europe, and found fewer incidences there, although those, too, were statistically perfect. Going back a hundred years, he found higher incidences in England; he figured that was probably where the scam originated.

Thomas spent weeks analyzing the information and figured that the hideout was in the United States where the pickings were good. There were probably several subhideouts, but the main one—if he were the guy planning all of this—had to be centrally located.

Unless . . .

He paused, hands over the keys, as inspiration struck again.

All those greeting cards, posters, t-shirts. *Images* everywhere of Santa in swimsuit and loud floral-print shirt, lounging in a beach chair on the sand, chubby ankles crossed while he stared at a pristine ocean. Those pictures never depicted Santa on a Hawaiian beach or relaxing on California's sultry sands.

Santa was always in Florida, generally Miami Beach, and he was always grinning at the camera.

Taunting someone—taunting Thomas—to find him.

Thomas scanned the Florida information. The farther south he went, the more evidence he found—in the lack of evidence, of course. Fewer Christmas fires (statistically attributable to the warm weather, the lack of heaters, the fact that Christmas trees didn't dry out as quickly), fewer suicides (statistically attributable the advanced age of the population; if they lived that long, they wouldn't throw what was left away), and surprisingly, given the wealth of the area, fewer robberies (statistically attributable to the fact that most people traveled *to* Florida during the holidays; fewer vacant homes). Heart attacks were up, but they didn't fall into his mathematical model because very few of those were a surprise, again given the advanced age of the population.

He went to his hardcopy cabinet and pulled one of his many Santa souvenirs out of the postcard file. Santa, wearing sunglasses five sizes too big, a red-and-orange-checked shirt a size too small, and matching orange shorts which revealed pale hairy legs, waved out of the image. *Wish You Were Here*, said the red lettering across the top.

"I will be," he promised the Jolly Old Elf. "Soon."

For some reason, the thievery began again in Gainesville. Orlando was safe—maybe because Santa liked it there, or spread out his Florida vacation spots—but anything north of Gainesville was as fair a target as the rest of the western world.

He spent the months before Christmas studying the maps, searching for patterns. He finally found them. Simple, elegant, and difficult to see. The thieves worked in an alphabetical or numerical pattern by street name. Each state was assigned a letter or number, and then the pattern shifted clockwise from year to year. In other words, if Maine was the "A" street in the first year, the next year it would be the "Z" street. The pattern worked the same with numbers.

Once the state's number or letter had been assigned, the thieves picked the exact street according to housing prices and quality of neighborhood. Then they probably staked a few houses out. It sounded like a lot of work, but it wasn't.

If he was right, that year, Florida was the "D" and "30th" state. Gainesville was a number town—there were a lot of thirties. Southwest thirties, thirties with streets, thirties with avenues. Thomas scanned all the possible thirties and came up with what he considered to be a jackpot—30th Terrace, an area where the homes were worth a half million or more with lots of acreage, right in the middle of the city. Right smack in the center of that region was a house that had been owned for a couple of decades by the same people, philanthropists by their profile, who didn't believe in home security systems.

He did a bit more research, discovered the home's owners boarded their dog and canceled their newspaper delivery every year just before Christmas. He didn't even break a sweat to find out that information. He imagined the Santa Stealers had all of this down to a science.

On December 18, he had lunch with fiancée number three—for old times sake, he said—and told her he was going out of town. He gave her a key to his safe deposit box, and told her to open it if he wasn't back by the first of the year.

She looked at him as if he were crazy, which was how she had been looking at him for the last year or more. But she agreed, which was all that mattered.

Then he flew to Orlando, rented a black sports car, and drove to Gainesville.

He hadn't done a real honest-to-god stakeout in nearly five years. Back when he was young and hungry, he got a lot of his information just spying on people. The older he got, the more he used legal information obtained through records, and then as he learned his way around computers, he found more and more fascinating things illegally.

But this was no longer a computer sort of case. This required diligence, wakefulness, and quick-thinking.

He slept during the day at a cheap hotel on the highway and watched the empty house at night. No neighbors nearby to report him, no big dogs to bark. By December 22, he was beginning to think the house was too perfect, or his research suspect. He hadn't seen hide nor hair of a sleigh or eight tiny reindeer or anything else near the target house.

But he knew that these Santa Bandits struck all the way through December 25. He just had to be patient.

And finally, at 4 AM on the morning of December 24, his patience paid off. He was keeping himself awake by making condensation rings on the driver's side window, when he heard a car engine, a sound he hadn't heard after midnight in this neighborhood since he started his vigil.

He slumped down in the sports car's bucket seat, and watched as a dark colored late model minivan with its lights off pulled into the house's long gravel driveway. When he was sure the occupants could no longer see his car, he grabbed his binoculars and climbed over the shifting column to the passenger seat. There he leaned against the dash and watched.

A chill ran up his spine, and for a moment, he touched his six-year-old self.

Instead he focused on the movement he saw on the empty house's roof. Three men, just like he had seen twenty-four years before, dressed as Santa, carrying black bags over their shoulders—empty bags. The men balanced precariously on the steep roof, climbing to its peak. Then the first man reached over and pulled open a window that probably led to an attic. He slid in, headfirst, as if he were diving into a pool.

The other two followed.

And Thomas, his six-year-old self still closer to the

surface than he wanted the boy to be, slipped out of the car to pee.

Less than an hour later, the men emerged the way they entered, full bags over their shoulders. They slid down the back roof, presumably to the van, which he hadn't been able to see.

Then, lights out, it left the driveway.

Thomas waited until it was nearly a block away before he started the rental. He followed, his lights out, too, keeping a discreet distance.

The van's lights came on at the end of 30th Terrace, and from then on all driving was normal. Thomas tailed them, mentally congratulating himself for a) practicing that skill a lot before and b) renting a sports car. He was able to keep up.

As he drove, he called 911 and reported the break-in.

Step one of his plan.

Just as he expected, when they hit the highway, they headed south. But they didn't go to Miami, like he expected.

Instead, they went to Orlando, where the waiters sang, men dressed like giant mice, and make-believe was part of the air.

His enemy was craftier than even Thomas thought. He should have known that Miami Beach was a ruse. It was the Florida part with the grain of truth to it.

When they finally stopped, he felt a surge of disappointment. He couldn't help himself. He had been hoping for something interesting, something unique.

Instead, they pulled into a strip mall in one of the outlying areas of Orlando, where the rents were cheaper and the businesses cheesier. They drove around back and he followed, but he knew where they were going. He didn't have to be a rocket scientist to figure that one out.

The biggest store on the strip. It had a candy-cane striped door, giant toy soldiers guarding either side. Decorated Christmas trees stood in front of each window, and a couple of plaster elves looked like they had just finished painting the store's name on its sign: *The Christmas Cottage.*

But that wasn't the biggest giveaway. The biggest giveaway were the Santa statues—all three of them. On the roof.

Thomas had his video camera, his microcassette tape recorder, and a digital camera with a telephoto lens. As he got out of the car, he called 911, said he saw some suspicious activity at The Christmas Cottage, and that he was getting out of his car to investigate.

The dispatcher urged him not to, of course, but he hung up, as if he were a zealous citizen. Which, he supposed, he was.

He left the digital zoom in the car, clicked on the microcassette recorder, and headed toward the back. The sun was just starting to come up, sending pale yellow light across the flat Florida landscape.

As he expected, the van was parked directly behind The Christmas Cottage. The store's back doors were open, and no one was in sight.

He slipped inside. The back of the store was bigger than he thought, almost a store in and of itself. There was an assortment of boxes, all of them clearly merchandise, some open with ornaments or tinsel hanging out. But an open storage door on the left side revealed items that didn't belong in a Christmas store.

He moved toward it as quietly as he could. Voices were coming from the storefront, talking amiably, as if someone were telling a story. Probably relating the events of the night.

When he got closer to the storage door, he stopped and made sure he was in shadow. He needed a place to hide if the thieves came back. He found the perfect spot behind a man-sized box, and set to work.

With shaking hands he raised the video camera to his right eye. Mentally, he cataloged as he went: coin collections, artwork, and jewelry—so much jewelry that his entire body felt numb. Then there was silver—from flatware to pitchers, the antiques (all small enough to carry), and the occasional high-end television.

He was nearly done with a white-gloved hand grabbed his wrist, pulling the camcorder down.

"Ho, ho, ho," a deep voice said with more cheer than seemed appropriate to the situation.

Another hand took the camcorder away. Thomas started to protest, but stopped. He was busted. He had to think clearly now.

He turned slowly, and tried not to let his surprise show.

The man standing behind him was no more than five feet tall, with white hair down to his shoulders and a fluffy white beard. He was wearing a red suit with real fur, and shiny black boots. He ho-hoed again and his stomach jiggled, just like that infamous bowl full of jelly. He had an unlit pipe in his bow-shaped mouth, and his blue eyes did twinkle merrily—at Thomas' expense.

All of the images of Santa were on the mark—if one ignored the height problem.

"Little Tommy Ulrick," the man said. "I wondered if you would be a problem."

"H–How do you know who I am?" Thomas asked.

The man tsk-tsked. "Tommy, of all people, you have to ask? I'm Santa. I know everything."

"Yeah," Thomas said, blessing his own forethought in having the microcassette recorder running. "That's why you have to steal for a living."

Claus—or whoever he was—sighed. "Ah, an explanation man. Somehow I would have thought you had it all worked out, Tommy."

"Thomas. And all I want to know is why."

"Not how? Not all the particulars?"

"No," Thomas said. He finally had control of his voice again. "Only why."

Claus' twinkling eyes narrowed. "I wouldn't have figured you for a true believer."

"I'm not," Thomas said. "I'm a reporter. I have a Need to Know."

Claus made a rude sound. "A need to spy, you mean. Which I would have thought that incident when you were six cured you of."

"Naw," Thomas said. "Just made me even more curious. So why do you do it?"

Claus sighed. "I hate this part."

His friends came through the doorway. They were even shorter. Even though they were wearing jeans and ratty Marlins t-shirts, they looked like Santa's elves. Which they probably were.

"Another one, Boss?"

"Whatcha gonna do this time?"

Claus ignored them. Instead he stared at Thomas. "Look, I'll split the loot with you fifty-fifty if you just don't ask for the explanation."

"Too late," Thomas said. "I already did."

One of the elves laughed. "Gotta tell him, Boss. Don't you just hate those magic rules?"

"How much time do we have?" the other elf asked.

"If he called 911, maybe ten more minutes."

"Plenty of time, Boss."

"Someone trained you, right?" Thomas asked. "This is like a worldwide scam that's been going on for centuries. The original Santa was, what? a real Fagan? A man who trained his cohorts from childhood?"

"I am the original Santa," Claus said.

· This time it was Thomas' turn to make the rude noise.

"I *am*," Claus said. He turned to the elves. "I really do hate this part."

"Get it over with, Boss," the first elf said, then crossed his arms and leaned against the wall. "I'm keeping an ear out for the coppers."

"Pigs," the other elf corrected.

Thomas frowned at them. Coppers? Pigs? Was their slang really out of date? Or were they faking it just for him?

"You figured it out," Claus said. "You know that part of the myth is true, and part of it is convenient. Well, I'm just a jolly old elf. Really."

"More like a leprechaun," the elf said.

"Or even that Coyote character," the other elf said.

"A trickster?" Thomas asked. That part he hadn't figured out.

Claus put one finger beside his nose and pointed at Thomas with the other hand. Thomas ducked, as if he expected something magical to happen to him.

Claus chuckled, a deep rolling laugh that seemed to fill the room. "You *do* believe."

"I knew something was up," Thomas said. "I figured you were in Florida."

"But you don't know why, and it bothers you." Claus let his fingers drop.

"Yes," Thomas said. If he could keep the trio talking, they'd stay here until the cops arrived. Then he'd have everything on tape. "If you have magic, why steal?"

"Magic requires belief. A few people still believe, but for the most part, rationalists have taken over. About the time Claus started, don't you know."

Thomas did know. He just hadn't put it together.

"So," Claus said, "if I can get people to believe in a jolly old elf for part of a year, why then, I have a bit of my powers. Not all, anymore. Just enough."

"But why use them to steal?"

Claus frowned. "An immortal has-been needs a way to maintain his lifestyle."

"At the expense of people's homes? At the expense of their lives?"

"Oh, crap, Boss," one of the elves said. "This is a live one."

Claus continued to ignore them. "Mistakes happen," he said. "The deaths are always regrettable."

"Regrettable?" Thomas' voice rose. Then he cleared his throat, too late, of course. They'd probably already heard the panic.

"I think I hear sirens, Boss," one of the elves said.

"Me, too." The second elf's ears—which really were pointed—started to twitch.

"You go," Claus said. "I'll handle this guy."

"Boss, we're going to need a new hideout," the first elf said.

"We'll worry about that later. Just go."

They scurried out the back and closed the double doors. After a moment, Thomas heard the van start.

Claus was smiling at him. It wasn't a nice smile. "I have so many options. I could let those cops you called find you here with the loot. I could kill you. Or I could make use of you."

"You'd make me a part of your thieving band?"

"Don't be silly," Claus said. "You wouldn't last a year. I can see through to Naughty and Nice, and you got waaaay too much Nice in you. That's probably why you searched me out, even though you say it's for the story."

He squeezed Thomas' wrist just a little harder. For an old man, he was very strong.

"Story," Claus muttered. "I wish I could use you for the story. But times have changed."

"Is that what the elves were alluding to? Someone else has caught you?"

"You'll kick yourself when I tell you." Claus grinned. His teeth were pointed, almost fanged. Thomas wondered how he ever found this face pleasant.

"Clement Moore," Thomas said softly.

" ' 'Twas the Night Before Christmas.' Same day, different year. Different century." Claus tilted his head, looking thoughtful. "Didn't have computers then. We weren't as accurate in knowing who'd be home and who wouldn't be. *He* had children I could threaten. You keep losing your fiancées."

"You know that?"

"My mind is full of useless information, all of it relating to goodness or badness. You'd think magic would be great—and it probably would if someone got the stuff of stories, you know, the ability to make things disappear, being able to fly things across a room. But no. I get stupid talents. Seeing people while they sleep. They lay in one position for a while, sigh, and roll over. Nothing exciting there. And the naughty and nice stuff? Good for the occasional blackmail, but nothing more."

Claus rolled his tiny eyes. Thomas strained to hear those sirens. But he couldn't, not yet. How good were those elfin ears?

"I'd like to pat you on the head and tell you to write a nice poem, filled with *my* lies, of course, and a little bit of the truth," Claus said. "But these days, the myth-making machine is self-generating. Who'd've known what a boon television would be?"

"Who'd've known?" Thomas asked. He swallowed, wondering if he could shake himself free, and get out of those double doors before the Jolly Old Elf caught him. Probably. It would be worth a try.

"So," Claus said, "I think I'll just let you go."

Thomas had been concentrating so much on escaping that he almost missed what Claus said. "What?"

"I'm letting you go." Claus dropped Thomas' wrist like it contaminated him. "Toddle on."

"But they'll catch you."

"No, they won't," Claus said, going to the storage area, dropping, and locking the door.

"I'll tell," Thomas said.

"Of course you will." Claus grinned. "But who's going to believe you?"

No one, it turned out. Not the cops who showed up, only to be greeted by the big man himself ("Sorry to bother you, officers. We got an early morning shipment and this man was worried."), not Thomas' old editor ("Tom, I say this only as a friend. Counseling.

Lots of counseling.") and especially not fiancée number three ("Don't ever call me again. Ever!").

In the end, there was nothing he could do. Oh, he called and reported a few break-ins before they occurred, but that only brought him to the attention of the police—and not in a good way. And then he tried to warn potential victims, which only made his police surveillance worse. He soon figured that if he continued along this path, he would be arrested for the crimes himself.

And to make matters worse, every January, he got a postcard from Florida—that year's Santa postcard, which always had the happy "Wish You Were Here!" on the front. On the back was just a scrawled number.

That first year he had no idea what the number meant. But the second year, after he mapped the robberies, he knew.

Total profits, after expenses, of course. Never less than ten million dollars. Tax free.

The old guy could have quit years ago. But he didn't. He wasn't doing it for the money. He was addicted to the belief.

And Thomas, whom everyone doubted, understood why.

THE WHITEVIPER SCROLLS

by David Bischoff

David Bischoff has been a professional writer for twenty-five years, and the number of his books is nearing the century mark. He has written teleplays and nonfiction and has recently been called "The best wrestling writer in the world" by *The Washington Post* for his article work for *Rampage* magazine. His new novel is *Philip K. Dick High*. His new story collection is *Tripping the Dark Fantastic*, both from Wildside Press. He can be reached at: DaveBisch@aol.com

I guess the most satisfying thing about skewering an elf is the way those damned pointed ears wiggle when you run the bastards through.

I mean, dwarves just grunt and shit themselves. Halflings? They shriek enough to burst your eardrums. Men? I try to stick to creatures smaller than me if I'm going to kill something face to face. (And as for women, I far prefer to skewer fair maidens with something other than my sword.)

But elves . . . ah . . . like take that Robin Goodfellow Junior fellow back in the Rainbow Year, back in my prime when King Arkok's army was lootin' and rapin' the Willowlands. I sneaked up on the guy watering the foliage (I tend to skulk around the peripheries of battle . . . lots safer!) and put my sword between his backbone and shoulder so hard, it pinned him to a spruce tree! Damn me, if those fey pointy ears of his didn't turn and wiggle and flap like they were wings trying to drag that offal offspring to Elf Vahalla along with his song-chirping soul.

Maybe the first elf I ever killed was the best, though, and that's what I want to talk about today—

Grompole! Is that Dictation Gem fading? Yes, I believe it is. Dunce! Troll dropping! Have a taste of this with your breakfast!

Now stop your screaming and put a new one in! I said, stop mewling! A little blood is not going to stop me or you from getting my memoirs down! They belong to the Ages! King Vincemole Whiteviper will be celebrated for ages to come. He will be (cough cough) . . . Necromancer! . . . Essence of Toad Vomit! Immediately . . . cough cough . . . I don't want to finish this in hell! (cough) That damned sorcerer didn't say that living over two centuries would be so damned tirin' and so bloody filled with infirmities. Glad I fed his brain to my pig-dog. . . .

Gods! What nasty stuff . . . Wine . . . wine!

There. I'm half-drunk most of the time anyway. Maybe we'll try this chapter totally snookered. Or work toward that lofty goal anyway.

Bottomserf! Throw another jent on the fire. Getting a bit cold in here.

Yes. Where was I? Elves? Oh, yes! Ears! Quite! The first ear wiggles! Yes, how true—but the Pointy Ear Waltz wasn't the only marvelous music I heard in those days!

I guess this all starts with Lady Foxvox. Gods, I suppose lots of my chapters start off with beautiful women. My life would have been a hell of a lot safer and more to my taste if I'd been able to navigate through the years without the old loindragon pulling me into trouble. For one thing I'd have been able to stab more elves in the back instead of the front, that's for certain!

But Lady Foxvox! What a vision!

I remember the first time I ever saw her, trailing along beside Lord Foxvox. The preening fool was inspecting the troops, and I was just a lieutenant then, standing at attention. By Crob, when she floated into reach of these very orbs, there was more at attention than King Hagbow's army!

Maybe it's senility that's gripped me, but I just don't see women as beautiful as she was these days. She had this creamy skin, and these lofty blue eyes and golden hair that make lesser men than me want to die for her. Stuffed inside her ermine robe beneath all that sparkling jewelry was a body that could raise the dead. Young Vincey was a fine horseman in those days, but he was thinking about more than mounting a horse that day.

So here was Lord Foxvox, moving around us like a priest with a broom stuck up his arse. You know the type. Born with a golden wand in his mouth. High society victim. (And from those wall eyes of his, my guess was that in his High Society there was a bit of inbreeding.)

"Lieutenant!"

I snapped to even finer-tuned attention. "My Lord!"

"You may kiss my ring!"

He extended his pinky my way, and damned if there wasn't a flashing blue gem there the size of an apple.

"Sir!" I bent over and planted a wet one on that

ring. I guess I've got a weakness for jewelry, because I fancied M'Lord's glowstone as much as his wife.

"Well done, Lieutenant." He eyed our troops loftily and not without a slight touch of distaste. "Do you think this army, Lieutenant, is capable of helping my people deal with this wretched business?"

"Indeed, sir," I said, and allowed a slight smile of pride to sneak onto my face. "We've got the best trained troops on the continent. Good stock, too, sir. Well fed, well trained, and loyal—and elf-haters to the last of 'em."

"Is that true, troops?" said Lord Foxvox.

Five hundred voices rang out. "Yes . . . M'Lord!"

"Excellent!" Lord Foxvox spun to Sheriff Narxton and Baron Brill, the two authorities who maintained this hold—and this army—for the King of the Lofty Lands, Narco the Bald. "His Majesty always spoke well of this army, and I must say these are fine looking lads. With the two hundred I've brought along and the battle magicians, I do believe we can handily extend the emperor's territory."

I kept my face unmoved, but inside my spine was hot oatmeal. Training, dueling, sporting—all this business with pikes and swords and maces and lances and what have you, charging about on horses, maybe even dodging the odd bit of wizardfire. . . . Well, I mean, it keeps one in shape and sometimes it's excellent fun. However, what this blasted ninny was talking about was obvious:

Old King Baldy was getting the hankering for yet more territory. And the territory in question was obviously the vast amount owned by the Green Elves of the Central Kingdom, cheek to jowl with this king-owned county, where I was currently hiding from the Death Orcs. The sum of the equation: we were going to go into battle with the most brilliantly skilled swordsmen of the Low Kingdoms: the Green Elves. We, alas, included myself and Young Vincey, who could match blades with the best of men, but when it came to elves—well, truth to tell, a good elf with a blade stood an excellent chance of reducing me to Vincemeat!

"At your service . . . m'lord!" I cried out, thinking, *Damn fool! And I'll bet you'll be back here playing hide the sausage with the wife while we're watering the grass out there with our blood.*

"Hmmmmf!" he said. He spun around, his spurs jangling behind him, the smell of expensive cologne fogging me.

It looked like doom for sure, and I was trying to remember the best way out of the barracks by night, when Lady Foxvox changed my destiny with a twist of a smile.

"Baron Brill," she said, her voice a genteel tinkling of charm. "Is it not true that a good portion of the elflands are totally unpopulated?"

The Baron, a hairy piece of work, rumbled a bit. "Aye. 'Tis true milady. Got some hills and mountains and a nice bit of plain, just adjacent to my Barony."

"Although my husband does not agree, I cannot help but think that the elves might be persuaded to sell this portion of their vast lands. The King certainly has suitable funds in his treasury." I couldn't help but notice that even as she said these words, she was taking my measure. I could feel her eyes go up shin, thighs, crotch (tingle!) right up my slender waist and broad chest and strong shoulders. I could almost feel my mustaches bristle as I thought I saw a twinkle of feminine approval in those sky-blue eyes of hers.

"The elves? They've got plenty of money!" answered the Baron gruffly. "Gems galore and several dragonholds worth of treasure. What use would they have for money!"

"Ah, but they value their soldiers' lives, I believe. Take a healthy payout and prevent disastrous battles that could lead to a horrible war? Plague, perhaps. Misery. Famine?"

The Baron, the old warhorse, smiled and growled. "Y'mean, like the Good Old Days?"

The beauty shrugged. "I have come along because I believe that I have diplomatic skills. I thought it might be prudent to parlay. The elves are known for their hospitality. Before we charge in to the land with a bunch of soldiers, why not negotiate? Why not make an offer?"

The Baron scratched his head, no doubt dislodging some lice. He eyed us. I happened to know that although the bastard was damned bloodthirsty, he was far more interested in gold than land.

"Perhaps we should adjourn inside, milady, for a cup or two of wine, and talk about his subject a bit."

"As you please," she said, all female courtesy. But she bowed, her eyes flashed my way, and I could see the vixen was made of hotter stuff than lace and veils and curtsies, and damn me if my blood didn't boil a bit.

Truth to tell, when the general dismissed us, I should have just bolted right then. Hightailed it right into the hands of the Death Orcs! Bribe elves! Nonsense! The sons of bitches have got their noses too high up in the air! My reason screamed to me that we'd be in the battlefield within the week.

But those eyes and that body, I admit, had stirred

up some irrational juices and the noggin and eyes were damned beclouded.

I had some grog with the lads, all of whom thought it would be grand to hack and slash at some elves and I honestly thought about going back to the room and then leaving by moonlight. But with all the parading and practicing for the royals today, truth was I was tired, and so when I went back to my humble officer quarters, I promptly fell asleep.

I was awakened by a tap-tap-tapping at the window.

When I peered out, squinting and mumbling, who should I see but the Lady Foxvox, all bundled up in a fur robe, shivering.

"Lieutenant!" she whispered. "Please open your door. I must speak to you!"

Well, I was too bleary to wonder if this wasn't a Dream Demon, come to suck my life's juices. I just stumbled over to the door and lifted the latch.

She came in like a warm breeze out of the cold, smelling of flowery daylight and sweet feminine musk. Her eyes were wide and there was actually innocence and fear to them that somehow touched whatever sympathy was left in a cynical and magic-scarred soul.

In short, I bloody melted into a puddle, if you must know.

"Oh, thank you so much, Lieutenant. I had to speak to you on the most vital matters," she said. "It's matter of life and death . . . and perhaps even more!"

I closed the door behind her. "I wish I could offer you some hot tea, milady!" I said, still damned flummoxed.

"Brandy?" she said, shivering a bit. "Do you have brandy?"

I did and I got us big beakers of it. She gulped hers down even while I was lighting up some candles and getting a small fire going. I poured her more, and she drank it and sighed.

I took a big sip myself and knocked enough sleep out of me to realize that I was in a room alone with maybe the most beautiful stack of woman I'd ever seen.

"I am honored by your visit," I said, still keeping up the gentlemanly front. "But, milady . . . coming to bachelor's quarters in the middle of the night. It seems to smack of impropriety!"

"Propriety be damned," said Lady Foxvox. "The old sot is snoring away back in bed and won't be awaked till lunch, I'd bet. It's so hard . . . it's so very hard . . ." She wept into a lacey bit of something she'd pulled out.

"Hard, milady?" I said. "What's hard?"

"Being a young woman . . . so much . . . in need. . . ."

"In need, milady?"

"Yes, dammit! In need!" She got up and shed her furs. I found myself facing a goddess in a translucent waterfall of not-much-at-all, her golden hair shining in the firelight.

"These lips, Lieutenant! This face—is it not full of need? But that is not what people see!" Her arms went to her chest. "This bosom! Is this not the bosom of a healthy young woman, made to be sucked! And, Lieutenant! These hips!" She smoothed her hands down her belly to between her legs, rubbed a moment and then slowly, tantalizingly moved out to the edge of her hips. "Tell me! Do these hips not look as though they have vast wants!"

I tried to speak, but my mouth was dry. I knocked back the rest of my brandy. "You are the loveliest lady I have ever seen, but your husband—" Of course I didn't give a bit of griffin snot about Lord Foxvox. I was just thinking about my neck, of course.

"The impotent bad joke is dead to the world. And oh, Lieutenant—I have never seen a handsomer man . . . nor male attributes and soul so attuned to my instinctual . . . needs. . . ."

The next thing I knew, her lips were on mine, her tongue was playing with my tonsils, and her hand was exactly where I'd fantasized it being when I saw her saunter into the courtyard.

Say what you will about magic. But when it comes to persuading certain activities, good old-fashioned methods sometimes will do just fine.

"Vincey?"

"Yes, Matilda, my dear."

We knew each other's first names by then, of course. And gods, a great deal more. The woman knew more moves than a dancing basilisk, and damn me had gotten more of my life's juices out of me than a Dream Demon could ever suck. It was only two hours since I'd let her in and the Galloping Cocksman was spent as a shilling in a crooked card game.

"You are the strongest, most vital man—I wonder . . . But no!"

"Wonder what, my darling!" I knew there were gods, but this had been my first taste of the upper heavens, and stupid wretch that I was, I was besotted.

"I cannot ask."

"Kill your husband? Where's my sword?"

"No, no silly. That would be so messy." She smiled and giggled. "No, Vincey. If you must know . . ." She played with my chest hair and started getting shivers out of me that I thought would never come again. "I have persuaded the Baron and my husband to journey to the Castle Keep of the elves and to parley—offer money for land. That sort of thing. I feel I should have a bodyguard. I thought . . ."

I chuckled and nuzzled her long elegant neck. "But who will guard your body from me!"

Her laugh was sunlight on a green river valley. "Oh, you jester! I did not know studs could make jokes! But no, darling . . . seriously . . . You are good with ALL swords!" Her blue eyes glittered in the candlelight.

"I am!" I did not tell her, however, that my specialty was slashing while retreating.

"Well, then . . . I am so thrilled with your skills . . . and in truth, I don't know what I'd do without you now. I shall ask for a strong swordsman to come with us—someone who can also play the part of the dashing diplomatic aide. You will agree when asked to play that part. You see, if all goes well, I can argue for your being brought back with us as a special . . . bodyguard."

I had her meaning, all right. And damn me, if the idea of bathing in Lord and Lady Luxury didn't please the villain and coward in me as well as the sap in love. I could only agree.

"Excellent. I have a gift for you." I saw a flash of lovely buttocks and a wiggle of nipples in the firelight—and then she was with her fur robe, all

squirming enthusiasm. She pulled out a ring with an
emerald that looked like a green sun.

"My lady—"

"No. It's yours. I always promised myself I would
give the first man to truly please me something of
value from my paltry collection." Her mouth became
a moue. "However . . . Vincemole . . . it would make
me very happy to receive something of value in return. Something to rub against when the night is
cold." She rubbed against me, and, blast all, I was
convinced.

"Very well. I shall give it to you tomorrow."

A tear leaked down her cheek. "Oh, but I need it
now." Then she suddenly smiled. "I know! You've
got something in mind—but it's hidden away somewhere. If you've anything of value in this . . . this
dilapidated shack they make you stay in, you must
hide it!"

Spot on, of course. You don't go through a few
years as thief and cutpurse and mercenary without
picking up a few baubles. I bumbled about, trying to
think up an excuse, but suddenly she started rubbing
me in places I thought were all used up for at least
a week. I gasped and agreed.

"Good. Well, you must put that ring someplace
safe anyway. So you can go and get my present at
the same time. How economical!"

Well, I admit that at times in my long, shady career, others have had me by the short hairs. However, I can assure you that it's far more pleasant to
be had south of the short hairs.

I got out of bed, threw something on. I went to
some floorboards in the corner, drew a loose one up,
got my sack out. I knew what would work well
enough—a paste diamond that looked real to every-

one but the very best gemsmith. Love and sport are one thing, but I was still sane enough to not give up ill-gotten gain!

"Oh, Vincey—it's so lovely!" She put it on and admired it in the firelight. "Thank you! Now come back to bed. It's hours before dawn."

Figuratively, the Lady Foxvox led me back to the passion pit by my nose.

Literally, it was quite another matter.

It took about a week before diplomatic machinations landed the Baron, Lady Foxvox, and a party of other genteels in the elf keep to parley. I was along, of course, or there'd be no story here, would there? Lord Foxvox, the arrogant coward, had managed to contract a cold, which kept him behind. It was all the same to me, as his illness had also allowed the Lady Foxvox plenty of time to romp with me in my night bed.

Still, as much as my pride was preened-up by my new position as royal bodyguard and diplomatic aside, I did not care for the elf keep one jot. And the Elf Prince? A puffed-up pansy. And the food and drink they gave us was not to the taste of my tongue or my innards. I somehow managed to immediately contract a bad case of both constipation and gas from the sorry stuff.

At first it seemed a simple enough task. I just hung around as the party of twelve traipsed into the keep. Solemn pronouncements were made. Elves danced about doing their fey shenanigans. The Elf Prince was in charge of negotiations and I can tell you, he did nothing to help my digestion.

"Now then," he said, narrow chin up proudly at table, eyes not on us so much as to the ceiling as though making pronouncements to posterity, not a paltry bunch of human spawn. "This is a most interesting proposition you make. There are all kinds of factors which we must consult, not least of which is a visit to our temples for pray and to consult with the Higher Gods who keep a watchful eye upon us." His nose and mouth quivered a bit as he looked down at us. He was diplomatically polite, this Bravebrow Highborn—but I knew enough about the world to detect the condescension in his manner.

The thing about elves which make me hate them even more than most creatures is that they think their droppings don't smell. It's like they alone are the true keepers of sentience and intelligence, taste and glory, and the rest of us mortals are just botches the gods allowed to hang around on their way to perfection: Elfkind.

Just think about the way they speak. With "Thees" and "Thous" and elegant frou frou rahs. They don't walk from place to place. They dance. And if you don't watch 'em half the time they'll whip out lutes and start singing! Mind you, that elf keep had some nice tapestries and statues, and I confess, they have a way with elegant costumery. But all those damned bells and perfume they wear, and their damned tinkly language! It's not to my taste at all, and I think it's infected humankind all too much.

This Elf Prince was a prime example. He looked as though he were posing and acting, not meeting with people who could cause his kingdom a wagonload of trouble. His narrow face and long chin were ghastly, and those ears of his were the longest and most elegant I've ever seen on an elf. He was dressed to the nines and tens and with all that robery he had on, I was sure he was a stashing a lute somewhere.

"So if you'll excuse me," he said, "we will adjourn now to our cathedral of worship to consult. You will have your answer on the morrow. Good eve." And off goes the elf train, tra la la.

"Bunch of bloody prissies," said the Baron. He shrugged. "Probably just use the money for interior decoration."

I had no problem with the idea of getting back to the bed the elves were giving me. My insides were acting up something terrible, and the notion of sleep seemed as delicious as Lethe Candy.

I was snug in my snooze, though, when someone started to shake my rear end.

"Vincey! Vincey!" I immediately recognized the voice of Matilda, Lady Foxvox. "Wake up!"

"Matty! Matty, please! I don't feel so well."

The rumbling of my innards also made the case for my infirmity.

"I'm sorry, darling," she said. "But I need you!"

"I don't think I'm capable of the loving you deserve this night." The strumpet was insatiable!

"No. No. We are on an important mission. A vital mission."

"Yes. And we will get our answer tomorrow!" I said, rolling over and showing her that I preferred hugging my pillow to hugging her.

"We have total victory within reach! And you shall be very rich. That ring I gave you? How would you like to have dozens and dozens more—and gems even larger than the size my husband wears."

Well, say what you like about Matilda, Lady Foxvox, but she knows how to go through a man's stomach problems, straight to his greed.

"Well—yes!" I said.

"We could buy our own kingdom. And I could

leave that wretched husband of mine. Just as we've talked of!"

Oh, excellent.

"Why haven't you spoken of this before?" I asked.

"I was afraid you wouldn't come. And I wasn't even sure it was possible! But now—the Elf Prince was right. All the Prime Elves have gone to their cathedral for prayer and mediation! The possibility is open—"

"Possibility!"

"There is a tower in this keep—and the top room of this tower holds marvelous gems. And Vincey—the most marvelous of these gems is the Gem of Valarium. It is High Magic, Vincey. Should we procure it—why, we would have the power to not only control the Elves—but to spread peace through all the Lofty Lands!"

Well, I didn't care much for peace in the Lofty Lands. But there were a few nonpeaceful folk on my trail that a little bit of that kind of magic might go a long way to bog down. And when it came to treasure unguarded, I must say, even my cowardice fades.

"I don't know . . ." I said, stiff and foggy.

"Here. Have a drink of brandy. It will calm your stomach and steel your nerves." She sighed, and I felt the sting of wet tears blubber down on me. "And to think. I thought that I had finally found a true Man."

I may have little bravery, but I do have my share of arrogance. I took the brandy and drank it down, and it was strong. So strong, that suddenly the tower seemed an easy thing to deal with. Still there were questions.

"How do you know what's up there?" I asked.

"A woman of my means can hire sorcery, my

love." Her teeth were pearly marvels in the largest smile she ever gave me. "Nor am I unprepared." She pulled out a piece of parchment, marked with a map and the unmistakable scrawl of a dealer of the Dark Arts.

"And you trust these masters of Dark?" I said. .

"The question, my darling," she said, smile disappearing, teeth clenched like a steel trap, "is do you trust me?"

In matters of such intimacy with women I've found it best to immediately answer in the positive, and such I did then:

"Oh, yes, my love!"

"Then get your swords and your breeches. We're off for more treasure than can be contained in your dreams."

And I thought, *Quite excellent.* Because that was a lot of treasure!

She was right about the castle. The drafty, dainty place was practically deserted, and so it was no problem skulking through chambers and corridors to the opposite end, where a large door stood, adorned in elegant patterns of elvish design and inlaid elegantly with silver threading. Alas, there was also a huge padlock upon it.

"Well. That's it," I said. "Come back to bed with me, Matty. There's more to life than treasure." The brandy was wearing off, and I was remembering that where there was treasure there was usually danger.

"Silence. Please. You think I'm unprepared?" From the fold of her robe she drew out a glowing key, far too small for the hole of the padlock—yet which unlocked the damned thing. My stomach turned over. I could smell the stench of magic. I gripped my blade and gritted my teeth and followed her.

We strode up steps, to a small antechamber. There, standing, waiting for us, was an elfin guard, sword drawn.

"No trespassing, humans," he said. He was a big elf, too, about a foot taller than I was. Most of the things were a head shorter and slender, so when this giant reared above me, I was quite prepared to take his advice.

"Kill him, Vincey!" said milady, and she shoved me forward.

Well, I'd like to say that I fought with finesse and talent, but truth to tell I just fought to save my sorry buttocks. And I think the fellow might have had my head but for Matilda, who snaked around to his rear and stuck him in the back with a dagger. It put the fellow off his slash and hack just long enough for me to drive my sword through his gizzard.

And that, posterity, was the first elf I killed and the first time I saw those pointy ears—and these quite large enough to produce a breeze-flapping as said elf expired. I laughed so hard I was almost grateful for my constipation.

Milady dragged me on. Up we went on a coiling set of stone steps. Up and up—and then into a large round chamber. There were torches in sconces there, but the light was great, because there was a dragon's share of gems in piles and batches. My fear gave way to my greed and I stuck my hand in a pile of rubies, diamonds, opals, and gems beyond my ken.

"I hope you brought bags!" I whispered.

"Oh, yes." She took out a couple of large burlap bags and tossed them to me. "But those are just baubles, Vincey. This is what I truly came for!"

I looked up as she started striding for a corner. There stood an idol carved in what appeared to be jade. It was a god, and male, I know that because only male gods have nether parts of those dimensions. All of him was stone green as well, save for his nose, which was a huge and odd bit of geometry, crystallized. It pulsed and glowed, and I didn't really have to smell it to know that it was magic. Matilda took out her dagger and started digging it out.

Well, good for her, thinks I. For in truth, although magic has been both friend and enemy often to me, I far prefer what treasure and money can bring a man.

And so, I started shoveling gems by the handful into my bags. My, my, my, these were gorgeous, fine pieces of work as well—and I knew in my heart that with just one of these bags I could travel far, far, far from the Death Orcs who would have my soul, clear around to the fabled island of Stralia—and there live like a king.

"Thieves! Wretched thieves!"

The strident voice caught me up short. I turned and my heart leaped into my throat. Standing there, blade shining in the torches was none other than the Elf Prince—looking self-righteous and full of indignation and holding up a mighty shiny sword. Behind him were a few more big elves, gripping even mightier swords.

"Milady!" I said, standing up, holding onto the bags of gems. I smiled, expecting to be whisked off upon the winds of sorcery to a better, safer place.

Instead, Matilda rushed to the Prince and prostrated herself. "Oh, my Prince! Thank the gods you've arrived. I was entranced by this fiend's spell. He forced me up here to steal the Crystal of Valarium!"

The Prince gasped. "The Crystal of Valarium!" He rushed forward. "Yes! It's gone!" He turned an angry face my way and an accusatory finger. "Where is it, devil?"

I'd like to think my tongue is quick, but Matilda had it all over me. "He used sorcery to transport it to another dimension, where he can retrieve it at will!" she said approaching me.

"Liar! Bitch!" I said, my brain spinning wheels upon wheels and not getting anywhere. I turned to face the Prince, imploringly. "I am only a—"

Alas, Milady Foxvox must have grabbed a nearby piece of iron or bludgeon and brought it down upon the back of my head, because suddenly the Prince dissolved in pain and astrology and the floor reached up for me and gave me a large cold kiss.

When I awoke, the pain was still there, and the cold was still there, and not only was I not entirely sure where I was, I was not sure WHO I was.

"Vincemole Whiteviper," intoned a deathly black voice.

"That's who I am!" I said.

It was cold comfort, and enough consciousness crept into the situation for me to get the setting picture. I was tied by ropy thongs, which alone supported me over some kind of stone pit. I looked down at myself and by the fluttering light of some oil in a sconce I could see why I was cold.

I was naked as the night I first sported with Milady Foxvox.

"Vincemole Whiteviper." That dead voice again. It sounded like snake slithers made vowels and consonants. "You will tell us where you magicked the Crystal of Valarium."

"Magicked . . . what?" I looked up. A dark figure approached, covered by a cowl. The cowl pulled back and I could see by the flickering light that a wizened elf with vicious eyes was staring upon me. He was one of the shorties, thank the gods, but he didn't look exactly harmless. Bastard had filed teeth and those pointy ears looked sharp enough to gore someone.

"Play stupid with us, foul one . . . and suffer!" I was suddenly aware of a poker coming my way. The tip glowed like a red-hot coal. It touched my shin, and exquisite agony raced up through me.

I gritted my teeth, though, and was strong. "Oh please. Please! I'd tell you! Honestly I would! But I don't know. It's that villainess Lady Foxvox! She seduced me and forced me into her service. She has—"

"Liar!" Another sizzle. "Tell me!"

Well, torture normally does it for me, but the pain was enough to lose consciousness again. Next thing I knew, cold water splashed into my face and I was awake again.

"There are other ways besides pain to produce needed results," said the torturer. "I am Quadric, Dungeon Keeper of Elf Land, and I hold the keys to dimensions as well. In these dimensions live creatures, Vincemole Whiteviper, who love the taste of human flesh. You dangle over an opening to one of those dimensions at this very moment."

"Oh, yes, I thought. The pit. I hadn't had the time to wonder about this pit, but my new friend here was explaining it to me, and I wasn't very excited at what he was telling me.

The elf priest or dungeon keeper or whatever the deuce he was brought some sparkling powder out of a pouch and dropped it over the edge of the pit. Then he muttered some kind of magical mumbo jumbo.

"It will be easy enough to remember now, I think.

And when you tell me what I need to know—I shall have you hauled up, put in a nice cell, and fed a delicious meal." He smiled snidely. "We elves, you see, are a civilized lot!"

I was about to comment on what I thought about the elvish civilization, when a roar thumped up from the dark beneath me, and a cold blast of something foul blew up onto my bare behind.

A kind of lizardy growl echoed up through the pit, and I thought I heard words sounding as though a quagmire was trying to speak to us.

"Ah. I believe that persuasion is coming your way!"

From up out of the pitch, came a snaky thing, lifting above me—I could see that it was no lizard or snake, however, but a tentacle, as though of some sea creature. Only the purple suckers that lined its death-pale flesh were filled with tiny, sharp teeth. The thing wriggled about languidly as though tasting the air—and then it whipped over me, winding around my midsection.

The stinging brought tears to my eyes, and I would have screamed except that my innards were in such turmoil I lost control of all vocal expression. Indeed, I believe a spot of terror and a speck of horror were in the mix as well.

That infernal coil, after constricting, began to pull on me, tugging me down toward the darkness. Only my bonds, tied around embedded chains, kept me in check.

"Now, then. That should loosen your memory somewhat," said the grinning elf sorcerer. "Well— tell me where the crystal is?"

"I . . . don't . . . know . . ." I managed to spit out.

The miscreant frowned. "Oh, dear. I do hate to work but it would appear some dark sorcery is in order." He went off to some sort of bench to the side. Pestle and mortar. Grind and dump. His fingers danced over the bottles of eyeballs and troll warts, and the next thing I knew he was carrying a tray over, holding a candle and a large pile of glittering dust. "You see, Vincemole Whiteviper, there is agony beyond your comprehension. I have but to sprinkle this dust upon your legs and your privates and light it . . . and oh, my . . . I have never seen it fail to produce secrets from the most recalcitrant of souls. I—"

I would like to say that what happened next was planned cleverly by myself. However, that would not be the truth and as much as I've lied in my life, I am endeavoring to tell the truth in these texts. Although the intestinal activities I spoke of earlier seemed the lesser of evils to which I was now victim, that did not mean they had gone away. And although my nether parts seemed sealed with constipation, the massaging and squeezing of that tentacle had the most remarkable effect.

One more tug of the thing did it, right in the midst of the sorcerer's speech.

I farted.

Nor was it any ordinary fart. Gases built up over hours and hours did not escape my rear so much as they were propelled by a blast that echoed mightily throughout the chamber. The gigantic fart traveled directly into the face of my oppressor—but not before catching hold of the pile of sorcerous dust and the candle flame. The result was an explosion even louder than my tremendous rear-end eructation . . .

. . . plus, one flaming sorcerer.

The fellow screamed his lungs out as he fought at the fire, but the magic stuff engulfed him. He hopped and skipped about, and then teetered over the edge of the pit. He lost his footing, and I was for the first time, quite happy that my feet had been splayed so widely apart. He tumbled right through my legs, right on down and down upon the monstrous tormentor below.

The thing roared and screeched. Almost immediately, the tentacle about me unwound and let go of me, and fell back into the heart of the pit, from which I heard the most unearthly thrashing and shrieking. The fire from the sorcerer had caught onto the bonds tied to my ankles and was now burning. However, before they could burn off, yet another explosion sounded from below. This blast was so powerful that it pushed me up and tore off the foot bonds and thrust me into a cartwheel straight up and onto the edge of the pit.

I did not hang onto consciousness. The next thing I knew, I was lying on the cold stone floor, wrists burning something awful. Amidst the smoke and smell of fried monster and sorcerer, I could see flames playing over my bonds and my hands, scorching me rather awfully. I pulled away, and scrambled for a dank corner, moaning and groaning and smoking a bit myself.

I took in some gasps and got hold of myself. Miserable as I was, I was still alive and had to make the best of it. I got onto my feet and managed to find my clothes and my sword that had been tossed into a corner. Although it hurt something fierce, I got them on, and stumbled for some sunlight.

Outside, however, was chaos as well.

I had expected to have to slink through halls and streets and then steal a horse in order to gallop away. But as soon as I pushed through a door to the basement from the odorous dungeons, I heard noises I was far too familiar with: the terrible havoc of battle. With my worldview and mind, it did not take me long to add two and two. This diplomatic mission had just been a ruse to put the elves off guard. Some of our people must have sneaked to the gates and kept them open, to allow the human armies to invade.

It was the first good news in a while, and my first thought was to just hide in a closet somewhere until it all blew over, then cut off a dead elf's head and carry it triumphantly out to the victors, with some wild and wooly tale.

However, there was, after all, the matter of all those gems I'd taken the trouble to stuff into those bags. Moreover, I recognized where I was—and knew I could easily find my way now back to the tower where they lay. I hurried there.

Along the way, it was made quite obvious to me that my surmise was correct. A glance out a window showed men and elves in the street doing battle. From the looks of it, the elves were getting the worst of it, which was quite fine with me. I heard the screeches and clamor of rape and pillage, music to my ears these days but frankly not really to my taste in those times.

I hurried to the tower.

The door was quite open, fortunately, and despite my wounds and burns, the prospect of the treasure awaiting me prodded me up those winding stairs at a goodly clip. Sure enough, the tower room was still there, as were the bags of gems—stuffed well enough to suit me. I took a moment to get some breath into my lungs and visions of luxury and debauchery danced in my head. What wine I would drink! What women I would have! Oh, yes, the wounds of my body and my heart—curse Lady Foxvox—would heal well enough, thanks to these beauties.

I turned to travel back down the tower, but was halted by an awful sight. There, blocking my way, was the Elf Prince. Blood ran down his face from a cut on his cheek, and his fancy clothing was ripped, but otherwise he looked in good heath and in one piece, damn his eyes. The worst part was that he had his sword out, and it was as sharp and wicked as they come.

"Lost!" he cried. "Lost . . . all this art and beauty . . . burning and under the thumb of sewer beings! And you . . . You scum . . . You deceitful buzzard . . . You are one of the causes! But you shall not live to enjoy the harvest. I shall have vengeance!"

He charged.

Well, I dropped the bags and got out my sword fast enough, little good that it did. I'd heard that elves were good with their steel, but that hardly describes it. I put up a quick defense and his blade skipped around, and although I'd got to my feet and was giving it the very best I could, fencing and parrying and thrusting and what-have-you that would have made my swordmasters drop their jaws and say, "This is Whiteviper?" It was clear that the Elf Prince was by far my better.

Desperately, I threw a candelabra at him, headed toward one of the windows, and pushed open the drapes. Those gems were all well and good, but they could not be enjoyed in hell.

My only escape was apparent. I would jump from the tower, into the moat . . . and swim to safety. It seemed so—well, right for me.

Alas, as soon as I reached the window and looked down, a shocking fact made itself apparent.

There was no moat!

And this tower was a lot higher than I'd remembered, situated as it was on the verge of some vertiginous cliffs.

Such was the vertigo that swept over me that I flung myself away from the very sight, hurling myself to the floor . . . and tripping the charging Elf Prince, who'd come to skewer me before I could make my leap.

He lost his sword and windmilled even as he was hurled through the window, balance totally lost. I got to my feet and turned around to see what had happened.

Hanging onto the ledge of the window were a pair of elfin hands. I picked up my sword and peered down. Sure enough there he hung, like a piece of elfin dung dangling from a god's arse. He glared up at me defiantly and would have spit at me, I think. In his place I would have promised the world, but he kept his damned mouth shut.

Too bad. Perhaps we might have worked something out. As it was, I quickly learned that elf ears could flap as fast as hummingbird wings.

But even so, dying elves cannot fly.

My wits and the bags of gems returned to me, it was easy enough to join in the fun at the castle. I refrained from any more elf ear experiments because I would have had to put my treasures down. As it was, with the chaos, I was able to show my wounds and get a wagon back home from the winning army—mine. There, in the warmth and safety of my quarters, even though I was half-dead with exhaustion, I took the time to secrete my newfound gain below the floorboards.

I did not even bother to take food or drink, but just tumbled into my blankets and the healing arms of sleep.

I dreamed. I dreamed a beautiful woman came to me. I dreamed she had ointments and salves, and glorious potions. And as only women can do, she nursed me and healed me and comforted me. She gave me water and I drank, and it was the most delicious stuff that had passed my lips.

And then this lovely woman bent to my ear, and she whispered to me, "Oh . . . I love you . . . so much . . . dear Vincey . . ."

Ah, sweet balm!

Was this a foretaste, I thought, of future moments in Stralia? Let it be, oh, let it be!

When I woke, the pain was back and the dawn had come and gone. However, the sweet lingering touch of that dream comforted me.

"I'm back!" I cried. "I'm alive!"

And soon . . . soon I would be on my way . . . a rich man . . . to the land of my hopes . . . and there, perhaps . . . I would be a better man. . . .

Perhaps.

Such was the sorrow, though, of that dream fading with the sunlight that I needed a taste of it again. I hurried to the corner to look at the vehicles that would carry me to the Kingdom of Vincemole.

I pulled up the floorboards, ready to be bathed in the radiance of my gems. . . .

The bags were gone. My box of coins and trinkets were gone as well, and with them the ring that the Lady Foxvox had given me.

In their place was a scribbled note in a flowery hand.

It read:.

Darling Vincey,

Oh, how proud I am of your prowess and wit. Escaped, and with bounty! Truly, loved one, I am honored to have crossed your crooked path. However, as happy as I am that you still live, I'm afraid that we cannot see each other for the time being, as My Lord would not understand. When you read this, we will have departed for our home—but with the powers of the Crystal that you helped me obtain, I have divined that certain parties (i.e. Death Orcs) seek you. I have, through the wings of sorcery, alerted them to your location. So, if you hope to ever see me again, do not seek me out now, but flee for your life!

All my love,

Matilda.

P.S. All this baggage will surely weigh you down. I will put it to good use for you.

The damned bitch!

Death Orcs or no, I'd get even, I raged. I would take this note and show it to Lord Foxvox. Or messenger it in any case. I would—

But even as thoughts of revenge swept through my head, the paper with the message burst into sparks and flame. I dropped it, and it was cinders before it hit the floor.

And then, as I thought about revenge . . . I thought about Death Orcs. And about the revenge they wished for me. Somehow that revenge seemed more relevant. . . .

I packed, managed to get my pay, bought a horse—and was off for safer climes.

And as for the Death Orcs . . . well, that's another story, and I'm tired.

What? A question? You've been listening, Grompole. Well, I am flattered. Hmmm? Oh, yes, one and the same . . . one and the same. And that is yet another story.

In fact, I believe she's calling me now. She does have a screech, doesn't she? Oh, well. Life could be worse.

Yes, Darling Dear.

I'm coming!

Yes, yes, I shall attend to all those things immediately. Yes, dear, I know your mother is arriving for a month and I must prepare for the pixie roast.

Coming, Matilda!

Coming, my dove!

A NEW MAN
by Ed Gorman

Ed Gorman has garnered acclaim no matter what genre he writes in. Britain's *Million* magazine called him "one of the world's great storytellers." Reviewing his western work, the *Rocky Mountain News* said, "Quite simply, Ed Gorman is one of the best western writers of our time." A review in *The Magazine of Fantasy & Science Fiction* said, "Gorman is a skillful writer (who turns) the reader's expectations upside down, which is refreshing and disquieting." He has won several awards, most notably the Shamus and the Spur, and been nominated for the Edgar, Stoker, and the Golden Dagger. His work has appeared in such diverse magazines as *Redbook, Ellery Queen's Mystery Magazine,* and *Poetry Today.* He lives in Cedar Rapids, Iowa, with his wife, children's fiction author Carol Gorman.

The way things worked out, it was kind of funny. It was a warm spring day as I wheeled into town in my Ford roadster. Every once in a while I'd glance in the rearview mirror and startle myself. That doc on the west coast had done a real good job. He'd charged too much, but I didn't have much choice. I could've killed him, I suppose, but—believe it or not—killing doesn't come easy to me. The papers and the radio would have you believe that I kill people all the time. But that's just hooey to sell newspapers and hair tonic.

The place was the sort of dusty little town I'd expected to find along the Mississippi River on the Iowa side. Three blocks of shopping, a town square with a bandstand, three or four churches, and a lot of small boats along the river, bobbing on the gentle waves. A lot of colored people along the dam, fishing. A bunch of white boys playing baseball in the parking lot of a small factory.

And some very pretty ladies sitting at a small outdoor café, drinking lemonade and smoking cigarettes and listening to Al Jolson on the radio.

Now that's the part of my reputation I don't mind. The newspapers always gussied me up as a ladies' man, and I guess that's true. They say I'm good looking, and while I'm not likely to argue with that, looks don't have nothing to do with my success with women. The gals like me for a simple reason: they know I really like and respect women and know how to treat them right.

I decided to have myself a lemonade.

I carried my glass out to the porch that overlooked the river. The four gals were all in summer linen dresses the pastel colors of flowers. They all wore their hair bobbed and they all smoked like Bette Davis, you know, with her wrist angled backward when she was just resting her cigarette. I had to smile. I was the same way. I go into a pitcher show and darned if I don't come out imitating the mannerisms of the hero. Sometimes I didn't even *know* I was doing it.

The gals looked me over and whispered and giggled among themselves like schoolgirls. They were small-town sweet, and I liked them. The way they smiled at me, I guess I must've passed muster.

I sat there and enjoyed the river. Though we were

in the shiny new 1930s, you could still easily imagine the old paddle wheelers making their way up here from New Orleans. Gambling boats filled with beautiful ladies and fast-shuffling men. Nights of music and reckless love. I guess every generation looks back on the previous times as better somehow.

It wasn't long before the law showed up. My instinct was to go for my gun. There were two things wrong with that. These days, I didn't carry a gun. And there wasn't any reason to get excited anyway. My new face didn't in any way resemble my old face.

He was young and he had just about the right amount of swagger. Too much and he would've been a punk. Too little and he would've been a coward. He wore a khaki uniform with a bright silver badge that glared in the sun. His gun was a Colt .45, the kind that Bob Steele and Hopalong Cassidy pack in the pitcher shows. He was probably twenty-five, and except for a broken nose he looked like a magazine cover. The altar boy ten years later.

He sat down. Didn't ask. Just sat down. He wore a white Stetson and doffed it to the gals. He must've passed muster, too. They sent him several flirtatious smiles, little invisible valentines.

"Those're the kind of gals who could get a married man in trouble," he said.

He was drinking lemonade, too.

"I imagine that's true."

He pushed his hand across the table to me. He had a strong but easy hand. He wasn't trying to impress anybody. "Name's Swenson. Con Swenson. I'm the acting sheriff. Hasty, Bob Hasty, the sheriff, he's laid up with some kinda heart condition, so I been sort of running things for the past two months. And you'd be?"

"Paul Caine."

"And Paul Caine would be from?"

"Milwaukee. I sell kitchen appliances there."

He nodded. "I've got a wife who's got every one of 'em. You should see our place." Then—still and always a lawman—"You're just passing through?"

"Staying a few days, then going on to Cedar Rapids. Got a cousin there. But he won't be back for a couple of days, so I thought I'd stay here and fish. Hear it's good here."

"Real good. Best fishing in the state except up near Devil's Backbone and a few places like that." Then: "Know anybody here?"

"Not a soul."

He watched my face, my hands, the way I moved. I knew I'd passed muster with the gals. With him I wasn't sure.

"You find a hotel yet?"

"Not yet."

"Hell, then, let me take you over to the Paladium. My cousin Ned is the desk clerk there. I'll get you a deal on a room. And it'll be a nice one, too."

I smiled. "You're a little bit of Chamber of Commerce, too?"

"Not Chamber. Not yet. But Jaycee and Rotary. Sheriff thinks we need to be part of our community, and I agree with him. The days of a peace officer just totin' a gun around and tryin' to scare people are over. At least around these parts. C'mon, I'll walk over with you."

He was a strange one for a copper, and he made me uneasy. I don't think he'd figured out who I was or what I was doing here. But something else was going on, and I wondered what it was.

I grabbed my one suitcase from the car and we

walked a block east. There sure were a lot of pretty
girls here. Wagons went by, horses hot in the Iowa
sun, leaving sweet-scented fly-specked remnants of
their passage in the road. Roadsters went by; trucks
went by; a big Packard with some fancy people in
the back and Chicago plates went by. *Flying Down to
Rio* with Ginger Rogers and Fred Astaire was on the
picture show marquee.

The Paladium was on the other side of the street.
Just as we were approaching it, a woman was coming
out of a dress shop next door. I couldn't get a good
look at her.

When Caine saw her, he shouted, "Hey, honey!"

And then she turned toward us and squinted into
the sun. And then her pretty face ignited into a smile
and she returned the wave. And then went on walking in the opposite direction.

"That's the little woman," Caine said. "My wife."

"Pretty," I said.

"She sure is," he said proudly. "I hope you get a
chance to meet her."

But I had met her. Many times I'd met her. And
that was why, in fact, I was here. Because I'd met
her and she'd betrayed me and now I was going to
kill her.

The fishing turned out to be all I'd heard. I spent
two days collecting sunrays and catfish, and two
nights drinking bathtub gin and squiring about a
young woman who wore just a wee bit too many
pieces of Kleenex in her bra. But her earnestness en-
deared her to me, and so we spent several sweet
moonlit hours in a hushed cove next to where the
water ran moon-silver at midnight.

Not until Tuesday did I start following the law-

man's wife. When I'd known her, her name had been
Ann Sage and she'd lived in Chicago. Here her name
was Karen Caine. She'd put on ten pounds and
dipped her hair a little too often in the peroxide bottle. She had a nice life. During the day, she went to
the beauty shop and the picture show and the
bakery.

Nights, her appointed rounds became even more
interesting. I found a hill on the right side of the
isolated Caine house on the edge of town. Through
my field glasses, I saw that hubby, apparently tired,
usually went to bed around 8:30, leaving Karen
downstairs to read movie magazines, smoke Chester-
fields, and listen to the radio.

He came from the woods in back of the house, her
lover. He was a big man with a handsome but fierce
face and a lot of girly-curly dark hair. He went
straight into the darkened garage. She came out
promptly at ten. It was all pretty sensible, when you
thought about it. You go anywhere with somebody,
folks are bound to see you eventually. But if all you
do is go out to your garage—and she carried a small
sack of garbage as a pretext—who could see anything? If lover boy kept his mouth shut, who would
ever know.

And hubby was upstairs asleep.

On my fourth day in town, I rolled out of bed an
hour later than usual. That bathtub gin can do bad
things to your system, especially your head.

He knocked and then came right in without my
invitation. He had on a crisp new khaki uniform that
would be sweated out and dusted out by day's end
and he had this strange smile on his face. One of

those smug smiles that said he knew something I didn't.

"Morning," he said.

"Morning," I said, still in my boxers, still sitting on the side of my single bed. I fired up a Lucky.

He had a glass in his hand. A plain six-ounce drinking glass.

"Recognize this?" he said.

Something was sure up. He was so excited he kept licking his lips and breathing very hard.

"Looks like a glass to me."

"Yeah, but what kinda glass?"

"Drinking glass." The hangover had left me irritable. "Look, I always like to have some breakfast before I play parlor games."

The grin came full force now. "This ain't no parlor game I'm playing, Mr. Dillinger."

So then I knew. "The glass I drank lemonade from?"

"One and the same."

"You're a bright lad."

"Bright enough to match the fingerprints with the WANTED poster J. Edgar sent out when they thought you were still alive. I didn't know who you were, so I had to look through a lot of posters. You got a real funny whorl on your right thumb."

"I cut it on a scythe when I was a kid."

"Too bad. It's real easy to spot you."

"You tell them where they can find me?"

His wife Anne Sage had told the federales where they could find me on the night of July 22. She'd be wearing red when we left the theater, and she'd be standing next to me. She'd pitch to the left, and they'd open fire. What they hadn't counted on was me figuring that something was going on. She'd been

acting jittery all night. Just as we were leaving the
theater, I grabbed her and used her as a shield.
J. Edgar wouldn't want his boys to gun down an
innocent girl. It'd look bad in the press. So they
didn't have any choice but to let me get in my car—
her along for the ride—and get away. That was three
years ago. Since then that west coast doc had worked
on my face, turning me into a new man. And I'd
been looking for Ann Sage.

Or I had been.

I'd outrun J. Edgar once. I doubted I'd do it again.

"They've probably got this hotel surrounded," I
said, suddenly feeling a lot wearier than my thirty-
seven years.

He shook his head. "Nah. I haven't called them yet."

I took a deep drag of the Lucky. The stream of
smoke I exhaled was a perfect ice blue. Beautiful in
its way. "You want all the glory for yourself, huh?
'I Captured John Dillinger.' Make you a regular
folk hero."

He looked kind of dopey, then. And I realized just
how young and unsophisticated he was. Despite all
the tough talk, I mean.

Standing right there, a badge on his chest, a gun
on his hip, for all the world a cold and serious lawman, he got tears in his eyes and said, "I can't take
it anymore, Mr. Dillinger."

"Can't take what?" I said.

So he told me.

I slept in again the next morning. This time it
wasn't the fault of bathtub gin. I was just tired. It'd
been a long and industrious night.

The desk clerk, as I handed him the two dollars I

owed him for my last night, said, "You must've slept through all the excitement."

"Oh?"

"You met Deputy Caine."

"Sure. Nice young man."

The clerk, who had a mole, slick hair, and breath that could peel onions, leaned forward on the desk and said, "His old lady was bangin' this here young buck of a farmer, see? The way folks surmise it is the farmer wanted her to leave Caine and marry him. They musta had an argument, see, and the farmer killed her and then hisself."

I shook my head. "Boy, what a sad old world."

"I hear ya, brother." Then: "Caine didn't hear about it till this morning. He took a prisoner over to Dunkertown and stayed there all night right on a cot in the police station."

Hard to find a better alibi than that.

I was just tossing my bag in my roadster when I saw Deputy Caine coming out of his office and walking into the dusty street. Several people stopped him. The way they kind of whispered and gently touched him, you could tell they were trying to console him.

I whipped the roadster around so that I'd drive past the sheriff's office as I left town. When I got even with the small stone building, I stepped on the brake. Caine came over and put his foot on the running board.

"I guess we both got what we wanted," he said.

I guess we did. She'd betrayed me with the feds, and she'd betrayed him in bed. We'd both gotten what we wanted.

"So everything go all right?"

"Just fine." The farmer had been big, all right, but dumb. Faking his suicide hadn't been difficult at all.

"She say anything, you know, before she died?"

I knew what he wanted to hear. What any man would want to hear. That she was sorry she betrayed him. That she still loved him.

"I could lie to you, kid, but I'm not sure I'd be doing you any favors."

"Yeah, I suppose not." He squinted up at the sun. "That funeral parlor's gonna be hot as a bitch tonight, with the wake and all."

"Yeah," I said.

Hot as a bitch.

"Good luck with everything—Mr. Thompson," he said. And grinned.

That had been my part of the bargain. I kill his wife for him—something he couldn't bring himself to do—and he let me go without informing the feds. Seemed reasonable to me.

"Good luck to you, too, Deputy."

We shook hands. Then I gave the roadster some gas. With any luck I'd be in central Iowa by nightfall.

SOULS TO TAKE

by Gary A. Braunbeck
and Lucy A. Snyder

Gary A. Braunbeck is the author of the acclaimed collection *Things Left Behind,* as well as the forthcoming collection *Escaping Purgatory* (in collaboration with Alan M. Clark) and the CD-ROM *Sorties, Cathexes, and Human Remains.* His first solo novel, *The Indifference of Heaven,* was recently released, as was his Dark Matter novel, *In Hollow Houses.* He lives in Columbus, Ohio and has, to date, sold nearly two hundred short stories. His fiction, to quote *Publishers Weekly,* ". . . stirs the mind as it chills the marrow."

Lucy A. Snyder has coauthored another story with Gary A. Braunbeck that appears in the anthology *Bedtime Stories to Darken Your Dreams* (in case you were wondering: no, they don't have the same middle name). By day, Lucy builds Web pages, by night, she writes fiction, publishes *Dark Planet* Webzine (http://www.sfsite.com/darkplanet/) and writes the occasional interview or book review for SF Site. Lucy was born in South Carolina, grew up in Texas, and currently lives in Columbus, Ohio.

Dr. Louis Cohen nervously pulled the collar of his overcoat up higher around his cheeks, and tried not to stumble under the weight of the yard-wide aluminum case that was slowly dislocating his left shoulder. His back itched, anticipating a bullet.

Act casual, he told himself. *Don't look around.*

He wished he was somewhere, *anywhere*, besides Over-the-Rhine. Despite Cincinnati politicians' attempts to renovate the area, Over-the-Rhine had sunk only deeper into decay and gangland terrors. Graffiti covered virtually every surface. Moldering trash ranging from rusted car parts to dirty diapers to syringes lay in the gutters, mounded at the sides of buildings. It was a good place to get anonymously murdered by someone who'd decided you were wearing the wrong clothes, had the wrong skin color, or simply looked like a nice bit of target practice.

Of course, there were already plenty of people who wanted Cohen dead.

His sweating fingers slipped, and he nearly dropped the case onto the cracked concrete. Cursing under his breath, he began to lug it with both hands. It was a military design, something to be carried by two strapping young solider-medics running through steaming jungles or treacherous deserts. Cohen was no longer young, and had never been strapping, but he was aware from his guts to his pores that he was in a war zone.

He'd had an assistant who helped him carry the leaden case, a bright young RN named Susan, but she's been gunned down outside her apartment less than three months ago.

God, how he missed her. She'd been a quiet young woman, so he never really felt he knew her as a person . . . but as a nurse, she'd been exactly what the job required: calm, kind, efficient, and absolutely fearless.

The neighbors said she didn't so much as scream when the Lambs of God opened fire.

And she very literally could not be replaced. Neither Planned Parenthood nor the National Abortion and Reproductive Rights Action League had been able to find a single local nurse or EMT who was willing to do the house calls that had become critical now that all the city's clinics had closed. Over the past few years, three doctors, five patients, and ten clinic workers had been slain in the city. No one was ever convicted for those murders.

Cohen stopped at the entrance to the dilapidated apartment building and double-checked the crumpled paper in his pocket. Apartment 3-B. At least he only had to climb three flights.

Grunting, he hauled the case up over the threshold and began to plod up the grimy concrete stairs. When he finally got to the door, shoulder throbbing, he gave the steel two sharp raps.

A moment later, there was the sound of a deadbolt unlatching and the door cracked open. A sad, deeply-lined face, one that had seen far too much misery and disappointment during its time on Earth, peered out at him from beneath the door chain.

"Hello, Ms. Green?" he asked.

"Dr. White?" she whispered.

Green and White, he thought. Good Lord—when he'd first started medical school, he never thought he'd be reduced to using assumed names like some character on a television detective show.

"Yes." He reflexively glanced over his shoulder, then met her worried eyes. "May I come in? I have the samples that you ordered from my company."

She undid the chain and he stepped inside, the case bumping noisily against the door frame. As Ms. Green (whose actual name was Thompson) secured the door, he set down the case and took off his overcoat and bullet-proof Kevlar vest. He wore a good cotton shirt, gray slacks, and a paisley tie; he made it a point to dress as professionally as possible—hoping, as he did, that it lent everything an air of respectability, of compassion. He surveyed the tiny apartment, taking in the water-stained wallpaper, the threadbare carpet, the cockroach making its way down the ancient fridge.

A forlorn girl was sitting on the old couch, knees pulled up to her chin as she stared at a soap opera on the small black-and-white television. The sound was turned down. Cohen wondered if she was lost in some fantasy, imagining that the people on the screen were actually being kind to one another.

Then he saw the bruises that were fading to gray on the light brown skin of her face and arms.

An older, darker teenage girl in tight cutoffs and a t-shirt came out of a back room and stopped, staring at Cohen, her brow furrowed in fright and embarrassment.

"I'm outta here," she mumbled. "I'll be back when he's done with Toni, Mama."

And with that she hurried past Cohen out the door.

He distractedly watched her go. Did she know about birth control? Would she use it? No, he couldn't worry about her; she wasn't his patient.

Not yet, at least.

He turned his attention back to the bruised girl on the couch.

"That's my Toni." Ms. Green said. "She was playing outside, and some of the gang boys found her. . . ."

Cohen felt his stomach churn. Toni barely had any womanly curves yet; she was just black pigtails, bird-thin bones, and huge dark eyes, a child. And so small. She couldn't have weighed more than eighty pounds. He cringed at what a full-term pregnancy would do to her body.

"How long ago?" he asked.

"Three weeks. I took her to the clinic, and they looked at her some—as much as them overworked folks look at anyone who lives around here—but they didn't have any of those morning-after pills. When I took her back last Tuesday to get her tested for AIDS, they told me she was pregnant."

"Did she contract *any* diseases?"

Ms. Green shook her head. "She was lucky that way, I guess. Reverend Johnson says we have to look for the good in times like this."

"Did the police ever make an arrest?"

"No. We all know who done it, but those boys, their parents all say they were at home." A bitter laugh boiled in her throat. "I wanna kill 'em, but I can't do that. The cops'd take me and Toni and Janice wouldn't have nobody. We just have to put it aside and try our best to get on with our lives."

She looked at Cohen's case. "You got any of those pills?"

Most women wanted abortifacients instead of the vacuum, and Cohen didn't blame them one bit. "No, I'm sorry, we ran out two weeks ago when our supplier got cold feet. We're not sure when—or even *if*—we can get more. It's probably better this way; the pills take a long time to work; the procedure only takes five minutes. There's usually less blood and cramping, too."

He didn't like to call it surgery; people got awfully nervous to hear that they'd be having *surgery* in their own home. Of course, it all made Cohen nervous, too. He'd have felt a lot better if he had a nice, antiseptic clinic to work in, a place where he had nurses and a psychologist to help him care for his patients. He supposed all field doctors felt the same way.

But unlike most of them, he wished he could change his gender when he saw his patients. It had always seemed to him that pregnancy termination was something women should do for other women, especially in cases of rape. Half the time, he felt like an interloper, not a doctor.

When he'd started med school, he'd never intended to do anything besides deliver babies once he graduated. But along the way he'd been obliged to learn about the *other* way to finish a pregnancy. And when his friends and colleagues started getting killed for doing the necessary, he knew he had to do *something*, even if deep down he felt he was the wrong man for the job, even if he himself sometimes wondered about the morality of the act.

Now he was practically the only one left.

He walked to Toni and knelt down so that he was a little below her eye level. "You understand what I've come here for?"

She nodded, not looking at him. "You're here to give me an abortion. So I can keep going to school."

"That's right, Toni. Do you still want to go through with it?"

Another nod.

"It won't take long, and I'll do all I can to make sure you don't hurt. I won't do anything without telling you what's going on. Unless you'd rather sleep through it. You'd feel a bit woozy for the rest of the day, but I can give you a shot to—"

"No," she said sharply, surprising him. She looked down at him. "I—I wanna know what you're doing to me."

Cohen gave her a quick smile and gently patted her hands. "All right."

He opened the case and took out his equipment, then unfolded the case itself to make a small examining table. It was supposedly designed to hold 180 pounds, but Cohen found it tended to be a bit unstable after 150. Toni wouldn't be a problem.

He locked the last of the telescoping legs into place and set the table in the middle of the living room. He slid the stirrups into slots on the edge of the table and pulled a huge sheet of paper out of a two-foot-wide dispenser.

"Toni, I need you to take off your sandals and shorts and panties," he said as he fixed the paper to the top of the table. "You can leave your t-shirt on. When you're done, just hop up here."

He rolled up his sleeves and scrubbed up in the kitchen with a bar of antibacterial soap, then dried off with iodine-impregnated towelettes. When he finished swabbing off, he slipped on some latex gloves and started to break the heavy little vacuum unit and the rest of his instruments out of their sterile packages. He hated having to get the instruments out himself, since he ran the risk of recontaminating himself.

"Okay, Toni, I need you to lie on your back like you did for the lady doctor who looked at you in the clinic and put your feet in . . . yes, like that, that's good. Bend your knees a little more and scoot this way, good. You want your mother with you?"

Toni nodded, and Ms. Green moved up beside the girl and gripped her hand.

"Okay, the most important thing now is to try to relax. . . ."

He spoke to the girl constantly, tried to soothe her

as he tried not to retear her flesh with the speculum and dilator, both designed for a grown woman. She winced at the anaesthetic shots, but seemed not to feel the vacuum tube, though its roar made her eyes go wide.

Five minutes after he began, Cohen was staring at a quarter-sized spot of white-membraned tissue floating in a thimbleful of bright blood at the bottom of the stainless steel vacuum tray. Feeling a vague sadness, he slid the tray into a zippered plastic bag for later cleaning and sterilization.

"Okay, Toni, you'll be feeling a bit crampy right now, but that's normal, the uterus always cramps when it's emptied. You'll bleed for the rest of the day, maybe heavily, but if you see any brown stuff, don't worry, it's just iodine."

He cleaned up and left the girl with antibiotics, cramp medicine, a few mild painkillers, and an admonishment to call his answering service if she developed a fever.

The case seemed even heavier on the trek back to his car. He had to stop midway, gasping for breath at a street corner.

Then he noticed the van.

It was an old blue Ford, the homemade paint job cracking over rust spots. The windows were dark glass. It rolled slowly toward him, the passenger's window sliding down—

Cohen jerked the case off the pavement and lurched toward the nearest alley. He heard two loud firecracker bangs and then a bullet slammed into the back of his knee.

The pain didn't reach his brain right away. His leg buckled, and he saw dark blood running to the pavement. He dropped the case, tried to hop to the alley but tripped in some gravel. He fell face-first beside some trash cans, skinning his palms and ripping the elbow of his shirt.

The men from the van surrounded him before he could get up. He saw their grim white faces, hands gripping baseball bats and ax handles, white t-shirts emblazoned with red crosses. The LifeGuards. His heart froze. In the same instant, Cohen was glad no assistant would have to die with him, and was sorry his assailants weren't from one of the other Anti groups. The Lambs and the Christian Militia never deigned to touch their enemies with anything but a bullet. The LifeGuards liked to drive their message home a little before they sent sinners on to Divine Judgment.

"Fresh from the slaughter—how can you walk in God's *clean* sunlight?" demanded one of the men.

"One foot in front of the other, then repeat the process . . . until you so rudely . . . interrupted everything," Cohen ground out through the searing pain. He knew it was a mistake the minute the words came out of his mouth, but he couldn't help it; fanatics made him angry, and when he got angry—and scared, to boot—he tended to get sarcastic. Toss in the agony ripping up from his destroyed knee, and you had a heady combination.

"An eye for an eye," snarled another LifeGuard. "As you have torn the limbs from the innocent, so shall we do unto you."

"It didn't *have* any limbs, you Bible-thumping, scripture-screwing, Neolithic dipshits!" he shouted at them, deciding that if he was going to go down, he'd not do so quietly. "It also didn't have nerves or a heartbeat or a gender! Listen, satisfy my curiosity about something before you do what your god commands you to do: Why weren't you guys around to *protect the innocent* when the girl I just saw was raped? Or do you only protect those whose existence furthers your cause and gives you something to shout about from your soapboxes? Silly me—never mind answering that: your god doesn't bother with harlots, does it? And if she was raped, well, then, a harlot she must be. Am I right?"

"Hey," came a husky female voice from behind the group. "Shouldn't you guys be off adopting unwanted rug rats or something? Or did those nasty old psychiatric tests get in the way?"

Cohen peeked around the group of LifeGuards and saw a tall brunette in black jeans, low-cut blouse, and a red leather motorcycle jacket standing a few yards away. Addled as he was by pain and fear, he realized she was one of the most gorgeous women he'd ever laid eyes on.

The LifeGuards looked confused. "Where'd she come from?" one muttered.

"You wanna do the doc, you gotta do me first," she said, the corner of her mouth twitching into a faint smirk.

A couple of the men looked at each other uncertainly.

"We haven't got time for this Jezebel," said another, a hollow-faced man with a frizzy beard. He pulled a pistol out of the front of the jeans and fired.

Blood exploded between the woman's breasts, but she did not fall. She looked down at the wound, her expression an odd mix of shock and amusement. "Oh, lookee there. You went and gave me an owie. You guys don't believe in foreplay, do you?"

She was bleeding so badly, Cohen was sure the bullet had penetrated her heart. He felt faint.

The hollow-faced man screamed something about Satan and started to empty his gun into the woman. One, two, three, a hail of bullets ripped through jacket and jeans and flesh. Her body jerked, her expression twisted from surprise to agony to rage. Still she did not fall.

The gun was dry-firing now, an impotent metal click like a stopwatch ticking down.

The woman let loose a roar, loud as the vacuum tube, and in a flash her hands were around the gunman's neck. She tore his windpipe away, leaving his head lolling on a crimson spit of vertebrae as he crumpled.

She was already savagely kicking at the head of another LifeGuard. Her boot connected with his ear, a tremendous *whack!*, his whole skull deforming before he was knocked off his feet.

Cohen couldn't stand this. He squeezed his eyes shut, tried to plug his ears against the screams and cracking of bones. But when it all stopped, he couldn't keep from peeking out again.

The woman was crouched beside the body of one of the men, her hand flat over his heart. Her mouth hung open in a horrified gape, her eyes staring wide at something only she could see. Tears started to roll down her frozen face.

Suddenly she jerked away, fell on her back, shaking. "Shit shit *shit,* I *knew* better than to do that, bad brains, bad memories, shit, somebody take it away *justtakeitallawaybeforeitkillsme!*" She sat up, rocking back and forth, tearing at her hair and crying. "Shit. Can't even get a decent high these days."

She took a deep, shuddering breath and stared up at the sky. Her face was smeared with blood and mascara. "Okay. Okay, I'm cool. Right."

She got to her feet and looked around, seeming disoriented. Her body was a ghastly, holey mess, her blouse entirely soaked with blood. Her eyes focused on Cohen.

"Ow. That knee's *got* to hurt." She stepped toward him, wiping her hands off on the seat of her pants. He involuntarily cringed.

"Don't look at me like that," she said, frowning. "I'm trying to help you. *Really.*"

Before he could scoot away, her hands were tight around his knee. There was a brief pain, then a strange tingly-warm feeling that spread up his whole leg. He watched, astonished, as she tore open his pants leg and worked his raw flesh and shattered bones like clay.

"Bad neighborhood for a guy like you," she said as she pulled a ligament into place. "Bet you live someplace a lot nicer than this . . . yeah, someplace quiet, with trees. How'd you get here? Somebody give you a ride . . . no, I bet you drove yourself. Yeah."

The woman's chatter had him thinking of the rental house on Hariet Street, and of the car Planned Parenthood had lent him for the day, which he'd parked a few blocks away beside a ginkgo tree. He felt dizzy, and assumed it was blood loss.

She sealed his skin as though it was zippered, and suddenly his knee was perfectly healed.

"There. Better than new." She patted her handiwork, stood, and winked at him. "Say hi to the cops for me. Oh, by the way—I really dug it when you called them scripture-screwing, Neolithic dipshits. That took some stones, considering the position you were in. It's a real turn-on."

And with that, she dashed out of the alley.

Cohen could do nothing but sit there staring numbly at the human wreckage, wondering if he'd lost his mind and was having some kind of grisly long-play hallucination. He was relieved to be alive, but . . . good God!

The police came a little while later, sirens keening and lights flashing. The officers pouring out of the squad cars were certainly real enough, smelling of cigarettes and coffee, voices short and black like the muzzles of their drawn revolvers.

They made him stand up, hands over his head, and demanded to know what had happened. He could only confess he wasn't quite sure. The cops stood around for a few minutes, muttering to each other and looking from the mess of corpses to Cohen's unstained hands and shirt. Finally, they told him he needed to come with them to the station to make a statement.

As they marched him to a squad car, he saw the rusty splatter that marked the spot where he'd been shot. His case was gone, probably stolen by a junkie looking for needles or pawnables. Another thousand dollars down the drain, a thousand the local Planned Parenthood didn't have. At least they wouldn't have to find a new doctor.

At the station, two cops grilled him for an hour in a drab, stinky little room walled in one-way glass. He judiciously left out the supernatural details of the incident. *The van came after me, and I ran and tripped in the alley. Yes, they wanted to kill me . . . you saw the bats. Look, am I under arrest? Like I said, a woman came, and she . . . yes, one woman, I only saw one. Yes, a red leather jacket and black jeans, I've told you this. Yes, she killed them all. Can I please call my lawyer?*

In the end, they said that, no, he wasn't under

arrest, they just wanted to make sure they had his statement down right. He was perfectly free to go, but shouldn't leave town anytime soon.

There was a knowing malice on their faces as they escorted him to the front of the station. Their smiles told him he'd be dead soon enough when the Life-Guards took revenge, thus saving them the paper-work involved in actually arresting him.

Nevertheless, the desk sergeant let him call his sister Ruth for a ride home. She'd been working for Planned Parenthood longer than he had, first as a clinic escort, later as a courier. She'd become quite an expert at spotting and losing tails, so he always called her for rides. When she arrived, he gave her the edited version of the slaughter in the alley.

"Why the hell weren't you carrying a gun, Louis?" she demanded as she started her Buick.

"I was wearing the vest—" he began.

"That's not enough! They almost *killed* you because you couldn't defend yourself."

"I don't like guns." Despite his sister's lifelong interest in target shooting, he'd always associated fire-arms with drunken yahoos in pickups, doped-up gangsters, and religious psychopaths. And he didn't want to give his zealous enemies *any* ammunition in their argument that he might be what they said he was.

"Dammit, you've got to lose that 'I'm no killer, I'm a doctor' attitude of yours," she said. "The Hippo-cratic Oath doesn't apply if you're protecting your-self against those nuts. If you don't start carrying a gun, you will be *dead,* Louis, D-E-A-D, dead! The Big Dirt-Nap, All Over, All Gone, Bye-Bye."

Having guns hadn't done much for the LifeGuards in the alley, but Cohen didn't want to go into all that.

"I'm sorry, Ruth, I just don't like guns. I'd rather just be able to drive away—oh, dammit!"

"What?"

"Oh, the car, I left the car when the police took me away. It's one of the loaners P.P. gets from that used car place so the Antis can't follow us. Some kid's probably stolen it for a joyride or stripped it down by now. Shit! I've lost them the car *and* the case, and they haven't got the money to replace any of it. Lord, this day has sucked eggs!"

"Way I understand it, that's part of your job, isn't it?"

Cohen—realizing too late the unintentional pun he'd made—glared at his sister.

"Forgive me for trying to inject a little levity into things," said Ruth. "Well, you're safe, and all things considered you can't ask for much more than that. And look on the bright side . . . at least for once a violent nut's on *your* side."

"And that's supposed to be a bright side? My God, Ruth! Do you see what's happening here? Your particular moral stance on the issue aside—because out here, your individual morality has no meaning anymore—this is a procedure that women have a *right* to. But it's been turned into a political issue so smirking Ken-doll senators can get voters riled up, clinics are closing down all over the country, and we're just a breath away from the bad old days of back-alley butchers doing this. I'll tell you the truth, if I had a choice, if things were different, I would choose not to perform this particular procedure. But choice has gone the way of individual morality, Sis. It doesn't factor in. This is simply something that *has* to be done, and I'm pretty much the only doctor left in the state who still does it, and I have to spend half my time looking over my shoulder. I deplore violence, so please don't try and make me believe that just because one violent psycho took my side that things are looking up!"

A few minutes later, they got to his current residence, a two-bedroom house in a quiet little neighborhood a few blocks north of Xavier University. Planned Parenthood was renting it from a sympathetic local realtor, and they moved him every few months to reduce the chance the Antis would discover where he lived.

"Do you want me to stay with you for a while?" Ruth asked as she pulled into the driveway.

"No, I'll be fine . . . I just have some things I want to think through. And I have to call my coordinator to tell her what happened."

"Okay, but there's something I want you to have." She reached under her seat and pulled out a pistol in a black nylon shoulder holster along with a slim booklet. "This is a Browning 9mm I've had for a while. It's an accurate piece, and reasonably light. This manual tells you all about handling it safely and cleaning and loading it. And it *is* loaded; the safety's on, but be careful."

She paused. "Don't look at me like that, Louis, just give this a chance. For me. I'll sleep a lot better knowing you have some way of protecting yourself."

"But—"

"No buts." She pushed it into his hands. "For me, please?"

He knew she'd never give up. His shoulders drooped in defeat. "Okay."

"Good."

She gave him a quick peck on the cheek before he climbed out of the car. And then she drove off, leaving him staring at the bundle in his hands. It was surprisingly heavy for something she claimed was "reasonably light." He imagined it must be all those bullets. The evening sun glinted off the deep gray-blue metal.

"Nuts." He didn't want to carry the thing, didn't even want it in his house. But he didn't feel right throwing a gift away. Besides, he knew it *had* to be expensive; he'd once asked Ruth how much she spent on her shooting hobby, and had been thoroughly horrified at her response.

The garage. He could stash the gun in the bottom of his tool chest, and then he wouldn't have to think about it again. He walked to the garage door, unlocked it, and heaved it open.

The big brown loaner car sat before him, tucked in beside his little red Honda hatchback.

His heart jumped in panic. He wanted to run after Ruth, but she was long gone. The door leading into the house was open, the kitchen lights on. He held his breath, listening for footsteps or voices. The house was silent.

Maybe whoever had broken into his house was gone. After all, if it had been the Antis, they would've either wired bombs to the front door and garage and left, or they would have waited in ambush and come out the moment he came into the garage. In either case, he'd be dead already. And besides, why would any of the Antis take the trouble to bring back the car?

Who had been in his house? And why? He looked down at the pistol in his hands. All his sister's exhortations replayed themselves in his mind as his curiosity overcame his fear. If it was stupid to go into the house, it would be far stupider to go in without a weapon. He clumsily pulled the Browning out of its holster and crept to the open door.

A naked black-haired woman was sitting on the dining room table, legs dangling, blowing smoke rings from a cigarillo. She had an extraordinary body, lithe and muscular like the female triathletes he'd seen on TV, except unlike all of them she had the huge, gravity-defying breasts of a pinup girl. It took him a few seconds to notice the small pile of metal fragments near her hip.

She arched an eyebrow at him. "I was beginning to wonder if you'd ever get here, Dr. Cohen."

He instantly recognized the voice. She was the woman from the alley. But what had happened to all those bullet wounds?

"Who are you?" he stammered.

"Me?" She paused thoughtfully, then emptied a handful of bloodied bullets into an empty glass sitting nearby—bullets Cohen realized she'd taken out of her own body somehow.

She smiled at him and said, "I'm your new assistant."

Cohen's jaw worked for a second before anything came out. "My new *assistant?* But you . . . you killed those men, and . . ."

"You're feeling really freaked out right now, I appreciate that. Speaking of that, why don't you put down that gun, love? You don't know how to use it; you're liable to hurt yourself. Or seriously annoy me. It was a real bitch digging these others out."

Grimacing, she picked up the glass and shook it, rattling its contents as she examined the bullets more closely. "Hollow points. Ugh. Got into organs I didn't know I had."

He took a deep breath and kept the shaking pistol

pointed in her general direction. "How do you know my name? And how did you get here?"

"Don't worry, the crazies don't know where you live, just me." She paused to puff out another smoke ring. "But you still look like you're gonna shit any minute now, so I guess I should explain myself. I've been looking for a doctor of your particular skills for a while, but they're in painfully short supply. So I figured, if you're looking for a duck, best thing to do is find some duck hunters. So I followed the Life-Guards for a week, and they led me right to you."

She drew her knees up to her chin and smiled a him. "And now that I've found you, things are going to be just ducky."

"But—but how did you find this place? And the car?"

"I'm a talented girl," she smiled. "And psychic to boot. I can just pick up surface thoughts, but it's pretty easy to get people to think about certain things, such as where they parked their car. You might have felt dizzy; some never feel me in there at all. Afterward, I got your kit," she pointed past his shoulder at the surgical case, which sat by the stove, "found your car, hotwired it and went to my motel to get some stuff, then came here. There's some blood on the car seats, sorry about that. Ditto your bathroom floor; I fixed myself up in there. I know of an excellent blood remover; I'll get you a bottle tomorrow." She shrugged. "A century of practice has made me pretty good at what I do."

She certainly didn't look a hundred. "What is it you do?" he asked faintly.

"I kill people. Mostly out of necessity, as you do. The price is too high to do it for sport." She slid off the table and approached him. "Actually, it's almost

always too high. I survive by taking a person's bio-
logical potential—their unexpired life span, if you
will—and converting it into energy. Unfortunately,
as I drain their time, I also get their emotional memories, whether I want them or not."

She paused, frowning. "There's a lot of people
walking around with absolute poison in their brains.
That last LifeGuard I killed this afternoon was definitely toxic. Let's just say that most of his childhood
was . . . extremely unpleasant, thus his mental state.
Unfortunately, I've never gotten used to the mind
bombs. I can't get that man's memories out of my
head, won't get them out until I take another life.
And then it might start all over again, unless I luck
out and take one of the rare happy ones."

"That's a vicious cycle," he agreed nervously. "But
what's it got to do with me?"

She smiled. "I've decided to conduct a little experi-
ment in better living, and you're going to help me.
You see, I realized last month—why it didn't hit me
sooner, I don't know—that not only do embryos and
fetuses have plenty of time, they have no memories
whatsoever. They're the perfect victims."

Cohen felt ill, and began to back up.

"Oh, don't worry, Doctor, you won't have to do
anything differently, and I promise I won't get in
your way. I just want to be there when they die."
She cocked her head at him, her black eyes boring
into his. "I have to kill *someone*, and these memories
are making me miserable . . . would you rather I
started prowling playgrounds, looking for innocent,
golden-haired moppets who'll fill my head with images of love and delight?"

"No! But . . . but you haven't got the medical training to be my assistant."

"Oh, but you're wrong. I've killed several doctors, and even if I hadn't, I know my way around the human body."

"But I told the police what you look like, and you'd be recognized for sure," he persisted, desperation cracking his voice.

"Wrong again." Her breasts began to shrink, muscles soften, face melt into round cheeks, blue eyes, and a cute, upturned nose. Suddenly, she was an extremely pretty version of his previous assistant. "Another useful hunting trick. I'll be a blonde by tomorrow morning. Tell everybody I'm Susan's sister Lita, come up from Houston to carry on her work."

Cohen made a choking noise.

"Oh, it's not *that* bad, Doctor. There's a lot of perks to having me as an assistant."

"Lita" came up close to him, so close he could feel her breath on his neck. Prickles ran down his spine, and he felt himself getting hard. The sudden lust cutting through his fear horrified the sensible part of his mind.

"Why me?" he managed.

"Aren't you ever lonely, Dr. Cohen? When's the last time you touched a woman without your gloves on?"

She kissed his earlobe, and the pressure at his groin swelled to an insistent ache.

"I'm lonely," she whispered.

She pressed her hand against his fly, making him gasp like he'd been burned. "And by the size of things, you'll be very entertaining."

Cohen couldn't stand it anymore. He grabbed her, kissed her. She pulled him to the linoleum and rolled on top of him, biting his neck and tearing open his clothes.

Cohen had always been terrified of roller coasters, and sex with the woman was like riding an enormous runaway wood-frame coaster, his body jolted and battered as he plunged down, down into oblivion, careening past terminal velocity.

When she finally let him come, the sheer sensory shock was like hitting concrete at the speed of sound.

He woke up when Lita sprinkled ice water on his face. Groaning, he sat up and realized he'd spent the night on the kitchen floor. His sister's pistol lay a few feet away from his head.

"It's eight AM." Lita flicked more water at him. She was perched on the kitchen table, already dressed in a blue skirt and blouse that were, if not exactly professional attire, at least reasonably demure. "Can't keep your patients waiting, can we?"

Cohen felt queasy again. How could he possibly let her near his patients? She was a *killer*, for God's sake!

On the other hand, what choice did he have? He could go along with her plan, or she would kill him. And judging by what he'd seen her do, she'd steal his memories, his form, and his place as the last abortion provider in Cincinnati. No. Better to stay alive. And try to do damage control where he could.

He watched her walk away, her shapely derriere sliding under the silky fabric of the skirt. He noted that she wasn't wearing underwear. The practical part of his brain reminded him he *did* need an assistant in a bad way, even if that assistance simply amounted to another set of hands.

And she was more than hands—she could stop a bullet, keep him safe. With her around, he could stop worrying so much about who was waiting around the corner and concentrate on the people he was treating. Maybe this wouldn't be such a bad deal after all.

He got up and sequestered the gun in the bottom of his tool chest in the garage, then went into his bedroom to get ready. The woman hadn't slept in his bed, but she had taken over his closet with an assortment of clothes, very few of which were suitable for a medical assistant. His bathroom was likewise cluttered with her stuff, mainly makeup and shampoo. He didn't see a toothbrush or any medicines.

Once he'd showered and thrown on some fresh clothes, he called his coordinator to find out what he'd be doing for the day and where he'd be meeting the equipment truck. He and the woman drove out to a side street near the zoo, where he got a new car and traded his case for another stocked with sealed, sterilized equipment. The woman, striding in stiletto heels, carried the cases as if they weighed nothing.

The morning's first patient was a thirtyish woman who lived in a brownstone in Mount Adams, long-time home of Cincy's yuppie elite. She was attractive, immaculately coiffeured, two months pregnant, and about thirty pounds too heavy for his case-table.

"You want to do it on my *dining room table?*" she asked incredulously, twisting her jade bead necklace around her fingers. "I have to eat on that thing!"

"Well, if you've got another table that will remain stable, we could use that instead," he replied. "Otherwise, I simply can't do the procedure. I'll do my best to make sure nothing gets on it."

"Well, okay, I guess. . . ."

"Do you want to stay awake dur—"

"No! Knock me out!" She shuddered. "I just wanna wake up and have it be *over!*"

Cohen ended up doing most of the preparations;

Lita seemed only minimally interested in the whole thing until he'd given the patient a shot to put her under.

"Is she out yet?" Lita asked.

"Yes . . . what are you doing?"

"You'll see."

She put her hands on the woman's belly. Soon those hands were quivering, arm muscles shaking, beads of sweat popping out on her face. Through the anaesthesia, the patient moaned, her womb starting to contract in miscarriage. Lita jerked away and staggered to the wall, her eyes glazed as though she were intoxicated.

"Oh, yeah." Her voice was badly slurred. "Plenty of time."

Cohen was busy trying to clean his patient up and give her a D&C so nothing would be left in her womb to give her an infection.

"You're not going act like this every time, are you?" he asked nervously. "People will get suspicious."

"So put 'em all under, and send everybody else out of the room. . . ."

"No, the decision to be awake or asleep should be up to the patient. Besides, the anaesthetic makes some people feel really bad—"

"Yeah. Whatever." She frowned at him. "Fine, I'll just eat it and try to act casual. But, man, what a rush! They usually try to fight me off, and I only end up getting thirty or forty years. I can't remember the last time I got a whole ninety!"

Cohen stared at the tissue he'd caught in his tray. Ninety years of potential. What if . . . ?

No. He shook his head. He was no theologian, and had been doing this too long to worry about imponderables now. The woman who'd been carrying the embryo was more than mere potential, and she had the right to bear or not bear children as she saw fit.

And if he'd been wasting the potential of the unborn all this time, well, now at least it was doing *somebody* some good.

He had three more patients that day, all of whom chose to stay awake. Lita showed better control, taking the embryos only after he'd dilated his patients, and he didn't think anybody noticed anything strange.

In light of the fact she was a supernatural murderer, she behaved very well. But though his knee proved she knew how to work with flesh, she didn't know how to work with people, not in a medical setting, at least. She handled his patients too roughly, and never asked their permission before she touched them. Her voice never seemed to find the soft, soothing range necessary to calm women going through a psychologically traumatic time.

He politely pointed all this out to her after the second patient, and though she nodded and agreed, she also didn't alter her behavior one bit.

That night, the woman left to go shopping while he ate his dinner, and seemed agitated when she returned.

"What's wrong?" he asked.

"The time's wrong!" She set down the Wal-Mart bag, which was filled with cheap novels and Sega cartridges. She began to pace, pulling at her hair. "I took 270 years today, right? I mean, I *felt* it, and the time felt like it always does, but now . . . now it's *fading* inside me, and it only feels like I've got eighty years. How could I have read their time wrong?

Damn! Maybe their potential's not really set yet when they're that young. . . ."

She sat down at the table and put her head in her hands. It was the first display of anything resembling human vulnerability that Cohen had seen in her. He decided to ask her some questions; his curiosity couldn't go unsatisfied for much longer.

"Lita?"

"*What?*"

"Please don't snap at me like that," he said with as much tenderness as he could muster; he had to be careful with her. "I was just wondering about a couple of things."

She smiled, but there was more weariness than humor in it. "I'll bet you are. I'm surprised it took you *this* long to ask me."

Cohen was taken slightly aback. "You say that as if you know what I'm going to ask."

"You want to know what I am, right?"

Cohen blinked, then remembered what she'd said about being slightly psychic. "Yes."

"You want the whole story or the *Reader's Digest* version? Keep in mind that I'm kind of tired right now."

"The condensed version will be just fine, thank you."

Her smile widened, but now Cohen couldn't read what was behind it at all.

"For lack of a better term, call me a soul harvester. I was created in 1904 by a dying god—I never knew Its true name—as a last-ditch effort to collect souls for It. The source of all the gods' power is the souls of those who are believers in their religion—my Master had so few followers It was dying, and It hoped to survive through my gathering of peoples' souls—

'converting' them by killing them for It. It didn't work. The god was too weak and I was still too young to gather souls to save it, so it faded away . . . died. But I was left behind.''

She shrugged. ''I have no master, no purpose. But I want to live. And I live to kill.''

''But . . . how do you—?''

''Live off someone else's soul? The human soul has two parts: the spiritual force, and the life force. The spirit is consumed by a god at death, or left behind as a ghost to wander or eventually fade. The life force is a finite quantity that is used up over the course of a person's natural life. I consume the life force, but since my Master isn't here to take the spiritual force away, I am haunted—in the most literal definition of that word—by the spirits of the people I've killed. Their memories become mine; their knowledge becomes mine also; I know every thought, every dream, every impulse, the structure of every cell—shit, Doc, I've got the precise DNA structure of over two thousand people that I can access any time I need to change form. So, unlike most women, I've always got something to wear. You can wake up now, I'm finished— No, scratch that, something just occurred to me.'' She turned to Cohen, her eyes shining with hunger. ''Can you take us to women who are farther along, say, six or seven months pregnant? Women who have real fetuses instead of those little jelly embryos?''

His breath caught in his throat. ''No. No, besides the third trimester being far too dangerous, I simply will not do something like that, understand me? I *have* to draw a line somewhere.''

''I thought individual morality had no place in the streets these days.'' She scowled at him, but then her face melted into an indulgent smile. She patted his arm. "You're tired. We'll talk about this later. You look like you need to go to bed."

She took him into the bedroom and seduced him much as she had the night before. When he was finally exhausted, she slipped out of bed and left him to sleep by himself.

Three days later, the LifeGuards tried to kill him again.

A man jumped out from the doorway of a laundromat as he and Lita were heading back to the car from a house call in Norton. As the man pulled a TEC-9 machine pistol out of his jacket, she jumped in front of Cohen. She caught most of the bullets full in her torso and fell to the sidewalk, bleeding from a dozen wounds as the gunman ran away.

A crowd gathered as soon as the shooting stopped. Cohen, who was unhurt, knelt beside Lita.

"Too many witnesses," she whispered through the blood filling her mouth. "Can't just walk away this time. Have to ditch this form . . . see you later when I've gotten out of the city morgue."

She reappeared that night in the form of a breathtaking Hispanic woman with full red lips, big brown eyes, and muscular flamenco dancer's legs. In such a marvelous flesh disguise, he expected her to affect an accent, or put a little extra strut in her step.

But in voice and action she remained as she had always been. Cohen began to suspect that although realistic mannerisms were not beyond her ability, they might be beyond her imagination.

They fell into a routine of house calls and sex. Sometimes she would lie beside him afterward, touching his face or playing with the hair on his chest, but in the end she always left his bed. He never saw her sleep. If he woke up in the middle of the night, he'd hear the TV or a video game. Every once in a while, he thought he could hear her crying, and he wondered if she was remembering.

On those rare occasions when she left him alone in the evening to go shopping, he would go out to the garage and stare at his sister's gun. But he would not touch it.

Two months after Lita first saved him, Cohen got a call that sent him back to Ms. Green's apartment in Over-the-Rhine. When he and Lita arrived, they could hear Ms. Green and one of her daughters arguing, their shouts muffled by the thick steel door. He had to pound hard on the door for a minute before anybody heard him.

"Doctor, come in, my daughter's being stupid!" Ms. Green exclaimed as she opened the door. "Maybe you can talk some sense into the girl!"

"Don't let that man in, Mama. I don't want him nowhere near me!" The older daughter crossed her arms protectively over her belly. From the looks of her, Cohen guessed she was three or four months pregnant, had already been pregnant when he took care of her little sister Toni.

"Stop being a fool, Janice!" her mother yelled.

"I wanna keep this baby, Mama!"

"I told you a hundred times, no!" She turned to Cohen, her face furious and sad. "How are we gonna keep a baby, Doctor? I work fifty hours a week cleaning the motel just to get us by as it is. Janice ain't got a job and she sure as hell ain't gonna get one if she has a kid! I ain't busted my ass all these years to provide for her so she can drop out of school and throw it all away 'cause she wants some live dolly to cuddle!"

"Look . . . I can't do the procedure if she doesn't want it. There's always adoption—"

"Ain't nobody gonna want this baby!" Ms. Green exploded, throwing up her hands. "That white boy who got her pregnant been giving her vodka, too, and before I caught on she was pregnant, I was yellin' at her for comin' home drunk. The kid's gonna be like my idiot cousin Alfred. His momma drank before she had him, too. There ain't *no one* gonna wanna adopt some little half-black retard baby!" She looked down at the carpet. "It'd be cruel to bring it into the world at all."

"Please, Ms. Green, calm down." He took her arm and pulled her aside. "I simply can't do the procedure without Janice's permission and cooperation. I can talk to her about it, but it's her choice. But there *are* people who'd adopt the baby, even if it does have Fetal Alcohol Syndrome—"

Janice cried out. He turned in time to see Lita release the girl's arm and stagger to the wall. Janice grimaced and clutched her belly.

"Goddammit!" Cohen hurried Janice into the bathroom.

She miscarried on the cold white tiles. He set up his equipment in the kitchen, then took the crying, confused girl to the table to give her a D&C to make sure her womb was clean.

Lita stumbled up beside him.

"I don't need any help here," he ground out. "Clean up that mess."

She looked nonplussed, but went into the bathroom and shut the door. He heard the toilet flush several times while he was working on Janice. His rage made it hard to even see what he was doing, but his hands remembered how to be gentle.

"What are you so mad about?" Lita asked when they were finally out of the apartment.

"Jesus Christ, you don't get it, do you?" He stared at her, incredulous.

"Hey, it was for the best—"

"That does not matter! That girl didn't want an abortion, and you had no right to decide she needed one! My job is to give these women choices, and you took that girl's choice away!"

He refused to speak to her on the way back to the apartment. He drove, eyes locked on the road ahead, jaw working furiously. Lita talked at him constantly, sometimes threatening, sometimes cajoling. By the time they pulled into his driveway, he knew what he had to do.

He marched straight to the bedroom and started pulling her clothes out of the closet, dumping them on the floor.

"What are you doing, love?"

"I want you out of here. Take your things and go!"

She scowled at him. "This had better be a joke, and you had better apologize, because you're pissing me off!"

"Are you deaf?" he roared. "Get out! I'm not going to be your supplier any more! Go get your fix somewhere else!"

"You seem to have forgotten who you're dealing with," she said ominously, stepping toward him. "I can kill you so slowly you'll think you've already died and gone to hell."

"And I hope you remember me well."

She stopped short. "I don't *have* to take your time.

I can just *waste* you. And then take your face and your name and have your patients all to myself."

Sweat trickled down the groove of his back. "Even if you looked like me, they wouldn't believe you *were* me, not for very long. You don't know how to take my place." He paused and licked his dry lips. "And yes, you can waste me. But I have the feeling you might remember me anyway."

She glared at him for a long moment, then started to pick up her clothes and shove them in the duffel bag she kept in the bottom of the closet.

"They'll kill you," she spat, hoisting the duffel onto her shoulder. "Without me around, you're just meat for the dogs."

She stomped out, and a minute later he heard her motorcycle tearing out of the driveway.

When he was sure she was gone, he went to the garage and lifted the Browning from the bottom of his tool chest. He pulled it out of the holster and held it up in front of his face. The pistol had a satisfying heft, felt good in his hand.

He slipped the gun into its holster and went back into the house.

She fell on him from behind like a curse from heaven.

"I missed you," she said, then rammed her hand through his chest cavity and gripped his heart.

Cohen could feel his life force being absorbed by her—his memories and knowledge, as well.

All his medical knowledge.

"Think about this, Doc," she whispered in his ear, "I can assume any form I want to—including yours. But you forgot one little detail—I assume all knowledge, as well. By this time tomorrow I could be walking around in your body, with all your knowledge and expertise, and despite what you might think, no one—your sister included—would know the difference. *You,* on the other hand, will be quite dead, and no one but me will know. And I won't even really *care*—except for missing the way you feel inside of me. But it might be interesting to try it from the other end, so to speak. I'm sure there are plenty of women out there—patients—who'd be willing to exchange certain physical favors for your specialized services. And if not them . . . I'm sure they've got mothers or younger daughters.

"Am I getting my point across to you, Doc?"

It was all Cohen could do to nod his head. He was slipping away, fading, dissolving into nothing. . . .

"Stay with me, Doc," she said, using her free hand to slap his cheek. "Got a proposition for you. I haven't actually *absorbed* your essence yet, I'm just gathering at the moment. It'd be real easy to just shoot all of this right back into you and heal this rather impressive hole I've put in your chest. Or we could go with my first scenario . . . but I'm guessing that's not much to your liking.

"So here's the deal. I stay on as your assistant, and we do the normal procedures, the early ones, and I'll take what I need from that. But you're going to . . . *expand* your patient base, got me? We'll put out the word that you will perform the procedure *at any time* during the pregnancy, right up until and including the ninth month. I *need* the older ones, their essence lasts longer.

"Those are your choices, Doc. Don't look at me like that, don't you dare think this makes you one of the bad guys—*everyone* is one of the bad guys, Doc. The world is full of nothing but villains. It's just a matter of whether or not you choose to be one of the villains who lose out, or one of those who emerge victorious."

She gave his heart a little squeeze. Cohen thought he saw Death on its pale horse riding toward him.

"Only a couple of seconds left here, Doc, and then it's all academic as far as you're concerned. Either way, I win; either way, I get what I want. Question is, do I do it alone or do we do it together? Think about it; together, we could become one—a new god of sorts. Fuck all the old-time religions—in fact, fuck all known religions. We'll be a religion unto ourselves. Not a bad payoff for a day's work, eh?

"All you have to do is just nod your head, and we're a team again. If not, then tomorrow Doc Cohen walks with a little more funk in his step and takes no prisoners.

"So what's it gonna be, Doc?"

He lifted his head.

Looked into her eyes and smiled and nodded.

She leaned down to kiss him.

"Good choice," she whispered, releasing his essence back into his body. "It's always more fun when the bad guys win, anyway."

NINA

by Pauline E. Dungate

Pauline E. Dungate lives in Birmingham, England, and
works as a teacher at the Birmingham Museum and Art
Gallery. Her stories have appeared in such anthologies as
The Skin of the Soul, Merlin, and *Narrow Houses.* She has
also written numerous reviews and articles under the name
of Pauline Morgan. Other interests include gardening, cook-
ing, ferret keeping, and truck driving.

This morning I got married. I was apprehensive:
who wouldn't be? Now, I am shit scared. You
see, despite the fact that I was born in Birmingham,
England, our family still follows some of the tradi-
tions of Indian culture, like arranged marriages. I
wasn't even consulted. It was all sorted out between
the heads of families.

At first, when father told me my bride was to be
Nina Chandha, I didn't think too much of it. In fact
I was quite pleased as I thought I remembered her
from school. She was two years below me in my
sister Mita's class, and reasonably pretty.

Then Mita started teasing.

"Hope you like girls with spirit," she said. "You've
got a right one there."

"What do you mean?"

"Nina likes her own way." She clammed up then,

Mita did, and no amount of cajoling on my part could get anything more than giggles out of her. Which just went to prove what I always thought: sisters are a creation of Kali sent to plague and annoy brothers. Not that I believe in that gods and demons stuff, though it does make an exciting tale.

Bali's sister, Jasveer, was a little more forthcoming. Balvinder and I go back a long way despite him being Sikh—we both started junior school on the same day. Bali wouldn't be wed for three or four years yet—his people liked to marry their daughters to mature men. Besides the scars from the beating he took almost a year ago still showed. Still, he was pleased for me, though he didn't really remember Nina either.

Jasveer did.

She was sitting at the big table in the kitchen of Bali's, supposedly doing her homework. She had declared that she was going to do better than Bali in her exams. Not difficult, since Bali only just passed in Technology and Art. Bali and I sat at the other end of the table, sipping lager. His mother would tut-tut about it, but his dad was more progressive. "We're in England now," he would say before going off to join his Irish workmates from the factory for a few beers.

We stayed in because Bali didn't want to be seen drinking through a straw—his jaw was still wired in places. That was another reason why his dad let me bring alcohol into their house. "Only the kitchen, mind," he would say. He reckoned Bali had suffered enough and deserved a few pleasures. Others would say Bali got what he deserved.

As I was telling Bali about my proposed nuptials

I could see Jasveer's ears prick up. Like young men do, we started discussing the wedding night. All innuendo, of course, and mostly for Jasveer's benefit. We pretended to ignore her, but I could see she was getting agitated.

"You're both fools," she eventually burst out.

"Little girls shouldn't listen to men's talk," I said, grinning.

Jasveer darkened and began to pile her books up. "It won't be like that, you'll see," she said. "Especially with Nina."

"What will it be like?" Bali croaked through his smashed larynx.

Jasveer looked straight at me. "Nina said she would kill any man who laid a finger on her."

Bali and I laughed—at least I did. Bali spluttered, but it was the same thing. How many times had we heard that line? It was straight out of an old movie, and every girl says it at some time or another.

"If you think it's so funny, go and talk to Anita Maini. She used to be Nina's best friend," Jasveer said.

Anita's not the kind of girl you take much notice of. At least, not when you are young and randy. She's plain and sensible, not a tease like my sister. Her uncle's got a supermarket down Ladypool Road and she works there Saturdays at the checkout. The shop seemed to be full of fat women lugging overflowing baskets and dragging protesting three-year-olds. The aisles were filled with boxes of dog food or washing powder, seemingly deliberately placed to trip you up.

I squeezed through the entrance and immediately realized that I'd have no chance of speaking to Anita unless I bought something and joined the meandering queue for her till. I could have got the packet of crisps and can of Coke in a fraction of the time at the newsagent's next door. More than once I was tempted to leave as Anita rang up yet another basket of rice, chapati flour, and bags of lentils. But I wanted to know more about the girl my father had arranged for me to marry.

Eventually it was my turn. Anita glanced up at me, surprised when I placed just the two items in front of her.

"I want to talk to you," I said.

She ignored me and rang up the bill. "52p, please."

"I'm going to marry Nina Chandha," I said.

Anita held out her hand, and I placed a pound coin in her palm. "Please," I said.

She slid the cash drawer closed and passed me the change. "Meet me in the park. By the swings. One-thirty," she said.

I feared she might not turn up, but hung around anyway. She was prompt. She had a six-year-old boy in tow, who ran off toward the playground the moment she released his hand.

"I've got an hour for lunch," Anita said. "What do you want to know?"

I shrugged. "Anything. I just don't like the idea of marrying someone I know nothing about."

"Don't, then."

"Don't what?"

"Marry. Get out of it. Get a white girl pregnant. Run away from home."

It sounded a little drastic. "Why?" I asked.

Anita watched her brother—or cousin—climb to the top of the slide twice before she answered. "I just get an itchy feeling between the shoulder blades when she's around. That's why I don't see much of her these days." Anita sighed. "It's probably my imagination, and I've no business questioning what your family have arranged."

"But?" Anita was sixteen, but she sounded like the kind of matriarch who quietly watches and absorbs information and then pronounces hidden truths. The kind of grandmother one respects and is a little in awe of.

"You know Nina's father killed himself?" Anita said.

I nodded. I'd heard something of it, about three years ago. That's why my father had negotiated my marriage with her uncle.

"Nina saw him do it."

That stopped me. There'd been rumors that Nina had found the body. I recalled that now and wondered what kind of effect that would have on someone. But to actually be there.

"Can you tell me about it?" Suddenly I felt different. A week ago I'd have laughed at Anita or made crass comments. Instead, a coldness settled in my stomach, and I was afraid. I remembered a story being read to us in junior school about a curious girl who opened a box and let out a lot of horrible demons. It was like that; only Anita was the box, and I didn't think I would like what was inside. I would have been relieved if she had refused.

"I have to tell someone," Anita said. She took a deep breath and plunged into the story. "You probably know that Nina and I were supposed to be best friends. It was more a case of our families being neighbors. We used to share secrets. We knew that Nina's older sister, Saira, was seeing a Muslim boy. We even helped them deceive both sets of parents.

For at time. Eventually a relative of Maboob, the boy-friend, saw them holding hands in the street and told his father."

It was a common problem, trying to follow the rules of our parents, but wishing for the freedom our English classmates had to pick and choose friends. It was a bit easier for boys than for girls.

"We were upstairs in Nina's room when Maboob's father came round." Anita said. "We could hear every word they said. Saira was called a whore and a slut, Maboob an evil seducer. Each father blamed the other for their child's behavior. I was surprised they didn't actually come to blows. Fortunately, Saira was out at the time doing some shopping for an elderly aunt, or I don't know what would have happened. The atmosphere was explosive. When Mr. Ali left, Nina and I tried to think of ways that we could warn Saira. If she could have stayed at the aunt's house overnight, her father might have calmed down. Just as we agreed that I should go looking for her, she returned. Nina leaned out of the upstairs window trying to signal her away, not daring to call out, but Saira didn't understand. Her father saw her standing bemused on the path. He dragged Saira into the house by her hair. Then he took his belt to her. Nina and I crouched at the top of the stairs, watching."

I saw Anita shiver as she remembered. I knew that kind of thing happened. I don't think that my father would ever treat either of my sisters like that. At least I hope not.

"Afterward," Anita said, "Nina told me that she would never let him do that to Saira again. She meant it, though I didn't see how she could stop him. He was within his rights—as he saw them, as our community would see them. Saira had brought shame on his family, and he had punished her. He also kept her confined to the house. Okay, she went to school, but he took her to the gate and was waiting to escort her home afterwards. When he was home, she had to be in the same room as him. I think he had arranged a marriage for her, in India. Saira refused to go."

"So he beat her again?" I said.

"Not quite. I was at Nina's house when it started. Nina's mother was out visiting, as were her two younger brothers. I followed Nina down to the back sitting room. 'I won't do it, Father,' I heard Saira say. She sounded scared. 'You can't make me.'

"Nina pulled me after her into the doorway. At the far end of the room a heavy brass curtain rail ran across an archway into the kitchen. Nina's father had fixed a length of washing line to it. The other end was tied into a loop. This, he held out to Saira. 'You said you would rather die than marry a decent boy,' he said.

"Nina stepped into the room. She told Saira to go to her aunt's house. Nina was nearly three years younger than her sister, yet Saira obeyed her. She walked out of the room, down the passage, and through the front door, slamming it closed behind her. Her father never said a word. Nina was watching him as he stood silently with the noose in his hands. She told him to put it over his own head, to see what it felt like. I expected him to lash out, to berate Nina, maybe even take his belt to her. But, no. Calmly, he put the noose around his neck, just as Nina bid.

"Nina must have remembered me, then, because

she told me to go home. And I went. I've never been back there."

I asked Anita, "Do you really think he killed himself because Nina said so?"

"I don't know. It was in the newspapers next day. Nina's father had hanged himself. Nina had found the body. She was off school for the next few months, staying with relatives, being counseled. I hardly saw her after that, except at school, and I always felt uncomfortable when she looked at me. I don't know what happened after I left that night. I don't think I want to know."

Anita called her brother from the playground. As she started to walk away she turned back. "If you can, Anil Patel," she said, "find someone else to marry."

I didn't think too much of Anita's tale. She was only a kid at the time and probably misremembered much of what happened. If anything, I felt sorry for Nina. It must be horrible to find any kind of dead body, but to find your own father swinging at the end of a rope must be extra awful.

When I got home later in the afternoon, I found my dad waiting for me in an agitated state.

"Hurry up and change," he told me. "We are supposed to be meeting your intended in half an hour."

"You should've told me earlier," I shouted, racing up the stairs.

"You're never in," he called back.

"Last night." I generally get on well with my dad. Especially now I'm working, he treats me more like an equal. It's only in this matter of marriage that he still expects me to defer to his wishes. I was glad though that I'd be given the chance to get to know

Nina a little before the wedding actually took place. I might even be able to take her out on proper dates. I looked forward to that.

This meeting was extremely proper. It was in her uncle's house as he was now her guardian. She sat on an uncomfortable, straight-backed chair on one side of the room. I did the same on the other. Her mother and aunt filled the sofa between us while the men, my father and her uncle, faced each other from overstuffed armchairs. Conversation was sparse and polite. Nina's mother poured tea which Nina, with properly downcast eyes, carried to the guests, and then she offered round a plate of sweet biscuits before resuming her seat.

The desultory chatter between the adults gave me a chance to study Nina. She wore a long, well-fitting tunic and trousers in a dark, chocolate-brown material, embroidered at the hem and ankles with gold thread. It might sound dull but it wasn't. It was exactly right for Nina. Her black hair was loose and covered by a gauzy scarf in the same color as the rest of her clothes. She wasn't quite as pretty as I thought I remembered. If anything, her nose was a bit large, but she had strong, pale-skinned features and incredibly long eyelashes. I could see her watching me through them. I sensed she was behaving impeccably for the benefit of the adults, just as I was. She wore plenty of gold jewelry as well—large hooped earrings, ankle chains, and an armful of bangles which clinked together as she sipped her tea. My father could have chosen a lot worse for me.

Nina had obviously been primed as to what to do. After about half an hour she collected the cups and plates.

"Why don't you carry the tray through to the

kitchen, Anil," Nina's mother said to me. "It will help Nina."

We were being given time together.

Nina didn't speak to me but ran hot water straight into the sink to begin the task of washing-up. Her movements were economical and tense, whether from being alone with me or from some other reason I don't know, but she seemed different.

"It wasn't my idea," I said, feeling someone had to break the silence.

"You didn't have to agree to it," Nina said.

"It's my father who arranged things. And your uncle."

"Do you always do what your father says?"

"No. But he probably knows better than me in this matter."

"You've changed since you were at school, then," Nina said. "Or was it all just for show?"

"What do you mean?"

"The crudity. The swearing at the teachers, the groping in the corridors. You probably don't realize how foul we thought you were, you and your friend Bali."

"That was more than two years ago. I'm different now."

"Are you? You revolted me then, you still do. I may have to marry you, Anil Patel, but you will never touch me. Do you understand that? Never!"

The look she gave me was withering. For a moment she looked sixty, not sixteen, and the only things I could think of were that her eyebrows met in the middle, and what it would be like to kiss her.

When my dad and I left, Nina stood next to her uncle on the doorstep, demure once again. As we turned out of the gate I glanced at her. She was staring at me with loathing, and I remembered I had seen her look like that once before, only then it had been Bali she was watching, not me. It shook me so much that I walked home in a kind of daze. If it hadn't been for my dad grabbing me as I stepped off the pavement, I would have gone right under a bus.

I admit it. Bali and I were pretty obnoxious at school. We weren't the only ones. Part of the problem was that neither of our families expected us to have girlfriends—nice girls don't go with boys—but our peers did. A lot of our schoolmates were discovering sex, so they didn't have to boast about it. We just pretended. We would swagger along the corridor wearing the tightest pants we could get away with, bulging at the crotch. Or lean past a girl to get a rubber and accidentally on purpose brush her tits with an arm. Bali got an elbow in the guts one time when he tried standing behind the maths teacher and looking down her cleavage. But that's basically all we did. We fantasized. And the opportunities for being crude diminish when you leave school. For a start, you're worked too hard to want to. My bakery job gets me up at five in the morning, and there aren't many girls in the garage where Bali works.

I suppose our male egos were a bit frustrated, which was why, about a year ago, we had decided to crash the school disco. The usual rule is that if you don't actually go to the school, you must be the partner of someone who does. It's not difficult to arrange.

Bali and I hung around near the entrance watching various groups going in. Black girls are usually the best bet. They've got a greater sense of daring, less respect for petty rules.

We recognized a couple in the group we picked, though Georgina and Evette had filled out considerably since we last saw them, when they were skinny third-years. Bali took the lead.

"Hi, Georgie. Remember me? Balvinder Singh."

"Who don't?" Georgina might be on the plump side, but she had a wicked smile. She used it on Bali. "You jus' passin'?"

Bali draped an arm about her shoulders. "Thought you might like to go to a disco."

"An' thought I might jus' take you with me? How you gonna make it worth my while, boy?"

Bali pulled a bottle out of his pocket. It looked like lemonade. "Vodka?" he said.

Georgina unscrewed the top, took a swig, and grimaced. "Okay," she said passing the bottle to Evette. It went round the group.

"That gets you in, Bali," Evette said, eyeing me. "What about your friend?"

I held my jacket open exposing the bottle in my inner pocket. "White rum," I said.

Evette slipped her arm about my waist. "Wicked," she said. "Shall we go?"

The girls didn't expect us to stay with them all evening. That wasn't part of the deal, though we might well have gone back to them toward the end if our luck was bad. By then they would've been too drunk to care since they either had their own booze in their handbags or had stashed it in the loo cisterns during the day.

Bali and I prowled.

I was actually getting quite friendly with this one girl, Harminder, her name was, when I noticed Bali was having a bit of trouble. If he'd had any sense he'd have backed off. It was mostly dark in the hall.

The lights had been covered with colored paper and the light show spat occasional streaks of red and blue across the dancers. The music was so loud you could scarcely hear yourself speak.

Bali's girl was pinned between a table and the wall. He was leaning close to her, I suspect he was touching her as well. She didn't like it. She had gone tense. He hadn't noticed because that's the signal to back off. He wasn't. She was staring at a group a short distance away. Nina was with them, but it wasn't her I noticed, then. It was the blokes with them. All three were older and bigger than we were, and I didn't like the way they were eyeing Bali.

I made an excuse to Harminder and took Bali's arm. "I think we ought to spread ourselves about a bit more," I said, indicating the watching blokes.

For a moment I thought Bali would ignore me, but then he tore himself away with a wave and a wink. "See you later, doll," he said.

All I wanted to do was to keep clear of those three. I don't court trouble as a rule. I know what I can get away with, but I know some guys can get very nasty if they think you are interfering with one of theirs, especially in our community. These gave me an itchy feeling.

We didn't hang around until the end of the disco. It was getting boring.

It happened fast. We were less than a hundred yards from the school gates. Someone cannoned into me from behind. I sprawled, hands grazing the pavement. I was yanked up and slammed into a tree. My head cracked against it. My vision swirled. A boot caught me under the ribs. I couldn't breathe.

Screaming assailed my ears.

My sight cleared a little.

They had Bali down. They were kicking the hell out of him. All three of them: Nina's friends.

Bali had his arms about his head. The boots went in anyway. Leather against bone crunches. Bali stopped screaming.

Then they walked away.

A shadow came between Bali and the streetlight. I looked up. Nina stood a few feet away, her arm linked with that of the girl Bali had been feeling up. Nina was staring at Bali. Her expression was one of hatred and loathing. A killing look. She turned, and they disappeared.

Clutching my stomach, I crawled over to Bali. I thought he was dead. His face was unrecognizable. There was blood everywhere.

Why he didn't die, no one knows. His skull was fractured in two places, his left cheekbone shattered, his nose destroyed and his upper jaw had been kicked loose from his skull.

The look Nina gave him that night was just like the one she gave me as I left her house after our first official meeting. I don't believe in the evil eye. It's just a load of superstitious nonsense, but that's what it made me think of.

I tried not to let it worry me, but it was hard. Over the next few weeks, I was thrust into Nina's company on several occasions. We almost avoided speaking to each other. I did try. After all, this was supposed to be the woman I would spend the rest of my life with, and I thought it would be useful if we started out liking each other a little bit.

"Forget it," Nina said when I asked her what kind of music she liked.

"You are not the first Nina's been betrothed to," Bali's sister said one evening when I was complaining to Bali about the way she always put down my efforts.

"What happened to the other guy?" I asked, as casually as I could.

"He was arrested for stealing cars," Jasveer said gleefully. "He was let off with a caution, but her uncle said they didn't want that sort in the family."

I wondered briefly what I could get nicked for. I would probably upset my mother more than anyone else. That wouldn't be fair. I resigned myself to following my father's wishes.

Two nights before the ceremony was supposed to take place, I tackled my sister Mita again. She was stitching gold braid to the sari she intended to wear.

"What was Nina like in school?" I asked.

She must have realized how nervous I was. "Why do you want to know?" she asked.

"I've been hearing all sorts of rumors. And Nina doesn't seems to like me much."

"What kind of rumors?"

I told her what Anita and Jasveer said, and how Nina had been around when Bali was hurt.

Mita made a show of tying of her thread and bit through the cotton. "She always gets her own way," she said. "Nina rarely did her homework. She got away with it with most teachers—for some reason they never pressed her. But Miss Gordon insisted. She seemed to be immune from whatever guile Nina had. So Nina copied the chemistry homework from one of us. No one ever refused her twice."

"Were you scared of her?"

"Not really. You just got an uncomfortable feeling when she looked at you. Things would go wrong. Nothing you could ever pin on her. Silly accidents."

"Did she ever do anything to you?"

"Nina never did anything. But I did fall in the river on a geography field trip the day after I refused to let her borrow my pen. Jasveer cut herself badly in chemistry when a beaker broke, the same day she refused to tell Nina the answer to a maths question. Coincidence probably, but coincidences happen when Nina's around."

"I don't think I want to marry her," I said.

"Don't worry," Mita said. "After the first night, she won't be able to do anything to you."

"How can you be so sure?"

Mita laughed. "Why are witches always unmarried? Why are unicorns attracted to virgins? They want to steal their power."

"I don't believe in witches—or unicorns," I said doubtfully.

"No?" Mita looked pointedly at my crotch and giggled before gathering up the cloth of her sari and heading out of the room.

Somehow, I got through the marriage ceremony. I can only presume Nina was as nervous as I was. I don't think we looked at each other the whole time. The wedding celebrations were held in the dining room of the school we both used to attend. It felt peculiar going back there legitimately. Eventually, we were escorted, separately, back to my house. Someone had removed most of my possessions from my bedroom, moved in a double bed, and hung decorations from the ceiling. I arrived first.

I heard them on the stairs, a shrillness of female voices. Then the door was pushed open and Nina came in, along with a cloud of flower petals. I felt extremely nervous. Unsure what to do. Nina, however, closed the door and looked at me. She had the same expression of loathing on her face that I had seen before.

"Shall we get it over with?" she said.

"What?"

"Let's finish this farce. Hit me."

I didn't think I had heard her right.

She took a step closer. "Hit me," she said again.

"I don't hit women," I said feebly.

"Yes, you do. Especially women who refuse to have your filthy hands pawing all over them."

My mind was stunned by bewilderment, but I felt my fingers balling themselves into a fist. I tried to relax them. I deliberately attempted to stretch out my fingers. They were frozen.

"I am refusing to submit to my husband," Nina said. "I need to be punished. Hit me."

I did. I couldn't help it. My arm just raised itself to eye level and straightened sharply. The shock jarred up arm as my fist struck her face. I felt sick. I couldn't believe what I had done. Nina took an involuntary step back, recovered her poise, and smiled. She unwound her scarf from her hair, and knotted one end into a loop.

"Tie the other end to the light fixture," she said.

"Why?

"Because I cannot reach."

In a haze, I climbed onto the bed. The mattress flexed under my feet. Her request seemed very reasonable.

"Now put your head in the loop," she said.

"Why should I?" I tried desperately to break out of the spell she seemed to have cast over me.

"Because you are ashamed. You don't hit women, remember? You feel you have to atone for your wickedness."

She was right. I had to do something to wipe out the shame. A feeble voice at the back of my mind suggested that this was a bit drastic. "I'll do whatever you want," I said. I was getting scared now.

She smiled. "Yes, you will," she said. "You will set me free."

"Yes. I will set you free. I'll annul the marriage."

"You will set me free by dying. Put it over your head."

I couldn't stop my hands from lifting the cloth and settling the noose around my neck. I wanted to ask her why, but my mouth wouldn't work. I could feel my body trembling.

"If I am single, my uncle will try again to marry me off. As a widow, I can do what I want and no one can stop me." As she turned to the door, I could already see the bruise forming on her cheek. "Goodbye," she said.

I hear her running down the stairs. The sitting room door opens, and I briefly hear the sound of laughter. As it closes, I have this overwhelming compulsion to leap from the bed. I must wipe out my shame.

HORROR SHOW

by Tim Waggoner

Tim Waggoner has published more than fifty stories of fantasy and horror. His most current stories can be found in the anthologies *Civil War Fantastic*, *Single White Vampire Seeks Same*, and *Bruce Coville's UFOs*. His first novel, *The Harmony Society*, is forthcoming. He teaches creative writing at Sinclair Community College in Dayton, Ohio.

"It's over, Shrike!"

Seventeen-year-old Billy Barton stood within a nightmarish landscape, a distorted forest rendered in broad charcoal strokes in a white background. In his left hand he held a ragged-edged piece of paper, in his right, a lighter, flame burning, a startling splash of color in this stark world of black, white, and gray.

The cadaverous figure standing before Billy chuckled, a sound like splintered, grinding bone. "Go ahead, Billy boy—flame on! But if you torch that drawing, you'll end up a crispy critter, too. Because, you see, I've brought you *into* the drawing. You're in my world now, and the only exit is marked D-E-A-T-H."

Shrike's fingers—long, multijointed digits that resembled insect legs—flexed slowly, ebony talons seeming to grow even longer and sharper. His Ichabod Crane face grinned; wild, black Tim Burton hair waved in a sourceless breeze like some sort of undersea plant whose tendrils undulated in a lazy current. Tattered black rags served as Shrike's garments, more torn scraps of construction paper than cloth.

The lighter's flame wavered as Billy's hand began to tremble. "I created you, Shrike; you're only a fragment of my imagination, just like this place. But *I'm* real! If I destroy this drawing—" Billy shook the paper once for emphasis; an image of the charcoal forest with Shrike standing in the middle of it rendered on its surface. "—you'll die, but I'll return to the real world!"

Shrike grinned. "Think so?" he nodded to the drawing. "Take a look."

Billy did and saw that now Shrike had a companion in the forest: a crudely sketched figure that could only be himself, holding a piece of paper over an orange-crayon flame.

Shrike took a step forward, multijointed fingers flexing, talons clacking together like crab claws. "You're right about one thing: you did create me. You poured all of your adolescent anger and frustration into your art, and I'm the result. You made me so real that I was able to cross over into your world and take revenge against those who wronged you— your parents, your older brother, your teachers, the principal, the kids at school . . . I've fulfilled your every dark fantasy. And now you think you're going to get rid of me? Toss me aside like a crumpled piece of paper? I don't think so, Billy boy."

Shrike gestured, and the charcoal trees came alive. Their branches reached for Billy, the whorls on the trunks rearranging until they resembled the faces of the people Shrike had slain in Billy's name. Their mouths stretched wide as they howled in fury; it was their turn for vengeance now.

Billy ducked a tree limb as it snatched for him, and he touched the flame to the drawing. Shrike screamed—

The phone rang.

Damn it! This is the best part! Simon Karkull— whose name once had been Steve Johnston more decades ago than he liked to think about—looked longingly at the TV screen one last time before picking up the remote and hitting MUTE. Normally, he would've just let the call go to voice mail, but he was hoping to hear from his agent.

He picked up the receiver and hit the TALK button. "This is Simon Karkull." He spoke clearly and distinctly, using a lower register, which implied just a hint of malevolence. Even when he was merely talking on the phone, he liked to project a certain amount of presence; he was a firm believer in the dictum that an actor was never truly offstage.

"Simon! Great to hear your voice! Peter Winston here."

Simon sat straighter on his threadbare couch, suddenly aware of the shabby purple robe he wore and the stubble that covered his face like some strange species of fungus. It was foolish—the man was calling from the other side of the country, for God's sake, but Simon couldn't help feeling self-conscious. Peter Winston was a *producer*, after all. Maybe not a Producer with a capital P, but a producer nonetheless.

"So how are things hanging for you these days, Simon? It's been, what? Ten years since we've seen each other?"

Despite himself, Simon found his attention returning to the TV. Flame had engulfed the charcoal-drawing forest, and Billy was running toward a sudden fissure that had appeared in the air. Shrike, surrounded by a halo of flame, shrieked his rage and pursued Billy toward the dimensional rift. Simon smiled. He remembered filming this scene before a blue screen, just himself and Terrance, the actor who played Billy. No trees, no rip in space, no flames. It had been quite a challenge, but he thought he had done a creditable job of it. In Shrike's expression, one could read a complex mixture of pain and fury, along with a dash of fear that—

"Simon? You there, buddy?"

Simon tore his attention away from the screen. *Look alive, man! You've got a producer on the line all the way from Hollywood C-A!* For an (let's face it) all but washed-up actor, it was the equivalent of Jehovah ringing up from Paradise for a bit of a chat.

"Eight years."

"Pardon?"

"It's been eight years since we saw each other. At that horror film convention in Atlanta, remember?"

A half-second pause. "Riiiiiiight. The convention. Good times and all that, huh? Anyway, the reason I'm calling is I got a call from your agent the other day. He told me that you heard a rumor about another Shrike movie being in the works. Said you read it on the, uh, Internet."

"You needn't sound so skeptical. I may be an old dog, but I have picked up a new trick or two since the last time we worked together." Simon didn't want to admit the reason why he had learned to surf the Net was primarily to check on fan sites honoring himself—and, of course, Shrike. "Is it true?"

Another pause, several seconds long this time. "Yes, it is. The financing's in place and we have a decent script, though it could still use a little tweaking. We should be ready to start shooting in a month for a full-scale theatrical release sometime next year, maybe around Thanksgiving or Christmas if we're lucky."

As Winston spoke, Simon's pulse quickened and he felt a familiar thrill in his gut. It was the same surge of adrenaline he experienced whenever he stepped onto a stage or in front of a camera. "So when do I get to see the script? I don't care how rough it is, just so long as I can start getting a general overview of where—"

"That's the thing, Simon."

Winston's tone stopped Karkull dead. He flicked his gaze to the television, watched as Billy made it through the dimensional tear a split second before Shrike could grab him. Watched as Shrike—as himself—screamed in agony as he was devoured by flames. No matter how many times he had seen this part, Simon had never got used to seeing himself flash-fried.

"Simon?"

"Hmmm? Oh, yes. About this script. I hope it's better than the last couple. The first Shrike film—" Simon gestured at his television without thinking, "—was an effective little piece of psychodrama. The way Billy's inner torment was embodied in Shrike, how the boy based the monster on his serial killer stepfather, named him after a species of bird which impales its prey on thorns. Hardly Shakespeare or Ibsen, of course, but all in all, not a bad representative of its genre. Not like the sequels . . . little more than slice-and-dice pornography, especially the last two. Of course, I tried to turn in the best performance I could, but without a decent script to work with—"

"You're not going to see the script, Simon. Not this time."

There was more, but Simon stopped paying much attention after that. Winston said something about how he was making this call purely out of courtesy, because of how many times they had worked together over the years. How the studio wanted a new Shrike, something more "modern" and "edgy," "younger" and "hipper." How Winston had lobbied hard to get Simon a supporting role, even a cameo, but the studio wouldn't hear of it, blah, blah, blah.

Eventually, Winston paused, and Simon muttered a "thanks for calling" and disconnected. He dropped the receiver to the couch, fumbled for the TV remote, and unmuted the sound. The film, titled *Dark Art* (but often referred to on the Internet as the First Shrike Film, the One That Doesn't Suck) had ended. Billy had escaped Shrike's trap—which in symbolic terms was the morass of his own anger—and been reunited with Heather, his supportive (and well built) girlfriend. Roll credits.

Now Simon stared at himself again, but this time it was a self twenty-some years older than the one who had met a fiery end only moments before. Dressed in a black turtleneck and seated on a papier-mâché rock before an amateurish painting of a cave wall with a few lopsided stalactites and stalagmites, Simon Karkull, host of *Karkull's Cavern of Terror*, grinned.

"What did you think of that ending, fright fans? Myself, I always get a little hot under the collar when I watch it." A quick tug on said collar for emphasis. "That's all the time we have for bad puns this afternoon, I'm afraid. Join me next week as together we face the disco horror of *The Rollerboogieman*. I'm

Simon Karkull, and I hope you have an absolutely terrifying week." The camera panned back as Simon released a burst of mad laughter.

The real Simon Karkull—the one sitting on his couch, still in his robe even though it was four in the afternoon on a Saturday; the one who had taped that cheesy ending bit at a local TV studio several days ago; the one who had just been informed by a Hollywood producer that he wasn't hip or edgy enough to reprise a character he had originated and played in seven films from 1978 to 1987—turned off his television and stared at the blank screen for a long, long time. When he was finished, he got up, made himself a rum and Coke minus the Coke, came back, sat down, and stared some more.

When Simon was drunk enough, he staggered into The Room.

His condo, while not exactly on the luxurious side, was large enough for a bedroom, a guest room (not that he ever had any guests), and *The* Room—the place where he kept the memorabilia of what could only laughingly be called his career.

Simon managed to flip on the light after only two tries, and found himself surrounded by framed movie posters and play programs, photos of himself in character, posing with directors and costars and occasionally someone far more famous than himself who got a kick out of having a picture taken with a cheeseball horror actor.

The shelves were filled with bound scripts—beginning with faded typed pages containing the lines for his role as Santa in the play *Wrong-Way Reindeer* in which he'd starred back in third grade, and ending with the script for the last film he'd been in, a direct-to-video stinker called *Cannibal Coroner*. There were a few awards displayed, though nothing major. All had been earned before he first donned Shrike's makeup—with the lone exception of *Arterial Spray* magazine's Bloody Good Show award for Best All-Time Actor in a Horror Film Series. The award, a brass representation of an anatomically correct heart, was covered with black scorch marks. Simon had taken great delight in stubbing out cigarettes on the hideous thing back in the days before his doctor had made him give up smoking.

But the crowning piece of his collection rested framed on the wall just above the brass heart. It was the sketch that had appeared in the climactic scene in *Dark Art*, the very same scene he had been watching when Peter Winston had told him with exquisite politeness to go straight to hell.

Simon had kept it, framed it, because to him it represented the last time he had truly been an actor. Not long after *Dark Art* became a hit—after the Shrike posters, action figures, and video games—Simon Karkull became a joke, a ludicrous man who put on a fright wig and went "boogah-boogah!" for a living.

He peered closely at the drawing, examining the figure that represented Billy Barton. The artist had worked in broad strokes—out of either laziness, incompetence or both—and the boy's features were indistinct, little more than a hint of eyes, nose, and mouth. It was a cipher's face, one that could have belonged to anyone, really.

Standing in front of the drawing, gut churning from too much rum, throat sore, bitter taste in his mouth that had nothing to do with alcohol, Simon looked at the roughly sketched face atop Billy Barton's body and imagined that it instead belonged to a bastard of a producer named Peter Winston. It did look kind of like him, Simon thought, if you squinted your eyes, tilted your head, and hated with all your heart and soul.

Screw it.

Simon turned and left the room, switching off the light and closing the door behind him. And if, as he pulled the door shut, he heard a dark chuckle that sounded like splintering, grinding bone, he told himself it was just the booze.

Simon woke to the electronic warble of his phone. He opened his eyes and pushed himself off the couch, swaying and nearly collapsing as a fierce pounding erupted inside his skull. He looked around the room, desperately trying to orient himself. He was Simon Karkull, Has-Been, and this was the living room of his condo.

He picked up the phone from the coffee table, hit the TALK button, and held the device gingerly to his ear.

"Yes?" More of a frog's croak than a word.

"Mr. Karkull?"

"Yes." Another croak, slightly closer to human speech than the first.

"This is Suzanne . . . from the Limelight Players?"

The throbbing in his head picked up tempo as if following the lead of some unseen, malicious conductor. He sighed. "I missed rehearsal last night, didn't I?"

Among the many humiliations he found himself faced with as he approached old age, Simon had been stupid enough to agree to direct a play for the local community theater group—a production of *Fiddler on the Roof*, nonetheless.

"We tried calling, but there wasn't any answer."

That's because I was too damn drunk to hear the phone. "I wasn't feeling very well yesterday afternoon, so I thought I'd take a little nap before rehearsal. I must have slept the entire night through. I'm so sorry. Did you still have rehearsal? How did everything go?"

Simon wasn't especially interested, but he was being paid a modest sum to direct the show, and he had to at least keep up the illusion that he gave a damn. As Suzanne rattled on about last night, he found the television remote, turned on a cable news channel, and sat back down on the couch. If he were lucky, his hangover would kill him any minute now.

He sat through a segment on a pharmaceutical company accused of unfair trade practices, muttering an occasional *Mmm-hmm* or *Uh-huh* to Suzanne, until the entertainment news came on. A helmet-haired blonde with glossy pink collagen-puffed lips tried her damnedest to look serious as she presented her report.

"Peter Winston, producer of violent horror films such as *Dark Art* and *Blood Tide*, has fallen prey to the same manner of violence that fueled his movies. According to authorities, Winston was found dead this morning in his Beverly Hills home, mutilated almost beyond recognition."

". . . And then Constance said 'So I improvised a few lines. What's wrong with that?' And I said, 'You have to respect the text, Constance,' and she said—"

Simon pulled the phone away from his ear and disconnected, cutting Suzanne off in mid-sentence. He put the phone down on the coffee table, his gaze fixed firmly on the television, Suzanne and the rest

of the so-called actors who made up the Limelight
Players totally forgotten. Simon couldn't believe what
he was hearing; it was like some dubious plot con-
trivance straight out of one of Winston's films.

He listened as the anchorwoman related the details
with a self-righteous smugness seasoned with a dash
of ghoulish glee. Sometime late last night, an intruder
had broken into Winston's home and sliced him to
shreds in an attack that police said resembled the
killings in the Shrike films. The implication was that
a deranged fan was responsible, but the police admitted they had few clues to go on at the moment.

As Simon turned off the TV, he felt slighted. Why
hadn't a reporter called him up to get his reaction to
Winston's death? After all, he had starred in seven
of the man's highest grossing films—emphasis on the
gross. Maybe he should give one of the networks a
call. . . .

He realized what an ugly turn his thoughts had
taken, and he chastised himself for being so self-
centered. A man he had spoken to only yesterday
had died in a horrible fashion, and all he could think
about was himself. So Simon forced himself to think
about Peter Winston for the next several minutes,
and he especially thought about their conversation
yesterday. Eventually, he came to the conclusion that
he wasn't particularly sorry that the man was dead.
No, he wasn't sorry at all.

An hour and forty-five minutes later, as Simon sat
at a rickety card table signing autographs at Beyond
Comix, he decided that Peter Winston had gotten off
lightly. Given his hangover, he'd considered skipping
out, but after missing rehearsal last night, he didn't
feel as if he could afford to. Kingsborough was a

small city and word spread fast; the last thing he needed was a reputation as an unreliable drunk. Well, more of a reputation than he already had, that is.

A grand total of seven pimply-faced fan boys showed up, three of them dressed to resemble Shrike. Two of those three wanted to discuss such arcane matters as what sort of horror archetype Shrike was. They might as well have been speaking Urdu for all Simon understood, and fifteen minutes before the autograph session was supposed to end, he pleaded illness—which wasn't altogether a lie, for, after all, he was *quite* sick of this—and got the hell out of there.

He wandered the streets of Kingsborough for a while, enjoying the early spring weather despite the merry hob it played with his allergies. It wasn't Hollywood, and northern Ohio was hardly So-Cal, but it had been the only place with steady work, and so he had moved here in order to avoid becoming a homeless drunk. Three years later, he was still trying to decide whether he'd made the right choice.

After a bit, he found himself wandering into Schuyler Park. Once a centerpiece of downtown in years past, the park was now primarily a haven for drug traffic and men looking for quick, cheap sex. Simon had come here himself for the latter once or twice after he'd moved to town, but after being caught and let off with only a warning by an undercover police officer who luckily was a horror movie fan, Simon hadn't been back. But today the place suited his mood. Like him, the park had seen better days.

Actually, it wasn't that bad. True, scraps of litter were scattered about, and the grass could use a good mowing and weeding, and the brick building where the restrooms were located was covered with incomprehensible graffiti, but it was spring, and the green smell of new growth hung in the air and—

A figure exited the men's room and began walking toward Simon: a thin, almost emaciated man dressed in tattered black rags, with wild, raven-colored hair and extended clawlike fingers.

Simon's first thought was that one of the fans from the comic shop had somehow followed him here. His second thought was to question how the fan was able to get here before him and secrete himself in the restroom. His third thought, which was really more of a subliminal perception than a thought per se, was that there was something odd about the way the Shrike clone carried himself, a too fluid way of moving, as if he *flowed* forward instead of walking. And his elbows and knees didn't seem to bend quite right; they appeared to bend a few inches beyond what the joints should allow, and Simon had the impression that they could bend all the way backward, as if the man's bones were made out of rubber.

He felt a cold watery ripple in his gut as the fan approached. The man had a leer on his face—on his far-too-familiar face—that made Simon want to run, run, run and not stop until his heart burst. But he was too old to try, knew that the fan would be able to catch him easily, so instead he resorted to the only option left him. Like a chameleon being eyed by a hungry bird, he would change color, he would *act*.

Simon drew himself up to his full height and fixed the man with a haughty stare. "It's not a bad likeness, but I'm afraid it won't win you any points for originality."

The fan came within five feet, then stopped. Simon was going to utter another sarcastic comment, but the words died in his throat as he got his first truly good look at the man's face. It wasn't merely the makeup that made it seem familiar, nor the trade-marked Shrike leer. This just wasn't any face; it was *his*—Simon Karkull's, as he had looked over twenty years ago when he had first played Shrike.

"Surprised?" Shrike asked. The voice was the same, too. Younger, more vibrant than his, full of sinister intent and dark amusement.

Simon could think of nothing else to say other than the truth. "Actually, yes. Quite a bit."

He looked at those fingers, watched the way the multijointed digits moved, as if they were some manner of strange crustaceans growing forth from the man's wrists. They couldn't be artificial, not the way the skin stretched, the muscles flexed, the knuckles hinged. They were real.

He should have been incredulous, should have questioned his sanity, worried he was having a stroke or experiencing the first signs of senile dementia. But he didn't. Shrike—*the* Shrike, the movie monster that Simon had played in seven films—had somehow acquired physical, independent existence and now stood before him. In a way, it felt almost as if Simon had been expecting his doppelganger, as if he had come to this park for the sole purpose of meeting his other self.

"I suppose my next line is to ask how this is possible," Simon said. "How *you're* possible."

Shrike grinned. "It's an actor's job to bring a character to life, isn't it? You did your job well, Simon. *Very* well."

"You mean I created you? Literally?"

"In conjunction with various scriptwriters and di-rectors. And the fans, of course." Shrike grinned, displaying white shark teeth. "I wouldn't be where I am today without them. But you are my primary creator, yes."

"Why have you appeared now? It's been over twenty years since the first Shrike movie, thirteen since the last."

"I needed to reach a certain critical mass in terms of psychic energy before I could become corporeal. The Internet helped a great deal—all those fans setting up Web sites, posting on message boards, obsessing over trivia. . . . And of course, there's you, Simon. You've become more angry and bitter in recent years. Those emotions fed me, gave me strength until . . ." Shrike spread his arms wide. "Here I am; happy birthday to me. Although, technically, yesterday was my natal day, when you left your little memento room."

Simon remembered hearing dark laughter as he closed the door, but he had put it down to being drunk.

"You were sooooo angry at Peter Winston for casting you aside, for not even giving you a chance to read the script for the new film. Angry enough to wish him dead."

The spring breeze suddenly grew chilly, and did the trees in the park seem grayer, their edges less distinct, as if they weren't physical objects any longer, but rather sketches done in charcoal? Perhaps.

"I didn't kill Winston."

"Of course you didn't," Shrike said soothingly. "*I* did. Because *you* wished it."

Simon wanted to deny it, to tell Shrike that he was crazy, but how did one seriously accuse a fictional character come to life of insanity? No, he knew it was true. Last night, Peter Winston had become the lightning rod for all the disappointment and self-loathing that had built up in Simon Karkull over the years, and this morning he hadn't been sorry at all that the man was dead, not one bit.

"I suppose you're here to kill me now," Simon said. He was surprised at how steady his voice was, even more surprised at how little the prospect of dying bothered him.

Shrike shrugged. "If that's what you'd like. Don't have any illusions that your death would mean mine, though. I exist independently of you now, and the new film will only strengthen my reality. Besides, your death at the hands of a 'Shrike impersonator' would fuel fan obsession for decades, making me even more powerful." For a moment, Shrike seemed to consider the possibilities, but then he shook his head. "But I've come before you with a different agenda, Simon."

Shrike clacked his talons together—were there flakes of dried blood clinging to the nails?—in what Simon thought was a nervous gesture.

"It's actually somewhat embarrassing to admit," Shrike continued, "but now that I find myself imbued with existence, I lack . . . purpose. I'm used to having a script, a director—" he gestured at Simon, "—an actor to interpret me. Left to my own devices, I'm not really sure what to do with myself. I was . . . I was hoping you might have some ideas." He smiled hopefully. "Like you did last night."

Slowly, Simon Karkull grinned, and though his teeth were normal blunt human teeth yellowed by age and didn't resemble at all the ivory incisors which filled Shrike's mouth, the grin wasn't all that different than his other self's. Not so different at all.

"The script needs another rewrite, Cecile. Yes, I know it's already been through seventeen, but it's still crap. Hire another writer—someone who can actually put together a sentence this time—and tell him to fix the damn thing, okay?"

Simon didn't wait for his assistant producer to respond. He disconnected and set the phone down on the glass table next to his beach chair. He picked up his glass of sinfully expensive wine, took a sip, and gazed out contentedly across the beach and over the waves. Three million dollars, that's what his oceanfront home in Malibu had cost, and as far as he was concerned, it had been worth every last drachma.

His skin was a deep, rich bronze thanks to years of California sun, and his face looked like it belonged to a man twenty years younger, thanks to a highly skilled and very popular surgeon in Van Nuys. His body was a bit on the bony side for the navy blue Speedos he wore, but he was too rich to give a damn.

"Can I get you anything else, Simon?"

Simon looked up, saw Paolo—sweet, young Paolo who looked just fine in his Speedos, or out of them, for that matter—haloed by the afternoon sun.

Simon was about to tell Paolo *exactly* what he could get him, when he felt a familiar tingle at the base of his skull.

"I'm fine. I've got to make a business call, and it might drag on for a while. Why don't you take the rest of the day off? Provided, as Scrooge said, that you're here all the earlier tomorrow."

Paolo flashed a grin, showing perfectly white, perfectly straight teeth that had cost Simon more than a bit of money. "Thank you, sir." Paolo turned and trotted back up the beach toward the house.

Simon watched him go, enjoying the way the boy's muscles worked beneath his tanned skin. At Simon's age, the servant was primarily eye candy, but that was okay with him; it beat all hell out of being surrounded by pale, geeky fan boys in horror film t-shirts.

A few moments after Paolo had gone, there was a shimmer in the air, and Shrike appeared.

"Is it done?" Simon asked.

Shrike nodded. "I sliced and diced the brake lines on her Porsche last night, and she took an unscheduled flight into a ravine early this morning. She'll live, but she'll never tap dance again."

Simon took another sip of wine. "Serves the bitch right. That's the last time she'll ever be late to the set of one of my films. It means we'll have to recast her part, of course, but that's a minor hassle. With any luck, we'll find someone cheaper and a hell of lot easier to work with."

Thanks to his association with Shrike—and the publicity surrounding the mutilation deaths of various actors who had appeared in the original seven Shrike films—Simon had not only been able to resume his acting career in the new Shrike movie, but with a few more strategically planned murders here and there, along with some intimidating late-night visits by his alter ego to the right people, he had been able to work his way up first to director and now producer. Life, as the poet said, was good. Damn good.

"I've got another job for you. There's this accountant over at Paramount—"

"Not this time, Simon," Shrike interrupted. "I'm tired of being your supernatural hit man."

Simon sat up and worked to control a rush of panic. Without Shrike . . .

He smiled, playing it cool. "Let me guess; you

want a raise. Or you've decided that what you *really* want to do is direct."

Shrike ignored the joke. His elongated fingers flexed and curled, looking more than ever like crustacean legs this close to the ocean. "Do you remember when I first made my grand entrance a few years ago? How I said I didn't know what to do with my new life, and how I needed you to give me ideas?"

Simon could only nod.

Shrike smiled his shark's teeth smile. "I lied. I already had an idea—and it was a doozy. But I needed you to help me make it a reality." Shrike looked out over the ocean. "Do you know what it's like to be a monster, Simon? Not a real monster, like you; I mean a *movie* monster. Stuck forever in the same stupid stories, always hunted by the heroes, always losing in the end. Oh, sure, you get to off a few people, and there's a chance you'll come back in a sequel. But the sequels aren't any better than the originals, worse, really, because they usually suck so much. And you're forced to do it all over again every time some idiot grabs a tape off the horror shelves at his local video store, takes it home, and shoves it in his VCR. And cable television—" Shrike shuddered. "A hundred channels, on twenty-four a days, seven days a week. How many of those hours are filled by horror movies? Too many."

"But that's not your problem anymore, right?" Simon said. "You've been free for years."

Shrike raised a single eyebrow. "*Free?* To coin a cliché, how can I be free if even one of my people is still enslaved? We monsters realized a long time ago if only one of us could break through to your reality, could become strong enough, he might be able to open a doorway for the others."

Simon couldn't believe what he was hearing. "A . . . doorway?"

Shrike's lips curled back from his teeth in a half-smile, half-snarl. He pushed Simon back onto the beach chair and sat down on his legs, pinning him in place.

"Thanks to you, I've become very strong. More Shrike films, more mysterious deaths . . . people talk, you know. At conventions, on the Internet. Some even go so far as to suggest that maybe Shrike isn't a fictional character, he's *real*. And last night's murder finally put me over the top power-wise." Shrike leaned forward, licked his lips with a black lizard tongue. "Time to play horror movie host one last time, Simon."

Shrike extended an oversize index finger and pressed the tip of its ebony talon to the base of Simon's neck. He pressed down and there was a sound like paper being punctured. Simon felt no pain, could only watch as Shrike slowly drew a bloodless line down his chest and across his abdomen, the edges of the wound peeling back like drawing paper.

"It took time to find the right host," Shrike said as he worked. "We needed a human who could bridge the gap between worlds, someone who portrayed a monstrous archetype so effectively that he was looked upon by his fellow men and women as if he actually *were* the creature he pretended to be. But it had to be someone full of bitterness and anger, whose soul was ripe ground in which our evil could take root and grow. Someone who could not only help one of us attain physical existence, but who would be foolish enough to help that one continue to grow stronger so that one day he might do *this!*"

With a final flourish, Shrike finished his incision, stood, and stepped back.

For a moment, Simon felt nothing. And then he sensed *Them* inside, stirring as they began to claw their way toward reality—fanged, furred, scaled, stitched, wrapped in ancient cerements, encased in chitin, nightmarish malformed things which stalked and lurched and loped through endless hours of schlock cinema, all lusting to at last be *free!*

As the first clawed hand thrust its way into the light, Shrike's grin widened until it threatened to split his face in two. "Cheer up, Simon. Your last role is going to be your greatest. Simon Karkull, starring in *The End of the World as We Know It*—along with a cast of thousands."

As he watched them come forth one by one in all their dark majesty, Simon had the strangest urge to applaud. He might have, too—if only he could have moved his charcoal-sketch hands.

DEATH MAGE
by Fiona Patton

Fiona Patton was born in Calgary, Alberta, in 1962 and grew up in the United States. In 1975 she returned to Canada, and after several jobs which had nothing to do with each other—including carnival ride operator and electrician—moved to seventy-five acres of scrub land in rural Ontario with her partner, four cats of various sizes, and one tiny little dog. Her first book, *The Stone Prince*, was published by DAW Books in 1997. This was followed by *The Painter Knight* in 1998 and *The Granite Shield* in 1999, also from DAW. She is currently working on her fourth book, *The Golden Sword*, due out in 2001.

Cerchicava was on fire. The city's nobility, arranged in pavilions along the Ardechi River, applauded with enthusiasm as the skyline went from crimson to orange to yellow and violet and back to crimson again. Most agreed that the mages hired by His Grace, the Most Benevolent Duc Arturo de Marco, to honor the birth of his son Giovanni were the best in years.

Standing amidst a gaggle of brightly dressed men and women, twenty-year-old Montifero de Sepori leaned down to listen to the comments of the woman at his side. Her eyes sparkled a deep forest green, the mage color many of the upper classes were sport-

ing this year. Sepori's own eyes were a paler sea
green, suggesting his abilities were not as powerful
as hers. This had excited her as much as his broad
shoulders and handsome features. He'd not bothered
weaving the silver threading through his thick, black
hair as was fashionable this season, but he was
known to be one of the hunting set, and they did
not go in for too much frippery. This had also excited
her. The glow of a personal enhancement spell began
to rise around her body.

For Sepori's part, nothing involved in today's foolish display of trickery, either personal or public, interested him in the slightest, but he made a show of
increased interest in his companion as she artfully
suggested a late night supper together. He was agree-
able. She was young and beautiful and, as the niece
of Cerchicava's Arcivescovo, politically well connected. Besides, his work would be done by then
and he would be ready for a distraction as well as
an alibi.

The light show ended a few moments later. Taking
his leave of her, he made his way slowly through the
crowd, speaking pleasantly with one acquaintance or
another. Glancing across at the ducal box, he could
see that the city officials had already taken their
leave. Half a dozen priestly mages were hard at work
blessing the seating area.

Sepori gave a disdainful sniff. A decade had passed
since the Mage's War and the Church had grown
careless. A half-trained necromancer's apprentice
could have breached those wards. For a moment, he
toyed with the idea of teaching them the extent of
their folly, then dismissed it. It posed an unnecessary
risk and besides, he mused wryly, he had no half-
trained apprentice to expend. With one last glance at

the fist-sized holes in the priests' magical array, he
allowed the flow of the crowd to catch him up and
steer him toward the city proper.

His manservant was waiting for him by the or-
nately wrought San Nuvao Gate. Pocketing a clay
pipe, he fell into step behind him.

Piero Bruni had served Sepori for seventeen years,
ever since the third outbreak of plague in a decade
had swept through the city in 1412. Bereft of his parents, three-year-old Montifero had come to live with
his uncle, Matteo de Sulla, Cerchicava's most illustri-
ous general, but as he was often absent on the duc's
business, Matteo had given the task of raising his
nephew to his most trusted manservant. It was Piero
who had taught the young nobleman how to dance
and fence and ride, how to perform a variety of petty
magecrafts, and how to move in the circles to which
he was born.

He'd also instructed him in more deadly pursuits:
how to wield a jack and a garrote, how to set poison
on the tip of a needle or along the rim of a wine
glass. How to kill a man a dozen different ways and
how to dispose of the body. He'd taken him from
his uncle's glittering Palazzo de Sulla down into the
twisted streets of the Vericcio and Bergo housing dis-
tricts and introduced him to the breadth of Cerchicava's criminal classes, from the lifters, curbers, and
rampsmen who robbed the unwary to the brokers
and swagmen who disposed of their goods. He met
defrocked priests and unlicensed physicians, sailors
who sold cargo space aboard their masters' ships and
street mages who used their abilities to hide all manner of criminal activities. And when he was ready,
Piero, himself a senior cutter, inducted the boy into

"the trade"; the powerful underground community of the damned: corpse-cutters and markers who served a host of necromantic sorcerers called death mages. Here Sepori found his true calling. By the time he was fifteen, he was the most powerful and lethal necromancer in Cerchicava. By eighteen, he was their undisputed overlord. The only threat to his power was the Church and It had never shown much initiative against the trade.

Until recently.

In the last fortnight a dozen cutters and minor necromancers had been arrested and tortured in the cells beneath the San Dante Cathedral. All had died without betraying their masters, but all had given up the names of others in the trade. More arrests had followed including Mario Chigi, cutter and ex-soldier who had served under General Matteo de Sulla. He'd been hanging on a north gate gibbet for two days now; rumor on the streets said he'd been betrayed by one of his own. Publicly, Sepori gave no indication that he even knew the man had existed. Privately, he'd sent Piero to find his betrayer.

Now, as master and servant passed through the San Nuvao Gate and made their way along the wide, tree-lined Via Certani toward his uncle's palazzo, Sepori could sense Piero had news. He gave a sharp nod.

"You've found him."

"Yes, my Lord. Nico Urbi."

"One of Mario's own bodyguards."

"Yes, my Lord."

"He didn't take the usual precautions?"

"It seems Nico was Mario's nephew, my Lord. He must have believed family was precaution enough."

"Stupid. Was Nico himself taken or did he volunteer his information freely?"

Piero's expression grew wrathful. "He approached one of the Arcivescovo's people, Father Luca Orcicci, my Lord, and gave his uncle up for money. It's whispered that Orcicci will pay a high price to anyone who'll turn nose on the trade, and he'll provide protection against retaliation. He says it's the duty of the pious to welcome the penitent," he added with a sneer.

Sepori's lip curled in an identical expression. "Orcicci's not a pious churchman, he's an ambitious churchman. If he's targeting the trade, it's for his own advancement." His tone grew thoughtful. "But why now?"

Piero shrugged. "Maybe he feels strong enough with his new appointment to the Arcivescovo's table. He's been outspoken against most trades that fall outside the Church's pale at one time or another."

"And yet he's a man who's been known to dabble in whatever activity he deems necessary to enhance his career or whet his appetites."

"Yes, my Lord."

"I do not approve of dabblers, Piero, nor of hypocrites. A man should be what he is. Anything else is a contemptible weakness."

"Yes, my Lord."

Sepori nodded to himself. "We will deal with Father Orcicci, presently, but for the moment we have more pressing business. Who might Mario have given up under torture?"

Perio shrugged. "His contact, Filip Loddi, and he's been warned already. One or two markers he employed. No one else of consequence."

"Not yourself?"

"Mario's willingly carried my binding spell for years, my Lord." Piero's tone held a mild reproof and Sepori smiled faintly.

"Then all that leaves is the whereabouts of our most unfamilial Nico Urbi."

"Yes, my Lord. I have people out searching for him now. I worked a locate spell, and I'm sure he's still in Cerchicava, but he'll know he's hunted, and if the Church is really protecting him, it'll take more than my summoning abilities to drag him out."

"The Church's protection is a fallacy," Sepori replied with contempt. Staring out at San Dante Cathedral's copper roofs just visible beyond Via Certani's row of tall poplar trees, he nodded to himself. "Nico has a family?"

"A father, my Lord. Geneo Urbi, ex-guardsman, lives in Vericcio. He was crippled in Pisario's attack five years ago, but he's still a hard-nosed bastard by all accounts."

"Bring him to me at sundown."

"Yes, my Lord."

"Alive, Piero."

"Of course, my Lord."

"As for Mario, send Gino and Paulo to the north gate for watch change. Have them cut him down on my uncle's authority and bury him at Debassino's with the proper wardings."

"Yes, my Lord."

They walked in silence for a time, then Piero stirred. "I brought Mario into the trade," he reflected sadly. "He had good hands. Do you think Tino might say a few words?"

"No doubt. Offer him a beaker of brandy, and I'm sure he'll find a passage inside the pale somewhere that will serve."

"Thank you, my Lord. If you wish it, Talano can take over Mario's set jobs. He's a good cutter, there should be no delay in deliveries."

"Talano will be fine."

At the entrance to La Palazzo de Sulla, Sepori turned, the pale sea green of his eyes fading to be replaced by a blood red so dark it was almost black.

"Find out everything you can about our most holy Father Orcicci, Piero: his habits, his ambitions, and most especially his magecraft. If he's so much as imagined a working within my domain, I'll have him laid out on his own altar."

Piero bowed. "Yes, my Lord."

The manservant took his leave as Sepori made his way through the palazzo's carefully maintained entrance gardens. His Aunt Maria had loved the scent of roses and, at her death, Matteo had given the entire accession mall over to them in her honor. Sepori enjoyed them for their delicate perfection and often walked the gardens when he needed to think clearly. Today, however, he strode right past them. The sun was already beginning its trek toward evening, and he had much to prepare for.

Used to his routine, his uncle's servants had laid out a light repast in Sepori's study. He ate quickly, then crossed the room to the stout oaken door, partially blocked by a statue of his late grandfather. The standard protection and locking wards about the lintel gave off a dull blue glow, masking the darker warding beneath, but none showed any signs of interference. The house servants knew better, and Piero had his own entrance.

Taking a silver key from his belt, he inserted it into the lock, feeling the wards running up and down his arm with the feathery touch of a thousand moths. Anyone else would have had the flesh eaten off in a heartbeat. Sepori passed through without a ripple and locked the door behind him.

A heavily warded set of stone steps led down to a wide work chamber, lit and ventilated by magecraft. Pausing at he bottom, Sepori allowed the familiar odor of damp stone walls and stale magics to settle over him. Later, the room would reek of the charnel house, but that, too, could be a pleasant aroma in its way. Sweeping his hand in a tight arc, he sent a seeking spell out before him and the room was suddenly illuminated with a tracery of red light. Studying each one, he methodically searched the room for signs of tampering. They would not be difficult to detect; the chamber was tidy to the point of obsession, tools laid out in an equally spaced line on a high bench. The worktable, its twin side channels scrubbed clean and purified with spells similar to those the priests employed for their altars, ready for use. One shelf held neatly stacked jars of herbs, another, boxes and vials of various sizes. At the far end was a strongly warded door to the outside, at the near end, a tightly locked and warded bookcase. The seeking spell never so much as quavered and, satisfied, Sepori crossed to the worktable and picked up a leather apron. He could feel the sun sinking slowly beneath the hills west of the city. It would be soon.

The wards gave him ample warning of Piero's approach. Burdened by the body of another man, he opened the door with a complicated series of spells, then closed it again the same way before dumping the unconscious body of Geneo Urbi on the worktable.

Sepori took up a boning knife in one hand and a fistful of dried herbs in the other.

"Be ready to open the door," he instructed. "Nico will be arriving presently."

It took half an hour for the ex-bodyguard to make it from his hiding place in Bergo. His face and clothes were covered in dirt and sweat, and deep scratches lined his throat where he'd tried to claw the coercion spell from his breathing passage. The remnants of a priestly spell clung to him like tendrils of dying ivy, their external protection unable to contend with the internal necromantic summoning. He collapsed in a heap at Sepori's feet, his eyes rolling in his head. The working did not allow for speech, but one tiny moan made it past his clenched teeth when he recognized the bloodied corpse sprawled across the worktable.

Sepori, his apron and hands smeared with clotted gore, stepped forward and glanced dispassionately down at him.

"Hello, Nico."

His deep voice reverberated in the stone chamber, but all the ex-bodyguard could do was shudder in response.

"We've not met," Sepori continued in an almost conversational tone, "but you'll know me. I am Mario's master, and therefore ultimately yours." He picked up a wide piece of leather studded with barbed spikes. Nico's eyes tracked the movement, the strain beginning to break the blood vessels in his eyes so that they slowly grew as red as Sepori's.

"When you betrayed him," the death mage continued, "you betrayed me. In a moment I'll allow you to speak, and you'll have a few precious seconds to explain to me why I should not make use of your body's fluids and its organs to further the trade which you've spat upon."

Nico began to shake uncontrollably, but Sepori paid no attention.

"Be assured, you will die tonight, Nico, but what you say will ultimately decide whether you die damned by the taint of necromancy," he picked up a fine scalpel, holding it so that the magelight reflected off its cutting edge in a ruby red glow, "or die pure. Of course, most priests, including your protector, Luca Orcicci, would argue that by working for Mario in the first place, you've already damned yourself." He drew closer. "I say the day you approached a priest with betrayal in your thoughts was the day you truly became damned." He stepped back. "Speak."

The working eased from around the man's throat. Nico began to cough violently, but one look at the expression on Sepori's face made him bring himself under control enough to gasp out one word.

"Orcicci."

"Paid you."

Nico shook his head desperately, blood-flecked spittle spattering across the already bloodstained floor.

"Forced . . ." he choked out.

"How?"

"Sp . . . ell."

"A coercion spell?"

The ex-bodyguard nodded eagerly.

Sepori leaned down so that he could stare directly into the other man's eyes.

"Priests do not work coercion spells," he replied as if to a child. "Try again."

"Swear . . . it. Cosimo . . . taught him."

"Cosimo. Cosimo Sansovi, the death mage?"

Nico nodded.

Sepori glanced at Piero who shook his head. "Cosimo Sansovi is dead, my Lord."

"Alive," Nico managed.

"Did you do a working to insure that he was dead, Piero?" Sepori asked.

"No, my Lord; the priests interred his body at Debassino's three weeks ago."

"What priests?"

"The Arcivescovo's."

"Orcicci?"

Understanding dawned, and Piero nodded. Sepori turned back to Nico.

"Orcicci has Cosimo Sansovi?"

Nico nodded.

"And Cosimo is teaching him trade workings?"

Again a nod.

"Where? At the Cathedral?"

"At . . . Palazzo . . . del Cassti."

Sepori reached out and gently laid his hand on the ex-bodyguard's head. He spoke a word and red magefire began to spill from his fingertips, running down Nico's face to pool about his nose and lips.

The summoning snapped off.

With a surge of strength, Nico bolted for the door. Sepori let him go. The ex-bodyguard crossed the threshold and the wards took him. Their power jerked him to a halt, blood spraying from his mouth from the force of it. Magefire crackled along his body, outlining every straining tendon, then flung him back into the room to land in a crumpled heap at Sepori's feet.

Wrapping the leather around his fist, the death mage shook his head and, with a gesture, raised the man up until his feet dangled a few inches from the floor.

"Good-bye, Nico."

The first blow caught him in the abdomen, the spikes sinking through clothes and flesh. Blood began to spray across Sepori's arms, but he ignored it, aiming a series of methodical blows at the man's body. The magic about them grew hot as it held Nico up against the force of the necromancer's barrage. Finally, Sepori drove his fist into the mass of bloody tissue that Nico's chest had become, and, using magic to crack the ribs apart with the sound of violent thunder, and, without even the pretense of finesse, gripped the no longer beating heart and tore it from the body, then allowed the corpse to fall.

Piero glanced over. "He was lying, My Lord?"

"Only about his own coercion." Dropping the steaming organ in a shallow bowl, the death mage gestured. "Get him up."

The two men worked steadily for over an hour, eviscerating Nico's corpse and stuffing it with herb-laced straw. Once it was whole again, Sepori began the painstaking process of covering the body with rows of tattooed bindings. Several hours later, he straightened and stepped back.

"Rise."

The corpse began to vibrate. Snapping back and forth in a parody of human movement, it tumbled from the table.

"HOLD!"

The corpse froze in midair.

Sepori circled it carefully, then made an adjustment to a symbol by its left temple and the corpse slowly righted itself. The death mage nodded.

"Dress it, then wrap it in preserving cloth. Dump the other body in Vericcio where it may be found swiftly."

"Yes, my Lord." Piero turned. "And what of Cosimo, my Lord? And Orcicci?"

"I will deal with them soon enough. In the meantime, I have a supper engagement."

Stripping off the apron, Sepori laid it across the table, then made his way upstairs.

Later that night, Sepori attended Clarissa Malatesta at her palazzo. He was at his most charming, complimenting her on her magecraft and feigning interest in the host of small talk expected before supper. They touched on politics and the weather, the possibility of war with Pisario and his uncle's military successes. Sepori asked politely after her own uncle's health, then frowned as she voiced her concerns about his workload.

"But surely with the addition of this new priest to his table, what was his name?"

"Orcicci," she replied, her tone decidedly chilly.

He pretended not to notice.

"Yes, Orcicci, surely with his addition, some of the burden has been lifted from the Arcivescovo's shoulders. I understand he's quite competent."

"Yes," she agreed coldly. "Quite competent. And quite ambitious."

Sepori nodded in understanding. "I had heard that," he admitted. "He is . . ." he made a pretense of searching for the most tactful word. "There were some doubts about his piety, as I recall."

"There were indeed." Warming to the subject, she leaned forward. "Captain Visconti of my uncle's Holy Scourge spoke against his appointment. He believes his devotion is driven by personal ambition, and not by faith."

"And the Arcivescovo?"

Clarissa paused, her desire to voice her dislike of Orcicci warring with her loyalty to her uncle.

"He admires his intelligence and his drive," she said finally. "He believes he is young, and that his ambitions will . . ." her lips curled, ". . . cool with time and experience."

Sepori nodded, but his expression remained unconvinced.

The arrival of supper ended further discussion of Orcicci's character, but Sepori was well satisfied with the results. And later, as the nightingales began to sing outside the palazzo windows, he rose and escorted her to her bedchamber where there was no more need for talking.

He took his leave of her as dawn colored the eastern sky. The air was crisp, redolent with the scent of fruit trees in bloom, and he breathed it in with pleasure. He enjoyed the springtime in Cerchicava much more than the summer with its heat and overlying stench of sewage. Bodies kept fresh longer and workings could be given the time they deserved. Workings of all kinds, he mused as he passed through his uncle's rose gardens.

He took a light breakfast of quail's eggs dipped in honey on the palazzo's east portico. As he began on a second cup of strong, black tea, Piero brought him the morning news. Geneo Urbi had been found lying dead outside his rooming house in Vericcio last night, his windpipe carved from his throat. It was clear he'd fallen victim to the trade. The watch had called in the priests, but his only family, his son Nico, could not be found to pay the thirty soldi needed for his purification. He'd been interred at the Debassino Heretic's cemetery in the meantime, but, again there was no one to pay for the warding, so who could say how long his body would escape further defilement. Sipping at his cup, Sepori nodded.

An hour later he attended services at the San Dante Cathedral. The morning's news had reached the high church officials and the Arcivescovo's sermon was a blistering attack on the trade and any who allowed its operators to go unpunished. Standing behind him, Father Luca Orcicci looked suitably outraged. Sepori studied him carefully.

Orcicci was a handsome man with thick black hair and cold blue eyes. Piero had told him he was twenty-five years old, the third son of a long-distance trader and the daughter of the city's last mayor. Born and raised in Cerchicava's wealthy Carmina district, he had received a private education and entered the church at age sixteen. He had never known want or fear or even doubt. The death mage smiled to himself. Luca Orcicci was about to become very well acquainted with all three.

Like most of the congregation, Sepori attended the season's first service reception in the Cathedral's main gardens. The talk was all about the body found in Vericcio. Orcicci could be heard violently denouncing the killers, and Sepori moved up behind Clarissa Malatesta as she frowned into her wineglass.

"Pompous ass," he breathed.

She started and then smiled as she realized who had spoken. "Yes, isn't he?"

"Who's the man standing by the olive trees? The one whose expression matches your own in disapproval, though, of course, never in beauty."

She glanced over. "Captain Visconti."

"Ah." Leaning down, he brushed the back of her neck with his lips. "Introduce me."

Piero was waiting for him when he arrived home. "You have news?"

"Yes, my Lord. An old servant of Orcicci's, Rico Zeni's his name, tells me that the priest has a pale-haired man with scarred arms imprisoned below the Palazzo del Cassti."

"Cosimo Sansovi."

"It sounds like him, my Lord. Rico says Orcicci spends a lot of time in the man's cell. Sometimes Rico hears talking, sometimes screaming. And sometimes he says he can smell magics, foul magics."

"How so?"

"He says the cellars reek of death, but nothing has died."

"Hm. This Rico Zeni, is he a pious man?"

"He is, my Lord. And a frightened one. He's sure that his master has become tainted by the trade and fears that he will become damned by his service."

"Why hasn't he spoken of his fears to his own priest?"

Piero shrugged. "His priest is poor, and his master is rich. And a powerful churchman besides," he added unnecessarily. "He doesn't think he'll be believed."

"Likely he wouldn't be. Not without further proof." Sepori stood. "I think it's time we contacted Cosimo Sansovi."

"Yes, my Lord."

Together, the two men retired to the work chamber.

*   *   *

That night, Montifero de Sepori animated Nico Urbi's corpse.

Cerchicava awakened to chaos the next morning. A corpse had been seen stalking the streets of the Carmina District. Outside the Palazzo del Cassti it had begun to shriek and wail hideously, then disappeared before the watch could investigate. Father Luca Orcicci was enraged that the trade would dare attack him at his home and swore to bring the death mage responsible to judgment.

The next night the same event occurred.

For three nights running the creature shrieked its wordless torment outside the Palazzo del Cassti. Two of Orcicci's servants fled the first morning, two more ran the day after. On the third morning Piero bought Rico Zeni before his master.

The old man was shaking with fear, but Sepori sat him in the rear garden gazebo where it was quiet and took a seat across from him with a caring expression.

"Be at ease, Rico," he said gently. "My man tells me that you and your fellow servants are frightened for your souls, but that you are afraid to bring your concerns before your master."

The man seemed ready to faint, and Sepori gestured. "Piero, bring water."

"Yes, my Lord."

Sepori returned his attention to Orcicci's servant. "You're not to be afraid to speak your fears aloud here, Rico. I will not condemn you for any supposed disloyalty toward Father Orcicci, but you must tell me, why can you not go to him?"

His eyes fixed on his feet, Rico began to speak, hesitantly at first and then more quickly, the words tumbling over each other in his haste to spit them out. Throughout, Sepori listened carefully without interruption, finally nodding when the old man stumbled to a halt.

"Your manservant, my Lord . . ." Rico licked his lips and, at Sepori's gesture, took a deep gulp from the cup Piero had brought him. "Your manservant told me . . . he said you knew powerful priests who might help us."

"Powerful . . . ?'

"The Scourge, my Lord," he whispered.

Sepori frowned. "The Scourge is a terrible force to unleash," he said severely. "Take care before you name it." He leaned forward, catching the other man in a stern gaze. "Are you absolutely certain that your master is involved in this heresy, Rico? Be aware, the Church punishes a false accuser almost as harshly as they do an apostate."

The man seemed frightened out of his wits, but he nodded. "I have seen it, my Lord," he whispered. "He will damn us all if he continues. Please, my Lord, please help us."

Sepori made a show of thinking deeply. Finally, he nodded. "I will speak with Captain Visconti. Return to your master's house and wait on my word."

"Yes, my Lord, thank you, my Lord."

"Piero."

"My Lord?"

"Take him home, then find Captain Visconti and beg his indulgence to come to the Palazzo de Sulla at once on a matter of extreme urgency."

"Yes, my Lord."

The two servants departed and Sepori reached over to caress one tight crimson rose blossom growing beside the gazebo.

"All too easy," he murmured.

* * *

Once begun, events moved swiftly. An accusation of necromancy by a member of the nobility was enough to send the Scourge to Orcicci's home at once. They found Cosimo Sansovi chained to the wall in a cell reeking of necromantic workings. He cried hysterically at their appearance, lifting up hands covered in burned flesh and pus, and begging them to kill him. There was fresh blood and excrement all over his clothes, and the man screamed and cried so wildly that one of the younger priestly-knights put his sword through him just to silence him. Orcicci was immediately arrested.

The trial itself was nothing more than a formality. The Arcivescovo presided and Captain Visconti gave evidence along with three of the Palazzo del Cassti servants, including Rico Zeni. Montifero de Sepori was not mentioned.

Orcicci, beaten almost insensible by the Scourge, was unable to speak in his own defense. He stood as straight as the chains about him allowed, staring blankly at nothing as if he could not comprehend how swiftly his ruin had come. He was condemned and scheduled for execution the next day.

Sepori visited him that night. One gesture was all it took to freeze the guards where they stood and, taking up a lantern from the wall, he crossed to the cell at the far end of the San Dante dungeons and peered through the bars.

Luca Orcicci was crouched by the far wall, his blue eyes dull with despair. The dark bruising that mottled his face made him seem much younger than his years and the blood matting his hair and clotted on his hands cast deep shadows against the gray pallor of his skin.

Sepori raised the lantern.

"Luca."

Orcicci slowly looked up.

"Do I know you?" he asked woodenly.

"No."

"Are you a priest?"

Sepori shook his head. "The priests have abandoned you. They won't service the damned."

Orcicci's eyes cleared slightly. "I'm not damned."

"You were convicted by an ecclesiastical court, defrocked, and flung beyond the pale. What do you call that?"

"Wrongfully accused."

"Really? You never worked a necromantic binding spell to constrain and coerce Cosimo Sansovi in the cellars of your palazzo."

"It wasn't a necromantic binding spell."

"What about the summoning you worked against Mario Chigi or the coercion spell you threatened to work against Nico Urbi. Both were learned from Cosimo, a self-confessed necromancer. Where do you think the magecraft came from?"

Orcicci glared at him. "Who are you?"

Sepori came closer. "I am the premier death mage in Cerchicava."

Orcicci paled. "You killed Nico Urbi," he breathed.

"And sent his animated corpse to damn you in the eyes of your church, yes. I could just as easily have sent it to kill you."

"Why didn't you?" Orcicci asked bitterly.

"You needed to be shown the difference between the Church and the trade. I sensed you were confused. This business of damning necromancy with one hand and working it with the other. Did you honestly think you could use our own magics against us and escape the wrath of both Church and trade?"

Orcicci looked away. "I may have made an error in judgement," he allowed.

"An error?" Sepori asked harshly. "Be honest, Luca. You betrayed your faith by willingly committing the most abhorrent of heresies in the name of ambition, then you spat in the face of a trade so dangerous that most people won't even speak its name for fear the very word will damn their souls. I'm not surprised your execution is going to be the event of the season. Every person in Cerchicava, pious or impious, will enjoy watching them spill your guts out onto the street before they hang you."

Orcicci closed his eyes. "What do you want?" he asked wearily.

"To save your life."

The ex-priest's eyes snapped open. "Why?"

"Because you're one of us."

"No, I'm not."

"Really? Tell me, Luca, the first time you worked one of our spells, how did it make you feel? Strong, powerful?"

"Tainted."

"Damned?"

Orcicci met his eyes. "Maybe," he admitted.

"Then let me tell you a secret about damnation that might ease your heart. Once you've taken that first terrifying step you're free to live the rest of your life without constraint. The worst is already prepared for you. And you took that step the day you first spoke with Cosimo Sansovi. He was an eloquent man, wasn't he? Was it his idea to make use of his knowledge against the trade, or yours?"

Orcicci met his eyes. "It was mine."

"Then your damnation occurred even sooner than I thought. You are an ambitious man. A pity I didn't discover you before the eve of your execution. You might have made something of the rest of your life."

"And now?"

"Now you will die and your body will be flung into a heretic's crypt in Debassino's where not even your own family will pay to have it protected from the trade." Sepori's eyes glowed hotly. "How long do you suppose your body will last before the cutters bring it to my table?"

Orcicci made no answer.

"One night, Luca."

The ex-priest dropped his head into his hands.

"Do you want that kind of end," Sepori continued, "or do you want to escape death and take revenge on the people who destroyed your life?"

"You destroyed my life."

"I destroyed your illusions. The Arcivescovo and his Holy Scourge destroyed your life. Will you allow them that victory, or will you leave weakness and false piety behind in this cell where they belong and embrace what you are?"

"And what am I?"

"You're a death mage."

"No."

Sepori shrugged. "Then you're a fool who will die in denial, and I will take your corpse and employ it to stalk the families of my enemies. Is that what you really want?"

Orcicci stared up at him as if he were looking into the eyes of some terrible demon, but when he spoke his voice was stronger than it had been.

"No."

"Then stand up."

The ex-priest rose very slowly.

"Come here."

Orcicci's approach was painfully slow, but finally he stood before the necromancer.

"Give me your hands."

The ex-priest obeyed, putting his bloodied and broken hands through the bars, and Sepori placed a square brown object into his left palm. Orcicci squinted at it.

"What is that?"

"Flesh."

Before he could react, Sepori's own hands shot forward, catching the other man's up in an iron grip. The ex-priest jerked backward and would have fallen had a net of crimson magics not suddenly sprung up to hold him upright.

"Do you come to the trade of your own free will?" Sepori barked at him.

Orcicci's head snapped forward from the force of the compulsion.

"Yes."

The word took on a life of its own, twisting around and driving back into his mouth to burn all the way down his throat and explode in his stomach. He sagged against the bars.

"And will you obey me in all things, learn from me, and serve me until I deem you worthy of the name death mage?"

"Yes."

Again the word burned through his body, destroying the priestly paths his own magic had taken and carving new, darker passages in their wake.

"And do you willingly take on my bindings that you might suffer the most unspeakable torment should you ever betray your oaths made to me this night?"

"Yes."

This time it was as if a great conflagration had engulfed him completely. It shot from his fingertips and poured from his mouth and nose in a deluge of fire. When it guttered out he felt, if not at peace, at least no longer despairing. He stared wonderingly at the other man, his blue eyes crackling with crimson magecraft. Sepori nodded.

"Come out of there, Luca."

The newly inducted necromancer touched the cell door and it swung soundlessly open. His eyes widened.

"That's only the beginning," Sepori assured him.

"But the guards?"

"Will never know you've gone." Sepori gestured and Piero came forward from the shadows, leading a man who looked remarkably like the ex-priest.

"A construct," Sepori explained. "It will last long enough for tomorrow's charade."

The creature took Orcicci's place in the cell without a word and Sepori turned. "Come, Luca, it is time we left this place."

Without a backward glance, Luca Orcicci followed his new master from the cellars of San Dante.

The next morning dawned sunny and warm, but few businesses opened their doors. The area around the north gate gibbets had been crowded for hours— it wasn't often the common people of Cerchicava got to see a nobleman hanged—and the hastily erected pavilions were equally full—the nobility of Cerchicava rarely got to see a priest hanged. From his place beside Clarissa Malatesta, Sepori watched the proceedings with an even expression, nodding as she suggested another late night supper, then turned at the sound of the death wagon approaching the gate.

The execution was a disappointment. The priests tried to draw it out as long as possible, but Luca Orcicci was either in shock or drugged, for he made a very poor show and died without a word. Denied their spectacle, the crowd was in an ugly mood and dispersed quickly, but Scpori was well satisfied.

Glancing over the heads of the nobility, he could see that the city officials had already gone, once again leaving the priestly mages behind to bless their seats.

The irony of his thinking the last time he'd stood before the ducal box made him smile, and when Piero approached, he gestured him forward.

"You may bring Mario's body home now," he said, pitching his voice so that only the manservant could hear him. "Inter him in the de Sulla crypt. His death did us all a great service."

"Yes, my Lord. And Orcicci, my Lord?"

"Take him with you. He needs to get his hands dirty as quickly as possible."

"Will it be safe for him out on the streets so soon, my Lord?"

"Oh, yes." Sepori glanced up at the construct, turning slowly on its gibbet. "No one is looking for him now."

Turning, Lord Montifero de Sepori made his way back to his palazzo where Cerchicava's newest death mage awaited him.

KING OF THORNS
by R. Davis

R. Davis currently makes his home in Maine, with his wife Monica, their two children Morgan Storm and Mason Rain, and one psychotic cat. In addition to his own fiction and poetry writing, he is the managing editor at Foggy Windows Books. He coedited the anthology *Mardi Gras Madness* with Martin Greenberg, and his work can be read in numerous anthologies, including DAW's *New Amazons*, *Merlin*, and *Single White Vampire Seeks Same*.

The five remaining Thorns—four men and one woman—had been gathered in a small, plainly-furnished room beneath the auditorium. Silent guards watched over them. Speaking was allowed, but the Thorns sensed that now was not the time for talking. Above them, the sounds of the auditorium slowly filling up with people could be heard: the scuff of boots, the mutter of voices, all transmitted to the Thorns through the stone walls of their temporary prison. Were they weaker of mind, the sound alone might well drive them mad.

Kille Tempen heard everything, but ignored it in favor of watching the other four Thorns. Each movement they made, each flicker of personality that was visible, even in silence, told him something. Raine, his Master, had beaten the lesson of observation into

234

him long ago. "You must learn to watch the smallest habits of others," Raine would say. "It's the best way to learn how to kill them." Kille held himself absolutely still during this period, to give away nothing of the fear he felt. Or his plans. All the Thorns were afraid—in the auditorium above, death and dishonor were waiting like hooded skeletons with their hands held out.

They wouldn't be here much longer before the guards escorted them to the auditorium, and the Thorn Trials began in earnest. All five knew each other, or at the least, knew of each other. They had been together in the same group *of* apprentice assassins for fifteen years. In the Temple of Illhana, friendships were rare. It wasn't practical when so many of the Thorns would die long before their training was over.

The woman, Sarahkis, was the first to break the silence. "It will be time soon," she said.

At first, no one answered, and then, almost all at once, there was a chaos of nodding and mumbled "Yesses." Kille stayed silent.

When it quieted, she added with a grin, "So which of you wants to be the first to die?"

This sally was greeted with some laughter. The Thorns were confident in their abilities—after all, they had outlived the other twenty-five Thorns who had started with them during the Trials. Those who had died during the Trials had been resurrected, and were now toiling away as beginning acolytes for the Temple.

"For your humor," Kille Tempen said easily to her, "I will save you for last."

The others grew instantly silent. In their group of thirty, only five remained to fight this last battle to

the death. Those that died here would be resurrected
(the Temple didn't believe in wasting talent), but
their future rank as Master Assassins within the Temple would be determined based on the outcome of
this battle. It was rumored that of the twenty-five
Thorns killed during the Trial so far, Kille Tempen
had accounted for twelve. No one knew for certain.

Sarahkis smiled at him. Aside from the horrendous
scar running alongside her jaw, she was quite beautiful. "Don't save yourself for me, Tempen," she challenged. "For your threat, I will hunt you down first."

Kille smiled back, then turned to the group as a
whole. "Do you know what will happen up there?"
he asked softly. "Do you know what really awaits
you in the hall?"

Silence returned to the small room, and he continued. "We will be taken from this room, and our
weapons and belongings will be returned to us separately in small cells just down the hallway from here.
Once we are properly armed, we will be escorted up
to the auditorium, and from there to the center platform, directly beneath the High Seat.

"The Prioress will be sitting in her throne on the
High Seat, and from her vantage, she will recognize
us for our accomplishment of surviving the Thorn
Trials thus far. She will also indicate which of the
five of us is her personal favorite, and she will place
the traditional Dead Man's Bet of two silvers.

"A brief time will pass while the final bets are
placed, and then the hall will go silent and dark. The
only light sources will be those that we provide for
ourselves. We will be given five minutes to lose ourselves in the maze that now covers most of the auditorium floor. And then a final horn will sound, once,
and the real Thorn Trial will begin."

He laughed quietly, as the others stared at him, a little appalled at his bleak knowledge. "The audience will be able to see and hear us through magic, though we will not be able to see or hear them. They will be watching us, watching you, die one at a time. Interference in the outcome is forbidden. In that darkened hall, there will be traps, put there by the Masters. There will be magic and illusion and poison, all designed to test each skill that you may or may not possess." He paused, and then looked at each of the remaining Thorns in turn, his gaze settling on Sarahkis last. "And there will be me. In the darkness, Hunting for you."

None of the other Thorns were laughing now, though Sarahkis nodded grimly, thinking of all he had said. *It worked as I thought it would,* Kille thought. *I will let their fears do most of my work for me. Belief is a weapon of power. Raine has taught me well.*

For a long time, no one said anything more. Above them, the sounds in the auditorium grew, and then faded as the last of the clerics and assassins who made up the body of the Temple of Illhana filed in. Finally, one of the guards cleared his throat. "It's time," he said.

The Thorns stood to file out of the room, but before he reached the door, Sarahkis touched Kille lightly on the arm. "You almost had me there, Tempen," she said. The others stopped to watch this final exchange. "You don't scare me," she added.

The others mumbled in agreement. "We'll band together to hunt you down first," she finished for them.

He grinned at her. "Do what you will, Sarahkis," he said. "All of you. But the rumor in the Temple is wrong. Of the twenty-five, I took eighteen, and the five of you are next." With that final jab, he turned and strode from the room, leaving Sarahkis and the other Thorns to wonder at the truth of his words.

The Thorns climbed onto the platform below the High Seat while waves of sound, the steady rhythmic clapping of hands and the whispered and repeated chant of "Thorns," washed over them. This was an accolade in the Temple. To survive this long was a high accomplishment, and they were being recognized, however briefly, for their talents. Finally, the Prioress raised her hand for silence.

The Prioress sat on her throne, a large onyx-and-silver-wire chair said to possess magical powers. Within the walls of the Temple, the Prioress always sat on the throne—it was moved to wherever she desired. Directly behind and on either side of her, her two hand servants stood in silence. Many rumors were whispered about the two women who lived in the Prioress' apartments and never seemed to leave her side: some believed them to be her bodyguards; others said they were her lovers. That they were to be feared was unquestioned. No one could live so long at the Prioress' side and not be dangerous.

As always, most of the Prioress' face was unseen, covered by the traditional black cloth mask of assassins. Her hair was the white of a first winter's snow, her eyes, pools of lavender. She was dressed in a simple bodysuit of black and dark blue, and she wore no jewelry upon her long-fingered hands. What skin was visible was pale, almost bloodless. She exuded an aura of supreme confidence, power, and sex that had brought many men, and no few women, instantly to their knees.

When quiet had once again claimed the hall, she

raised her hand in salute. "As our goddess, Illhana, Mistress of Assassins dictates, only five Thorns remain. You have done well."

The Thorns bowed respectfully.

"The final Trial is upon you," she continued. "In a short time, the hall will be darkened, and you will fight amongst yourselves to determine your rank as Master Assassins. There are no rules, and those of us who watch you will not interfere in the outcome on pain of final death. Four will die and be restored to life as Master Assassins. One will live, conquering all others, and will have rank over the others—a Master among Masters, the King, or Queen, of Thorns."

The Thorns bowed again, to show their understanding of the rules.

The Prioress pointed at Sarahkis. "You are favored," she said, while the other Thorns looked at Sarahkis in surprise. "Though you haven't the largest number of kills in the Trials, you possess the strength and wit to prevail." The Prioress turned to the Betmaster, and handed him two silver coins. "I place the Dead Man's Bet on Sarahkis."

The Betmaster nodded, taking the coins and marking down the wager in his logbook. He called out the bet, and added that final wagers could now be placed. Scattered throughout the hall, his assistants gathered coins and bets. Sarahkis was now the odds-on favorite.

As the betting continued, Kille stepped forward and signaled the Betmaster, who stared in surprise. Warily, he called down from his place beside the High Seat. "Yes?"

Kille stepped forward and tossed him a small pouch. The Betmaster opened it, and gasped in shock. Inside were a number of rubies and emeralds. "Fair value?" Kille said loudly.

The Betmaster nodded. "Fair value, 1,000 gold." The crowd noise suddenly ceased. "You wish to wager this?" the Betmaster asked.

"Yes," Kille called. "All of it, on myself."

"Such a thing is unheard of!" the Betmaster said. "The Thorns do not wager on themselves during the Trials!"

"I have offered a bet," Kille reminded him quietly. Tradition held that a wager offered must be answered. The other Thorns remained motionless and silent. It had never occurred to them to place any kind of wager, or even to carry the money to do so.

The Betmaster looked helplessly at the Prioress, whose eyes lit up with interest. "It will be allowed," she said.

The Betmaster called out the bet, and a fresh round of wagering began. Kille listened carefully to the final odds. If he won, his wager of 1,000 gold would be worth 5,000, perhaps a little more. Finally, the ritual was complete.

The Betmaster signaled the Prioress, who nodded. "Let the final Thorn Trial commence," she said, then clapped her hands sharply. The room went instantly dark and silent. Each Thorn heard her voice, cold and ghostly, slide into their ears. "You have five minutes to do whatever you will in the maze. When the horn sounds, it begins."

Almost before the Prioress had finished speaking, four of the five Thorns leaped off the main platform and headed into the maze. They were used to the darkness, and moved with grace and confidence. The maze was a jumble of rocks, crevices, hidden passageways, and small rooms. There was no pattern to it, no discernable pathway to follow. For Kille Tempen, it was the ultimate game of cat and mouse.

Standing at the base of the platform, he chose the role of cat, and waited, listening to the others move off into the shadows. He calmed his breathing, and listened as Raine had trained him to listen, focusing on the little sounds that would tell him what he needed to know. They hadn't all banded together as Sarahkis suggested, he realized. Sarahkis, who had chosen to wear hard-soled boots, was with one other person. *An odd choice*, he thought, *but perhaps she feels that the added protection is worth the risk of being heard.* If he listened carefully, Kille could make out the distinct sound the boots made even when worn by someone as soft-footed as an assassin. The two others moved off in separate directions. *So, it is two and one and one.*

Smiling to himself, Kille moved away from the platform, his leather moccasins, chosen for just this event, making no sound on the stone floor. Within a few minutes, he had entered the maze, a cat among the mice, a hunter in the dark auditorium.

The small room was indistinguishable from any other in the maze. Kille had found it by the use of a quick spell that allowed him to see in the dark, and quickly decided that it was suitable for his first kill. There was a crack in the center of the stone ceiling, a fault line just large enough for his purposes.

Taking a silk cord and grappling hook from his pack, he quickly attached the grapple to the cord, then carefully wedged the grapple itself into the fault. He left the cord to dangle in the center of the room, playing out its remaining length along the floor to the exit. He whispered a spell to make the cord glow

a faint purple color, which began at the ceiling and
ended at the floor, making it appear as though the
cord was only seven or eight feet long.

His trap in place, Kille sat to one side of the doorway, a shadow among the shadows, the silk cord
wrapped tightly around his gloved hands. He also
released the spell that allowed him to see in the
dark—the faint glow of the cord provided more than
enough light for his purposes, and to maintain the
spell might cost him precious energy he would need
later. He waited, not moving the merest muscle, as
Raine had trained him. *Patience*, Raine had told him,
*will always be the assassin's greatest weapon. Learn to sit,
breathe, think, and plan without moving your body. Flex
your muscles slowly and methodically so they don't cramp
up, for they are silent and you will need them when the
reward for your patience arrives.*

It took nearly two hours, but his patience paid off.
In the opposite doorway, a shadow moved. To the
untrained eye, it would have been nearly impossible
to see. There was little sound to tell if it was a person
or his imagination, but then the nameless Thorn released a slightly pent-up breath, and Kille knew for
sure.

The Thorn stood, unmoving near the doorway, for
almost five minutes. Watching the cord, trying to determine its purpose, looking for whichever of the
other Thorns had put it there. Kille did nothing,
barely breathing. He couldn't see the other Thorn's
face, didn't know who it was, but the build suggested
a male.

Finally, convinced that the room was empty, the
Thorn stepped closer, one hand reaching out to grasp
the cord, then, thinking better of it, he stopped. Still,
Kille waited.

The Thorn looked up toward the ceiling, trying to penetrate the gloom and determine where or how the cord was tied off. At the same moment, Kille yanked on the cord with all his strength, and the grappling hook, barely secured to the stone, came tumbling down. The first hook drove itself into the other Thorn's cheek, the second hook lodged in his left eye, which made a peculiar popping sound, and the third grazed his temple. The Thorn screamed in agony, and before the echo had faded, Kille was on his feet. As the Thorn drew in breath to scream a second time, Kille drove a dagger into his straining throat, killing him instantly.

He cut the cord and left the grapple embedded in the other Thorn's face. As he quickly wrapped it up and stuck it back in his pouch, he pulled off the assassin's mask. The Thorn was Thomrine Calar, one of the two that Kille thought had gone off on their own.

He turned and left the room, knowing that any of the others could be close by, watching or homing in on the noise. *One down*, he thought as he ran. *Three to go*.

He didn't follow any specific path, but rather chose random routes around the boulder-clogged maze. When he judged he'd gone far enough, Kille stopped and began looking for another good place to spring a trap. Rounding a corner, he slammed directly into another Thorn, whose back was turned. The sudden contact in the darkness startled both, and Kille jumped backward, cursing. *Damn! I should have gutted him right then!* Now it was too late, as the other Thorn drew out a short sword and dagger.

Kille continued to back up for several paces, while drawing his own long swords with his right hand,

and selecting a small dirk from his belt with his left. Neither spoke, but both continued to circle warily. Sometimes, assassins in the Temple referred to this as the Dance of Shadows, when in the darkness, all you can see of your opponent is his barely visible silhouette, or perhaps a telltale flicker of light from his blade. The other Thorn quickly closed in and Kille met him halfway.

Their swords clashed, while their daggers rapidly clicked together, parrying and thrusting, looking for the smallest opening in the other's defenses. Kille felt a sharp pain in his shoulder at the same time as he parted the other Thorn's guard with his dirk. Ignoring his wound for a moment, Kille pushed his advantage, and stepped inside the other Thorn's guard. He left the dirk buried in his opponent's stomach.

The Thorn cried out, and Kille heard the short sword drop to the ground. Decisively, he stepped forward, and sensing the other man's position, he cleanly cut his throat. The Thorn dropped to the ground like a sack of grain, his scream cut off before it could begin. He hit the ground with a dull thud, and Kille grabbed him beneath the arms and pulled him into a small, cavelike opening in a nearby group of rocks.

Kille knelt down beside the body and removed the assassin's mask. It was Gavnar. Which left both Sarahkis and her follower, Tristan, somewhere in the maze. *So much for my hope that they'd have split up by now*, Kille thought. *How am I going to take both out at once?* As he sat there, he felt the first tingle of real pain from his shoulder. *I hope to Illhana he hasn't poisoned me.* He carefully peeled back the bloodied cloth, and using his fingers, gently probed the wound.

It wasn't as bad as he'd feared, though it was

bleeding freely. Kille contemplated the situation. He preferred to save his magic for combat and traps, rather than healing, but the wound might slow the arm somewhat, and that was a liability he couldn't afford. Shrugging to himself, he removed an herbed bandage from his pack and applied it to the wound, while mumbling a minor healing spell. The wound slowly closed, and the pain faded to a dull ache. It wasn't the most potent spell he could have chosen, but it would do. *Better to save the serious spells for when I'm truly desperate. Of course, with two of them teamed against me, I may soon be desperate.*

He paused to listen to his surroundings again. Silence. *I could spend hours in here playing this game with them. I wonder how they'd respond if I didn't play anymore?* He rose from his crouch, and began making his way back to the main platform, an idea taking shape in his mind.

Kille was known in the Temple as something of a showman, which perhaps explained some of his success. The ability to put on a show, the right face (or mask), even the ability to weave the right tale at the right time were all skills that were admired and even encouraged within the Temple walls. Many assassins developed unique "calling cards," subtle or not-so-subtle clues that marked a victim's killer, though the Temple Masters discouraged this practice as foolhardy. Kille didn't think of the small orchid formed of iron he usually left near a victim as a calling card, because he didn't always leave it. He knew that always leaving such an item, particularly for someone who killed as often as he did, might well lead to a massive manhunt. He also specialized in public assassination—a skill very few Temple assassins could boast.

Kille moved quietly through the maze, pausing frequently to listen or to watch the shadows. He had no desire to run into the last two Thorns before he'd had time to set the stage for his, or rather their, farewell performance.

Kille activated the spell, and light almost as bright as day illuminated the main platform. As a matter of course, the rest of the auditorium remained dark, but for the two remaining Thorns in the contest, it would be a beacon. "Sarahkis," Kille called out. "Let's not spend hours sneaking around in the dark. Come up here and let's fight it out."

When no one answered, Kille called again. "Sarahkis, are you afraid? Two of the others are already dead. Why don't you and Tristan come down here? We'll duel it out amongst ourselves."

The dagger sailed out of the darkness at the edge of the platform, and as it struck Kille in the throat, the light from his spell immediately went out. Arms flailing, his body fell in a heap on the wooden surface of the platform, unmoving.

Tristan climbed onto the platform first. "I got him, Sarahkis!" he called out. When he turned, her broadsword sliced him open from belly to chin. His scream was piercing.

"So you did, Tristan," she said as he fell. "You do good work." She kicked his writhing form out of the way, and stepped past Kille's prone form to take her accolades at the front of the podium, anticipating the return of light. The hall stayed dark, and she peered around cautiously. "Who's left?" she called out nervously. "He said the others were dead."

"Just me," said Kille from somewhere in the shadows around the platform.

"You . . ." she said, spinning to try and look every-where at once. "You're dead. Tristan's dagger took you in the throat!"

"Always check the body," Kille said. "I'm tougher than I look."

Sarahkis was turning in wary circles, trying to lo-cate him in the darkness, her sword held at the ready. "Come on, then," she called. "Let's finish it."

"In good time," Kille said. "Nice work with Tris-tan, by the way," he said. "I don't think I could have taken you both at once."

"You knew," she whispered softly. "You knew I'd kill him. How?"

"It's what I'd have done," Kille said, leaping onto the platform, and reactivating the light spell. *May as well put a spotlight on the stage*, he thought.

Sarahkis whirled to face him. "You're good, Tem-pen," she said. "But are you good enough?" She ges-tured to the blood on the shoulder of his robe, and overhead at the magical light source. "That where the dagger hit? Do you think it will slow you down in the Dance of Shadows?"

Kille smiled. "There are no shadows here, Sarahkis. And I don't feel any slower than normal." He moved his long sword to a defensive position, and they began to circle one another. "And actually," he said, "Tristan missed."

"I won't," she said, "now that you've given me light!" She charged forward, her sword twirling in a deadly arc. Kille parried, and backed away. They closed again, and as they attacked and parried, mov-ing forward and back, Kille quickly realized that she was every bit as good as he was, and maybe—at least with a sword—a little better. He'd have to do something to change the odds, and quickly.

In the Temple of Illhana, there were those who practiced the art of faith, pure clerics, those who trained as assassins only, and those who did both. While Kille was both cleric and assassin, Sarahkis was purely an assassin. Her strength was the blade, while Kille relied on both spells and weapons. Her extra practice with the sword was paying off.

He backed off several paces, and surprisingly, she didn't close the gap. Kille reached into a pouch and removed a small handful of powder. Stepping forward, he tossed it toward her face. However, when it should have caused her to have a coughing fit, she just stood there. *That always works!* Kille thought.

"I sincerely hope," she said, "that that's not your best trick."

"One of my better ones, yes," Kille admitted. "Guess I'll have to figure out something else."

She began to close the space between them, and Kille noted an amulet under her robe. "Magic?" he asked, pointing his blade.

She smiled. "What else?" she said as she took a cut at his head, which he parried as he continued to circle.

It figures, Kille thought grimly. *She doesn't use spells, but that doesn't mean she won't have a magical trick or two.*

"I'm going to take you, Tempen," she said. "And you know it."

"A lady of a thousand promises," Kille said. "But I've heard you never deliver."

Her eyes widened a little at the insult, and she pressed her attack. The sword threw prisms into the air as the battle continued. "Getting tired, Tempen?" she asked.

Kille didn't respond, saving his breath for fighting.

They closed again, and this time, Kille took a solid gash to his left arm, which fell to his side, useless.

"A piece at a time if I have to," she said.

Kille backed off again, gaining a few steps, his mind racing. Suddenly, a look of pure pain crossed his features. "Poison!" he hissed, grabbing for his left shoulder. "You bitch!"

Kille crumpled in a heap at her feet, the light from his spell slowly fading. Sarahkis stepped forward to finish the task, her sword raised. "I didn't use poi—" she said, then stopped, and screamed as she felt something pierce her boot sole and enter her right foot. The final bit of light fled the platform.

Rather than continue forward, she backpedaled, and promptly put her left heel on another weapon. She howled again and froze, then desperately cast a light spell of her own.

Kille lay sprawled on the floor where he had fallen, but the platform area all around him was covered in caltrops—small metal jacks with sharpened points. These, she noticed, were all shaped like miniature orchids. She realized he must have been getting ready to throw them when he died.

The lights in the hall brightened and Sarahkis could see the Prioress and all the other Temple clerics and assassins. Sound returned and she could hear cheers and clapping. Still afraid to move with the caltrops embedded in her feet, she turned slowly to face the Prioress directly and made a small bow.

Her face contorted in pain as the caltrops shifted in her feet. "I live to serve, Prioress," she said, in the traditional greeting of the Temple.

The Prioress' face showed no emotion, though her eyes were wide, as she replied. "No, Sarahkis, you're dead."

Sensing danger, Sarahkis tried to spin around as fast as her crippled feet would allow. Kille's sword met her halfway, and her head rolled onto the platform. At the same moment, the orchid-shaped caltrops disappeared.

The crowd, after a brief moment of stunned silence, burst into cheering and wild applause. *They love a good illusion*, Kille thought. His arm still hung at his left side, and blood soaked his robes. His left glove was wet with it.

He bowed to the Prioress. "I live to serve, Prioress."

"So you do, Kille Tempen, and so you shall," she said. "I name you King of Thorns."

The healers had finished their work, and the Betmaster had grudgingly paid him the wager money, when Kille was summoned to the main audience chamber of the Temple of Illhana for the final ceremony of the Thorn Trials. The others, those who had died today, would be there, relegated to minor, though celebratory roles. He motioned for the acolyte to wait outside and slowly rose to his feet. He was bone tired, and even though his injuries had been healed, he still ached all over.

A soft knock on his door was followed by the appearance of his Master, Raine. "You are well?" he asked.

"I am well," Kille said. "Though every bit of me hurts."

"That's usually a good sign," said Raine.

"Walk with me to the hall?" Kille asked.

"Of course," said Raine.

They made their way out of his chamber and began the trek through the hallways. Raine moved slowly, allowing Kille to take his time. "You did well today," he said. "Very well."

"Thank you," Kille said.

"I thought she'd taken you at the end there."

"So did I," Kille said, smiling grimly.

"How'd you know she'd buy the illusion?" Raine asked.

"Her boots," Kille said.

"Boots?"

Kille stopped walking and sat down on a stone bench. Though tonight's party would last well into the night, he wouldn't be staying late. "She wore hard-soled boots, which meant that she was either very protective of her feet or she had a fetish. Most assassins prefer lighter footgear." He smiled impishly. "And, she didn't really strike me as a fetish kind of girl."

Raine laughed. "You mean you didn't know for certain?"

"Didn't have the slightest clue," Kille said. "I was desperate."

Raine grasped Kille by the shoulders. "Don't ever tell anyone that," he said seriously. "They'll hate you all the more for it."

Kille nodded in understanding.

"Still," Raine said, "it was a damn fine guess."

They made their way into the audience hall, and people began applauding again. This time the chant was loud: "Thorn King!" The other four thorns were seated on chairs beneath the Prioress's dais. Kille made his way to the front of the room. He bowed to the Prioress, and then, quite diplomatically he thought, he bowed to the other Thorns. Other than Sarahkis, who looked quite a bit worse for the wear, the remaining Thorns nodded in return. As the applause died down, Kille said, "I live to serve, Prioress," and knelt.

"Rise, Kille Tempen," she said.

He did so, and waited in silence.

"You did well today," she said. "You used all of your talents—blade, magic, and wit—and you prevailed. You are truly the King of Thorns."

"Thank you, Prioress," he said.

She gestured to the two ever-present hand servants, who brought forward a large iron box, carved with runes. "Your reward," she said, as they opened it and stepped back.

Inside the box, Kille saw a beautiful long sword. The blade was an eerie white color that didn't reflect light, and the edge and hilt were etched in runes. "Thank you, Prioress. It is a priceless gift," Kille said.

"Yes," she said. "It is a fine blade, and highly magical. I'm sure you'll find it most useful."

"Yes, Prioress," he said. "I hope to."

The Prioress gestured again to her hand servants, who brought forth the badges of rank. The ritual was over quickly, and all five were given rank as Master Assassins. Kille's badge was different than that of the others, reflecting his higher status—theirs were simple iron lotus blossoms on a field of silver. Kille's was blood red on gold.

"There is but one task remaining to you tonight, King of Thorns," the Prioress said, when the ceremony was complete.

"Yes, Prioress?" Kille said.

"Start the celebration," she said. "For on the morrow, you will have killing to do."

Kille smiled in real pleasure, then turned to the room as a whole. "Let's get this started," he said. He signaled the acolytes who had drawn table service and they brought ale and wine to the celebrants.

Behind him, he heard the other newly appointed Master Assassins getting their glasses filled. Slowly, Kille raised his wineglass to the room. "To our Mistress, Illhana," he began. Then, a flicker of movement in the reflection of his glass caught his eye. The room was silent, all eyes on him. "May she—" he said, then spun suddenly to his left while ducking his head.

Sarahkis went flying past him, her sword just narrowly missing his skull. Kille dropped his wineglass and picked up his new sword almost in the same motion, then leaped down the steps behind her. The magical blade slid completely through her back and into the stone floor, pinning her there. He twisted it sharply, once, and Sarahkis twitched once and was still.

Kille pulled the blade from the lifeless body and climbed slowly back up the dais. He bowed again to the Prioress, and called for a new glass. Into the utterly silent room, Kille called out his toast: "I am the Thorn King, blessed by Illhana, and I serve at the pleasure of the Prioress. You don't want to lose your head around me."

The assassins, acolytes, clerics, and even the Prioress raised their glasses in return, and drank their fill. Raine was the first to take up the "Thorn King" chant, and it carried long into the night. Sarahkis was left on the floor and by the time the celebration was over, little remained but a red splotch and some hair.

THE USURPER MEMOS

by Josepha Sherman

Josepha Sherman is a fantasy writer and folklorist whose latest novels are *Highlander: The Captive Soul* and *Son of Darkness*. Her most recent folklore volume is *Merlin's Kin: World Tales of the Hero Magicians*. Her short fiction has appeared in numerous anthologies, including *Battle Magic*, *Dinosaur Fantastic*, *Black Cats and Broken Mirrors*, and *The Shimmering Door*. She lives in Riverdale, New York.

To: The most foul and villainous usurper who dares name himself Regis I

Know that your sins have been found out, and that vengeance will be both swift and—

To: Kregar, Captain of the Royal Guard
From: Regis I, Ruler of All Tavara
Re: The attached scrap of parchment

Captain Kregar, what is the meaning of this? I found the attached in my council room. My council room, Kregar! Look into this, and bring me the letter writer without delay. We shall have no more of this nonsense! We both know I am the right and just ruler of Tavara, as I have been since the late Etyk, false and self-styled king, met with his unfortunate accident.

*   *   *

To: His Most Puissant and Merciful Majesty, King
      Regis I, Ruler of all Tavara, Son of the Sun,
      Master of Destinies
From: Jertic Kei, Overseer of Qet
Delivered Via: Royal Carrier Pigeon #415
Re: Wheat Production in the Province of Qet

Know ye, O Most Powerful Ruler, the harvest has
not been, umm, quite as bountiful as it was in the
Year of the Purple Dragon. While this is not an agree-
able situation, the committee does not predict any
true difficulties. However, I feel it only prudent to
advise Your Most Puissant Majesty that there have
been some grumblings among the peasantry to the
effect that—dare I write it?—this decrease is the
land's own protest over the late king's untimely
death.

To: Jertic Kei, Overseer of Qet
From: His Majesty, King Regis I, etc. etc.
Delivered Via: Royal Carrier Pigeon #416
Re: Wheat Production, etc. etc.

Define "not quite as bountiful."
The peasants are always grumbling.
And I do not need to remind you again that Etyk
is only to be named the false or self-styled ruler,
never "the late king." Nor are there to be any more
mentions by you or anyone else of "untimely death."
He never should have been foolish enough to go
walking on the ramparts alone. The stones were slip-
pery, and it was surely the gods who punish all
foolishness.

To: The Hunter of Heads
From: Regis I
Delivered Via: Unofficial Carrier Pigeon

Interesting offer. Most. But you tell me why I should consider it. I have a kingdom to rule!

To: His Most Wondrous Majesty, Hammer of the Foe
From: General Whesten Gar
Delivered Via: Royal Carrier Pigeon #551
Re: Victory!

Rejoice! We have this day won our battle with the false Pretender with only minimal damage to our troops. The Pretender has been taken alive, as you commanded. Your Majesty, what are we to do with him?

To: General Whesten Gar
From: Regis I
Delivered Via: Royal Carrier Pigeon #552
Re: Victory!

Define "minimal damage." One man lost? One troop? How many, eh?

As to the traitor—what do you *think* you are to do with him? Bring him to me! And this time, I want him, or at least his head, undamaged. No more rumors of live Pretenders to the throne!

To: His Most Puissant and Powerful Majesty, Regis I, Lord of Tavara
From: Chamberlain Pitatalan
Re: Overdue Notice

Your Majesty, I beg forgiveness for such an interruption of the Most Royal's time. But has it, perchance, and pray forgive the assumption, slipped Your Majesty's mind that the pay due to the workers restoring the Northern Wall is now three months overdue?

To: Chamberlain Pitatalan
From: His majesty, Regis I
Re: Overdue Notice

Why, in the name of all the deities, are you bothering me about this? Contact the Chancellor of the Exchequer!

To: His Most Puissant and Powerful Majesty, Regis I, Lord of Tavara
From: Chamberlain Pitatalan
Re: Overdue Notice

I humble myself before Your Majesty, and I would not dream of contradicting Your Majesty, but I must remind Your Majesty that right now, there *is* no Chancellor of the Exchequer. Your Majesty had him executed last month for the treason of challenging Your Majesty's economic reforms.

To: Chamberlain Pitatalan
From: Regis I
Re: Overdue Notice

Sarcasm, I need not remind you, does not become you.

To: His Most Puissant and Generous Majesty, Regis I, Ruler of Tavara
From: Secretary Ekata
Re: Protocol

If it please His Majesty, the royal signature is required in triplicate on the enclosed documents, not merely in duplicate. And to complete the legality, the royal seal must be affixed to each copy.

To: Goldsmith Gearth
From: Regis I

Dammit, I need a royal seal! Haven't you finished the copy *yet?*

To: His Majesty Regis I
From: Goldsmith Gearth
  Surely His Majesty understands that such sensitive matters take time? And surely His Majesty understands that had he retrieved the seal from the former ruler's body, there would be no need for a counterfeit?

To: Goldsmith Gearth
From: Regis I
  Surely I understand that you're going to be joining your predecessor in that newly reheating batch of molten lead if the seal isn't on my desk by tomorrow.

To: His Most Glorious Majesty by the Will of the
      Highest Ones, Regis I
From: High Priest Tatuiat
Delivered Via: Sacred Carrier Pigeon
Re: Rites of the Seventh Moon
  Majesty, the Rites of the Seventh Moon are fast approaching, and yet the Temple has still to receive the standard donation of gold. I need not remind you that your late predecessor was most prompt in his donations.

To: High Priest Tatuiat
From: His Puissant and Merciless Majesty, Regis I
Re: Rites of the Seventh Moon
Delivered Via: Royal Carrier Pigeon #467
  While I appreciate that the gods must, as the saying goes, have their divine palms greased, may I remind you that mentions of the late Etyk, false and

self-styled king, are not appreciated? It would be most regrettable should even so exalted an individual as yourself meet with an unfortunate accident.

The donation will be made. *Through the proper channels.* Kindly contact the Chancellor of the Exchequer.

To: Chamberlain Pitatalan
From: Regis I
Round up the standard lot of bureaucratic idiots. Find one who can add two and two without adding four to his own pockets, and tell him he's now the Chancellor of the Exchequer Pro Tem.

To: The foul usurper who dares call himself a king, the self-styled and false Regis I
Beware! The forces of justice and liberty have not forgotten your sins, oh, most villainous of usurpers! You will pay for your many crimes of murder!

To: Kregar, Captain of the Royal Guard
From: Regis I
All right, Kregar, enough is enough. I don't know what you've been doing, and I don't much care, but put an end to this nonsense here and now, or I'll put an end to you!

Have a pleasant day.

To: The Hunter of Heads
From: Regis I
Delivered Via: Unofficial Carrier Pigeon
Yes, yes, I know the deal is still open. I'll get back to you.

To: His Most Puissant and Merciful Majesty, King
     Regis I, Ruler of all Tavara, Son of the Sun,
     Master of Destinies
From: Jertic Kei, Overseer of Qet
Delivered Via: Royal Carrier Pigeon #443
Re: Distribution

Behold, three weeks have passed without another
word from the royal presence. I regret to inform you
that the peasants are now flatly refusing to pay their
taxes. Your Majesty, they claim that the poor harvest
is to blame. *And* the rumors concerning the, ah, reason behind that poor harvest continue to spread. I
fear that these rumors cannot easily be blocked.

To: Jertic Kei, Overseer of Qet
From: Regis I
Delivered Via: Royal Carrier Pigeon #446
Re: Distribution

You do well to fear. So do the peasants. Enough
pampering of the idiots! If they fail to give up their
taxes, see that they give up their ears. Keep me advised of your progress.

To: His Most Puissant and Powerful Majesty, Regis
     I, Lord of Tavara
From: Secretary Ekata
Re: Protocol

I understand the pressures on Your Majesty, truly,
but I respectfully wish to remind you that while the
papers have been most satisfactorily signed in triplicate, they still do lack the royal seal.

To: Goldsmith Gearth
From: Regis I
Where the hell is my seal?

* * *

To: His Majesty Regis I
From: Warrik, First Undersmith
Re: Goldsmith Gearth

Your correspondence, Majesty, has been forwarded to my desk. I fear I must inform you that Gearth has disappeared from the palace, leaving behind only a note saying, "I'm getting the lead out—or out of the lead."

Please advise.

To: The Hunter of Heads
From: Regis I
Delivered Via: Unofficial Carrier Pigeon

All right, all right, I'm considering your deal.

To: General Whesten Gar
From: Regis I
Delivered Via: Royal Carrier Pigeon #543
Re: Victory!

Where is the Pretender? And where, for that matter, are you?

To: His Most Wondrous Majesty, Hammer of the Foe
From: General Whesten Gar
Delivered Via: Royal Carrier Pigeon #544
Re: Victory!

I regret to tell you that the Pretender is dead. He managed to escape briefly—that's what took us so long, tracking him down. And in the skirmish, well, one of the men got a little overenthusiastic.

To: General Whesten Gar
From: Regis I
Delivered Via: Royal Carrier Pigeon #552
Re: Victory!
  His head! Did you bring me his head?

To: His Most Wondrous Majesty, Hammer of the
      Foe
From: General Whesten Gar
Delivered Via: Royal Carrier Pigeon #544
Re: Victory!
  Rejoice! I am even now sending you under sepa-
rate cover the head you requested, Majesty—the head
of the soldier who so foolishly slew the Pretender!

To: His Majesty, Regis I
From: Chamberlain Pitatalan
  Sire, surely you would not have some uneducated
man as Chancellor of the Exchequer? We must have
time to study each candidate, and test his—*or* her—
qualifica—

To: His Most Glorious Majesty by the Will of the
      Highest Ones, Regis I
From: High Priest Tatuiat
Delivered Via: Sacred Carrier Pigeon
Re: Rites of the Seventh Moon
  I have, as you so advised, sought to consult with
the Chancellor of the Exchequer—only to be told that
there is, as of now, no longer such an individual. Is
it true that so high-placed an official was dispatched
without the customary religious rites? Kindly advise—and remember, O Mighty Majesty, that the
gods watch—

To: His Most Puissant and Merciful Majesty, King
Regis I, Ruler of all Tavara, Son of the Sun,
Master of Destinies
From: Matati, Second Overseer of Qet
Delivered Via: Royal Carrier Pigeon #445
Re: Distribution

Alas, Majesty, Jertic Kei is no longer with us. The
peasants are besieging the gates even now, and I
don't know how much longer we can—

To: His Most Puissant and Powerful Majesty, Regis
I, Lord of Tavara
From: Secretary Ekata
Re: Protocol

I would not dream of lecturing Your Majesty, but
I fear I must inform you that the supposed "royal"
seal imprinted on the documents is clearly not the
official version. It will become necessary for each
document to be completed anew, in triplicate, and
properly signed and sealed, with, of course, the official seal—

To: Regis I, Ruler of All Tavara
From: Kregar, Captain of the Royal Guard

We got him! We got the idiot who was sending
those rotten messages to you! A more formal report
is attached, in triplicate—but we got him!

To: The tyrant who styles himself Regi—

To: The Hunter of Heads
From: Regis I
Delivered Via: Hell, Who cares?
Deal!

To: The Entire Cursed Bureaucracy of Tavara
From: Regis I
Re: The HELL with "Re's!"

All right, you idiots—*I quit!*

That's right. I, Regis I, Ruler of Tavara, quit! Rather than be nudged and prodded and nibbled to death by you and your cursed memorandums, I hereby re-sign my royal office. Period.

But you haven't won. You're not rid of me. Oh, no. I have just taken a new position as Chief Executing Officer of Avian Transit and Transmission. That's right, you bloody bureaucrats—from now on, *I* control your carrier pigeons. There you have it: *I* control what memorandums you send, and where, and when.

In short: I win!

And may I but conclude in traditional fashion: *Bwahahahahahah!*

TO SPEAK WITH ANGELS

by Michelle West

Michelle West is the author of a number of novels, including *The Sacred Hunter* duology—*Hunter's Oath* and *Hunter's Death*—and *The Broken Crown*, *The Uncrowned King*, and *The Shining Court*, all published by DAW Books. She reviews books for the on-line column *First Contacts*, and less frequently for *The Magazine of Fantasy & Science Fiction*. Other short fiction by her appears in such DAW anthologies as *Black Cats and Broken Mirrors*, *Elf Magic*, *Olympus*, and *Alien Abductions*.

The old man had come to hell in a fashion different from most of its denizens: he had walked the narrow path, and although he stood upon the hot, red sands near the riverbanks, he felt no fear whatsoever. Eternity was not his concern; neither was imprisonment nor torment. He had form, and flesh, and these were not the province of the creatures that ruled the damned.

They were, unfortunately, the province of time and mortality; he was old, and he was well aware, feeling those years so keenly, that this would be his last great walk.

You are going to hell to die.

Well, yes.

He walked under red skies and storm clouds that

glittered like light-touched obsidian. The pleas of the damned filled his ears, although it would be many miles before he could see them.

Soon enough, he was almost upon the river. Once crossed, there would be no returning. Grabbing the tightly knotted pouch at his belt, he began to hurry. His steps were light and quick over the hot, sharp stones.

Gray bones were scattered across the riverbank like strokes of color laid against canvas by a madman. As the saint passed them, they trembled with feeble life, grasping at the hem of his robe and clacking as they shut tight around air. He could almost hear their cries of frustration and sorrow.

"You chose your place, and choose it still," the saint whispered softly. But he spoke to himself. Of all things he'd thought to find difficult, pity was not among them. He shook it off as quickly as he could and hurried to the river's edge.

There, carried by a hot, humid wind, the scent of death and decay did what the damned could not; it drove him back with its strength. Eyes watering, he lifted his sleeve to his nose and mouth, and began his wait. He hoped it would not be long.

Perhaps, had he belonged to hell, it would have been an eternity. But only a few minutes passed before he caught his first glimpse of the boatman and his slender craft. All of the river might be alive with the screams of the damned, but they did not touch the skiff or its owner. He came, cloaked in silence as much as black robes, until the very prow of his boat touched shore's edge. Then he nodded and lifted one hand, palm up.

Like the debris on the shore, the hand was skeletal.

"No, not yet my friend," the wise man said. "You've a task to perform first."

The boatman nodded. A glimpse of ivory peered out of his hanging cowl. He stood aside, and the saint muttered a quick prayer under his breath. The boat did not look like a water-worthy craft. Perhaps it would take the weight of those who no longer had bodies to worry about; what would it do with the living?

What indeed? The old man shook his head. There was only one way across. He listened to the planks creak as he took his seat on the spartan bench. The boatman's pole hit the shore and they drifted out into the river.

The current was as gentle as an arterial wound. The boatman provided no companionship and no idle chatter, which was a pity; this was the one time the saint would have happily endured it. The gurgling screams of perpetually drowning souls were the only conversation offered. It was not a sound that could be ignored, and as they moved toward the opposite bank, it grew louder, almost intolerable. The saint looked down to the boat's side, and beneath the thin sheen of red, he could see armor and weapons, slick as they might have been after too much use on too many battlefields. He knew why the river ran.

"You have no pity, have you?" the saint said quietly, although he knew that this boatman would never reply.

A hand as skeletal as the boatman's shot up near the side of the skiff, straining and grabbing at air as if to pull itself out of the water. As if in answer to the saint's question, the boatman's pole came up and down again. There was the sharp, hard crash of wood against brittle bone. Ivory splinters flew down in a pale rain, landing in the saint's lap.

If the sage shuddered, the boatman did not seem to notice. Instead he continued to do his duty: To deliver the souls of the damned—living or otherwise—to the farther shore.

The saint carefully collected the shattered wrist and examined it. *What were you in life? Were you a warrior? An assassin? Did you leave any mourners behind?*

But life had not been this soul's concern. The saint shook his head. *I am becoming old and mawkish.* he did not choose to speak. Instead, he stared at the shoreline as if it were a lighthouse, and he a storm-tossed sailor. It approached slowly; it became a torment, a small hell of its own. But they did reach it, the boatman and he. The prow struck red sand in silence.

The saint rose, anxious to be free of the river and his companion, both. But the boatman barred his way with a long, hard pole. Once again he turned to the saint, his skeletal palm demanding its price.

To the saint's surprise, he found himself hesitating, although he had the coin to hand and ready. The voyage across the river had troubled him more than he had expected it might.

"You want payment. Very well. You have shown me hell, my friend." His arms swept out, and he spoke a few words. For a moment, his palms glowed, unnatural and white—the only thing of beauty as far as the eye, or soul, could see. Light leaped like liquid from his fingers, a white river running into the red one.

Where it struck the waters, it bubbled brilliantly, and then began to take shape. Soft and warm, it grew and hardened until, where light had been, lilies floated in the troubled river. Only when the entire boat was surrounded did the saint once again close his hands.

"This," he said softly to the silent boatman, "this is the payment I offer."

The boatman gazed outward, watching the flowers drift away from the edge of his boat. One hand reached out of the water to grip and claim a lily, and the boatman lifted, and then lowered, his pole, without shattering fragile bone. The river fell silent a moment. Even the screams of the eternally damned seemed to be absorbed by the presence of lilies.

Then the boatman turned to the saint. His hood dipped, almost brusquely. He lowered his pole and raised his arm, granting free passage to the shore. The saint stood, bowed awkwardly, and left the boat When both of his feet were planted firmly on the shore, he turned back to see the skeletal figure standing in the center of his craft.

The wooden pole trembled slightly, held in a grip that was too tight. The cowl fell back onto black shoulders as the boatman raised his silent head to the red and clouded sky. He stood frozen, his silence a question and a demand. Then, lifting his pole, he snapped it in two.

That was the image that the saint carried with him as he turned away from the river. It hurt him, and again he was surprised. Shaking his head, he turned back, but the boat and its ferryman were gone. The damned remained.

He had come for his answer, and it would not do to forget it. If he let the pain of every denizen of hell—whether keeper or kept—stop him in his tracks, he would never reach his goal, never ask his question.

He walked.

The sand was hot against his feet, his face, his tongue. He did not take care when choosing his path, because he knew that from this point on, all roads led to the palace; all roads led to Lucifer.

But they did not lead there quickly, and many times during his long trek, the saint was forced to rest. Under outcroppings of rock black as slate, he tried to find shade and shelter, but the shadows of hell provided no retreat from the heat, and certainly no safety. Better to walk in the open, where most threats were obvious.

The fields of the damned were being sowed and tended; the attenuated cries of fading pain gave way to the tenor of new ones. There was a terrible music about it that filled the saint with awe and pity. Three times he tried to interrupt the singers in their torment, and three times he failed. He made no fourth attempt on the plains.

Only once did one of the keepers stop him. From high above, it sailed on the thermals of endless heat. Against the pitted, furrowed ground it cast a perfect shadow: two wings, spread in an exact inverted arch from tip to tip. It carried a sword, one grooved and edged with light.

"You are not of my demesne," the demon said as it touched ground.

"No, nor of any demesne of hell." The old man bowed. "That is a rather fine weapon."

"It is mine." He drew it closer. The leathery tip of bent wings curled over its edge.

"Is it? But I remember a different day, when it was forged to serve another master."

It was hard to tell if the demon's skin darkened, for it was already the color of obsidian. But he looked down at the tang and pommel of the sword. The glint of something more valuable than any gold or mortal jewel faded from his eyes as he stared. At last he looked up and met the old man's unwavering gaze.

"You are," the demon said, as his eyes sought the sky, "the serpent in Eden." With a push of mighty legs he took to the air, deigning once again to touch ground with nothing but his shadow.

A shadow, the saint thought, of his past.

"Why do you choose to serve?" But the old man's words were lost to the screaming of the damned.

The palace rose above red mist and redder sky to dominate the landscape. Towers and spires stood like solid night, with just a glimmer of golden light along their edges. Demons flew among them, carrying a banner that was both unreadable and unmistakable to the sage. Like the chorus of a reluctant choir, souls whispered their jagged pleas to faceless, perfect walls. They did not falter in their praise of hell's pain.

Nothing mortal could create such a palace, and no one mortal could truly appreciate it, not even the man who had come so far to visit. He stopped and murmured his prayers; the winds tore them away.

He was tired, but it was almost done. He had only to reach the palace and he would have his answer.

I understand, he thought, as he stopped to rest his blistered feet, *why curiosity is often thought of as a sin*. At the very least, it was, like any self-indulgence, costly in unforeseen ways. The road to the palace had not been straightforward or easily traversed, and everywhere he walked there was pain—so much so, that he wondered if any crime, no matter how hideous, could truly deserve hell.

Pity did not govern him in hell, as it often had in life. If he cried, stopped his ears with his hands, closed his eyes, or uttered a prayer, it slowed him down but did not stop him.

With such a determination he came to the gates of the palace. Fine, high arches were adorned on either side by living gargoyles that watched from their obsidian perches. The gates rolled open; the gargoyles, as one creature, looked down upon him as he passed beneath. They spouted flame, like breath, and he gestured, splitting it harmlessly into two orange fans that fell well away from his body. They snarled and growled, but did not pursue him. As he continued toward the doors, he understood why.

They were guarded by tall, slender creatures which wore shadows and flame for armor. Above their shoulders, hovering more than a body-length above them, were black, feathery shadows. He knew what they had once looked like. The clang of their swords as they met to bar the saint's entrance was the screech of metal against metal in hell's furnace.

"I have come," the saint said, without preamble, "to speak with the Bright Lord, and I will not leave."

They were still and silent as they contemplated him, their eyes widening in the hollows of their pale faces.

"It has been long," one said, as he slowly pulled his sword away from its defense of the door, "since I have seen a soul like yours."

"Do you remember when it was?"

"I forget nothing."

"Do you remember *my* Lord?"

Silence, then, the silence of the damned.

"We have no dominion over you," the other

guardian said, his voice brittle and chill. "And well do we know it, now. Go." He stood aside.

But the saint was not yet satisfied. "Only answer one question," he said, in as proud a voice as he could muster.

"Perhaps."

"Why do you serve? Why did you leave the fields of heaven for this?"

"This is the home that we have chosen. We made it. We fashioned it. We rule here in strength. The fields you speak of had nothing of interest to us."

"Oh?" He gestured, a sudden, graceful lift and sweep of arm. Light trailed like liquid into his palm, and, from it, spilled onto the oddly gleaming flagstones. Where it hit, the stones screamed, and the saint was reminded, yet again, of where he was. He shuddered, but the light had already taken root; it blazed a sudden trail across the air and then faded, leaving behind a bush of white roses, green thorns.

The breeze that carried their scent to the guardians was cool.

They stared at it a moment, and then each raised a hand, palm out, in denial. "We left for love of the Bright Lord," one finally said, his voice low and shaky. "Which would you choose, mortal? Would you choose father over brother, brother over father? Did not your Lord give Lucifer dominion over the host itself, and bid us obey and honor him?

"To the end of time, we pledged. To the ends of heaven itself." The creature straightened its black wings. "Go." He lifted his sword.

The saint did not tarry further. At his back he could hear the sound of swords, wielded as axes, against the rosebush.

*　　*　　*

He made his way through the winding passages of the castle, treading with care upon the upturned faces that lined the floors. They grunted or cried out as he walked, but they did not snap at his heels or seek to impede his progress. They could not; they had no teeth.

Souls were the bricks and mortar of hell.

He walked for miles, perhaps for days; there was no sun to mark time's passage. He stopped to rest, but the screams and cries of the damned were only that much louder, and in the end he chose to walk, however slowly, toward the palace's inner chamber. And no matter how long, or how far, he walked, he met no other demon, no other soul that was not bound fast into floor, wall, or ceiling.

At last he found what he sought: two arched doors whose peaks were so high they vanished into the shadows above. They were gilded and pale, and they alone of all the architecture of hell were not alive with the movement of the lost. He almost fell to his knees with relief at the sight of them, but the relief lent him strength and he walked more briskly to reach them.

They swung wide, one to either side, although what hand moved them, he could not say. He didn't even think to ask, because as the doors widened, the lord of hell was revealed.

The Bright Lord sat upon a throne that was glorious in its simplicity; it seeemed to be carved out of one piece of wood, seamless, perfect. His skin was pale but golden where it was revealed; his hair was almost white, but it shone with a luster of its own. Above his perfect shoulders, wings rose in twin arches. He cast light, but the light did not cast any shadow.

Lucifer, alone of all the denizens of hell, remained as he had been before the descent: The fairest and the brightest of the host.

"And should I not be?" The Bright Lord asked quietly. "I own hell. It does not own me." His voice was soft and pleasant, almost sensual in the way it touched the ear.

The saint sank to one knee then, and rested his head upon it; it was easier that way. He felt his mortality and his age as if they were sins. To look upon the lord of hell caused him pain of a type that he had never known.

"You have troubled my horde with your questing."

"Yes."

Lucifer smiled; the smile was gentle, full. "Why have you come here? You must know that you will not leave alive."

The saint nodded. "I know it." He wanted to add "my lord," but he stopped himself. The Bright Lord was not his and never would be.

"Good. You have dignity. I have not seen it in a long time." Lucifer rose, his wings fanning out in a glorious spray of white light. "But you have not answered my question."

"I came to satisfy a curiosity," the saint replied, aware of the way age had withered his voice.

"You wished to see hell?"

"No. I wished to see you." The saint glanced up and then down again, but not before he met the eyes of the angel. The vision was, indeed, almost worth a life. His own eyes teared; he could not look up again.

"I'm flattered."

"My life is forfeit. We both know it. Let me ask my questions, and if you will, answer them."

"If it pleases me," the Bright Lcrd said. He drew closer, slowly, to where the saint knelt.

"You were the best that the Lord birthed, the brightest and the fairest. How can you live in such a place as this, who once wandered the fields of heaven itself?" He raised his hands and began to pool light in his palms.

"Do not try such trickery here," Lucifer said, and the light died. "I have seen your progress, sage. I know what you offer, and you know that it has its effect. Do not sully my realm—not here."

"Lucifer—you who knew the love of God—how can you create so loveless a place?"

"You will never understand it."

The saint did not reply.

"Here, I am master. No love I feel, or have felt, will ever control me again. No love will make me slave to one who—" He drew closer to the old man. "To even God Himself. And if I am to turn away from such slavery and such a command—what love can there be here? A shadow of it. A mockery. Even I cannot descend to that."

"But you did love God."

Lucifer grew still. "Did?" His voice fell low for the single word, and he gave a soft, bitter laugh.

The old man understood all that he heard. His heart raced, and he spoke quickly. "There is no reason for you to remain here. God waits, and His love is boundless. Should you desire to return, He—"

"I made my choice. I am proud of it. And those others who populate the hells made their own choice of masters to serve, and they serve me well. They came for love of me, and they know now full well what the value of that love is. There is none here who would now return to God. None save Charon.

"Old friend," Lucifer continued, but in a different, distant voice. "You came to my domain for love of me, and love of God, both. Do you yet dream that one day you will take me back to the rivers of heaven?

"What you did to the boatman was cruel. More cruel than even I have been. The others, perhaps, deserve what you offer. But not he. He had almost forgotten and you have renewed his memory in a most bitter fashion. He hopes, again, that we two will walk side by side. For this he came, and for this he has waited, dwindling in time."

Silence enveloped them both, and then the old man felt an almost gentle pressure at his neck.

"Now, having satisfied your curiosity, I fear I must send you on your way. If you chance to see your Lord, tell him I am well satisfied. Tell him, for he and I shall never meet again."

The saint understood, for he thought he knew the answer to the question he had not yet asked. But because he thought he knew the answer, he asked, wanting to hear any answer but the one he felt was true. To hear it, even if it was only a lie, from the prince of lies.

"Do you miss him, still?"

But the Bright Lord was cruel. He had made hell, and if it did not own him, it held its torment for even its lord. As he exacted the death that the saint had earned for his boldness, he answered the final question with a single, lost word.

And it was thus that the saint was the first and the last of all souls to bring a thing unknown and bitter to heaven; tears for the pity of pride.

HEROES AND VILLAINS

by Peter Crowther

Since the early 1990s, more than ninety of Peter Crowther's short stories (plus a few poems) have appeared in a wide range of magazines and anthologies—and as individual chapbooks—on both sides of the Atlantic. Two collections of these stories appeared in 1999, one of them—*Lonesome Roads*—receiving the British Fantasy Award for Best Collection. A regular columnist and reviewer, he is also the editor or co-editor of sixteen anthologies and the co-author (with James Lovegrove) of the novel *Escardy Gap*. He lives in Harrogate, England with his wife, Nicky and their two sons.

(1)
"We will never have true civilization
until we have learned to recognize the rights of
others."
—Will Rogers
from *The New York Times*, November 18, 1923

"When all the world is young, lad,
And all the trees are green;
And every goose a swan, lad,
And every lass a queen;
Then hey for boot and horse, lad,

And round the world away;
Young blood must have its course, lad,
And every dog his day."
    —Charles Kingsley (1819–75)
        from "The Water Babies" (1863)

"You okay, Boss?"
    "Yes, Sidney, I'm fine."
Sidney Smolt frowned. His employer neither sounded nor looked fine, or even anything approaching it, but he knew better than to re-ask a question that had already been answered . . . even when that question was voiced with only the Comedian's best interest at heart. Despite his name and his trademark mischievous and even irreverent smile, the Comedian was neither a patient nor a lighthearted man.

The small, fat man shrugged, hitching his pants a little higher at the same time, and checked around the roof. Everything seemed to be in its place and nothing was there that he had not seen before. He keyed the CHECK button on his cell phone, gave a wave to the man standing over by the pool cabins, and walked to the south edge of the roof and glanced over the waist-high wall onto Central Park West. It was all clear, just the traffic edging its way up to Columbus Circle or down to the Plaza, mostly yellow cabs and cyclists braving the early morning rush..

As he walked back to the French windows leading into the penthouse apartment that controlled the Komerdie Building, Smolt glanced at his employer who was standing on the poolside leaning on the railings. The man was dressed only in his shorts, ready for his early morning swim, but, at least as far as Smolt could see, he had not yet been into the water.

Was it Smolt's imagination, or had the Comedian grown more introspective these past few months?

Pausing before going back inside, Smolt tilted his head and ran his eyes up the Comedian's tanned and muscular legs, over his firm backside, and on up the torso. Introspective or not, and no matter how many millions he had stashed away nor how much of the world he controlled, even the Comedian was unable to stop time. With a hint of regret and even sadness, Smolt saw a thickening around his employer's waist—love handles, his mother used to say of his father's girth back during Smolt's long-ago childhood in Cedar Rapids.

But that was before Captain Iowa had caused a building side to tumble onto Jack Smolt's rusting Ford Fairlane, while the so-called "Hero of the Heartland" battled it out with his nemesis, the Gargoyle. It had been an accident, of course, and the Captain was very apologetic—to the tune of an out-of-court settlement of more than $60,000—but Smolt's father was still dead.

That was twenty-five years ago this year, and the once little Sidney Smolt was now thirty-seven. That made the Comedian . . . how old? Must be getting on for fifty, Smolt guessed. And in addition to the love handles, the man considered by many to be "the biggest worm in the Big Apple" now had graying hair where once a thick thatch grew so black it was almost blue. It was thin hair now, too, thin around the temples and the crown, and the jowls and the chin on the face beneath it were droopy . . . looking tired.

Smolt watched the wind blowing the Comedian's hair and then, when the big man—he still big, at least—shifted over to the little wall looking out over

Central Park, Smolt saw the telltale whiteness of a piece of paper held in the Comedian's hand which was tucked under the other armpit. It was a piece of mail he had received just this morning: a piece of mail bearing a British postage stamp and a spidery handwriting addressed, simply, to Leonard B. Komerdie, New York, USA. Smolt knew who the letter was from, and he knew it wasn't good news. With a deep sigh he went inside.

The Comedian leaned on the small parapet wall of his pool area and looked out over Manhattan. He reached down and picked up his coffee, the mug feeling reassuringly warm in his hand. It seemed chilly suddenly, chilly for June in Manhattan. He looked at the one-page letter and its envelope again, then took a sip of coffee and lifted his face to the sun as he swallowed. Sometimes he felt that he alone of the city's denizens was in the sunlight; all others walked only in the shadow of the buildings themselves, scurrying the matrix of streets and avenues like ants, their lives filled with a curious purpose that, no matter how long he considered it, he could not fathom.

In front of him the park loomed green and expansive, its distant thrum of buzzing energy drifting onward up toward 110th Street where Uptown began, and where the rocky ridge that lifted the Upper West Side continued the gradual incline which started around 59th Street and went all the way to Washington Heights. He scanned the bright blue sky and, amidst the occasional plane moving off from or drifting into JFK or Laguardia and the ever-present advertising dirigibles that hovered over the park, he noticed a speck coming in fast from the east.

It was too small for a plane or a dirigible.

It was a hero, probably flying in from Queens where The Monitors had their East Coast HQ. The Comedian squinted into the sunlight reflected off the myriad car windshields and windows littering the streets below and tried to see who it was, but he couldn't make him out . . . if it *was* a "him." There were so many of them these days.

The figure was dressed in green, with a cape that flew behind, stretched out in the air. That meant it was probably Captain Chlorophyll, one of the Monitors—or Grassman, as he was more regularly called. The Comedian smiled at the audacious use of the name, coined by a one-time veteran of the streets who had been caught peddling mind-expanding drugs out of a Hells Kitchen basement. The boy, hardly out of his teens, had called to the smug Captain Chlorophyll as he was been marched away into the holding cells. "Hey, you all green," the boy had shouted, with that strange clipped delivery and the equally odd reverse-pointing gesture that characterizes and complements the argot of the rappers. "You ain't nothing, man. You just a *grass*man." After that, the green-clad flying wonder had started referring to himself by the new nickname . . . but that was the heroes for you. To them, nothing was sacred.

The figure swung around Roosevelt Island and lined up with the Queensboro Bridge, heading for Manhattan. Down on the street, people shouted and pointed up at the sky, waving.

Hey, Captain Chlorophyll! they called.

And, *Way to go, Cap!*

And other inanities dreamed up by the small people trying to make something of their small lives. Just like the stars of the celluloid adventures that played the local theaters, the heroes were considered the property of all and sundry. All the gossip magazines were filled with stories of who was dating whom, and the inevitable revelations of infidelity, same-sex relationships, and abuse were the order of the day.

Thus Desmond (*Slingshot* to his many adoring fans) Antigones' new and seemingly serious relationship with a balding and bespectacled bank teller in Carmel proved both a new rallying point for the West Coast's powerful gay movement and a popular front page feature across the country. And the sudden hospitalization of young Manhattan debutante Cheryl Heggler with "abdominal complications" following an alleged intimacy with off-planet electrical hero *Direct Current* promoted serious doubts for any possible cohabitation between heroes and normals.

Similarly, the lengthy court case promoted by the lawsuit citing mental and physical abuse brought against wealthy socialite Malcolm Benners—*Trapeze* to the world at large—by Benners' young ward, Arnie Leverson (AKA *The Acrobat*) questioned the inevitable effects of power and adulation on the stability of the nation's heroes.

There were more such instances.

The Comedian shielded his eyes and watched as the flying figure slowed down as it came over the park, and then stopped to hover. The Captain was replenishing himself over the green.

The Comedian heard footsteps behind him. Without turning around, he said, "How does he fly? You ever stop to wonder about that?"

"Who, boss?" Smolt asked, waiting for an appropriate moment.

"The good Captain Chlorophyll." The Comedian

leaned over the wall and watched men and women running through the park's entrances, some of them with kids in hand and others just by themselves. Laughter flooded up over the noise of idling engines—Central Park West had come to a standstill.

The Comedian turned around and leaned against the wall. "I mean," he said, hands thrust deep into the pockets of his shorts, "he has no wings, no jet-boosted rocket pack . . . how does he do it?"

Smolt shrugged. "Pills?"

The Comedian scowled and jigged his head from side to side. "Maybe. Everyone's on *some*thing, Sidney." He looked back over his shoulder in time to see the flying figure move off from the park, leaving behind in its wake a muted roar of applause and shouting.

"I wonder what it feels like."

"What's that, boss—flying?"

"No—well, yes, I wonder what *flying* feels like. But I was actually referring to *doing good*. Being wanted . . . being *loved*." The Comedian fingered the piece of paper in his hand.

Smolt frowned and shifted his weight from foot to foot. "You sure you're okay, boss?"

The Comedian gave a small smile and nodded. "So, you wanted me."

"Yeah." Smolt hitched his trousers and flicked his neck to one side. "The Dummy called. Said he was on his way over."

The Comedian nodded. "That should give the local boys in blue something to occupy them. Anything else?"

The little fat man hitched his pants again, an action that involved his shoulders shooting up a few inches, and clasped his hands. "Well . . ." he started, glancing back at the French windows where a couple of shadowy figures stood behind the drapes. "We was a little . . . concerned."

"Mmm? About what?"

Smolt nodded at the paper in his boss' hand.

"This?" The Comedian held it up. "It's a letter from my mother. My having a mother should surely not concern you."

Smolt flexed his fingers while keeping his hands clasped, and looked down at them briefly. "It's not that, boss. It's that we know you ain't spoken with your mom in a long time. And getting letters—" he waved a hand at the paper, " —like that always means bad news."

The Comedian nodded and allowed a small smile.

"Hey, we didn't mean noth—"

"That's okay, Sidney," Leonard Komerdie said in a tired voice. "I didn't mean to be antsy." He turned around and looked down into the street at the sound of a long blast on a car horn. "He's here."

"The Dummy?"

Komerdie folded the note and slipped it into his shorts pocket. "Are we all ready?"

"Yeah, boss."

"Have we heard from the Bomb?"

"He'll be here by nine."

"What time is it now?"

"Twenty before."

Komerdie walked across the roof to the lounger and sat down. "Show them out here when they arrive. Coffee would be good."

Smolt nodded and started to move off.

"And, Sidney—"

The small man stopped and turned back, his eyebrows raised.

"Thanks."

"Hey," he said, waving a hand and—if Komerdie were not mistaken—coloring slightly across his cheeks, "that's okay, boss."

(2)

"One murder made a villain,
millions a hero."
—Beilby Porteus (1731–1808)
from "Death" (1759)

Komerdie was only halfway into *The Times* when Professor Maximillian Skellern's henchmen strolled out onto the roof. The Comedian nodded and continued to read while the men checked the place over in a fuss of unsmiling faces, gray suits and snap-brim Fedoras. They looked like central casting walk-ons for Stanley Kubrick's *The Killing*.

After a few minutes, and having apparently satisfied themselves that it was all clear, the men disappeared and returned with a small trunk, which they laid almost reverentially on the mosaic marble area alongside the pool. One of the men flipped the catches on the trunk and opened the lid.

"Jesus Christ," a small voice whined. "I bet it is damned hot in here."

"And how are you this fine morning, Max?" Komerdie called, turning the page of his newspaper.

"Impatient," the voice said, though it didn't sound impatient. The Dummy's voice didn't sound anything: it was just words . . . always just words.

One of the henchmen leaned into the trunk and lifted the contents out.

The Dummy was "wearing" the body of what appeared to be an eight- or nine-year-old child. The henchman stood the figure down and held it for a few seconds.

"Yes, okay, okay," the Dummy said in what would have been, in the voice of anyone else, an emphatic snarl. "I am fine now."

The man let go, and the figure, after momentarily staggering slightly, walked across to the nest of chairs and sun loungers by the pool.

The head was slightly bigger than the body—all of which was constructed from wood and plastic, although skillful painting and the addition of a thick and unkempt thatch of hair had rendered it very believably human, particularly from a few feet's distance.

Inside the head, attached to a complex system of minute pulleys and levers, all operated by electrical impulses generated by the synapses, rested the brain of Professor Skellern, one of the country's foremost authorities on the human mind and, specifically, neuron research.

A tragic fire resulting from a laboratory explosion had left Maximillian Skellern with burns covering eighty-five percent of his body. In the words of the intern who examined him on arrival at Cabrini Med Center, the Professor was a chicken leg that had been left on the barbecue while the cook had gone to answer the telephone. All senses and nerve tissues had been destroyed and only a formidable course of pain-killing drugs had been able to keep him alive.

It was during that time, with his faithful brother Rudie by his bedside, that Skellern reflected on the fire and the fact that the need to cut corners due to a lack of funding had resulted in the loss—effectively—of his life. But perhaps, he had decided, that need not be the case.

Over the following weeks, Skellern had his brother assemble a motley crew of henchmen who more than made up for their lack of intelligence with a blind devotion worthy of the most faithful four-legged friend. Then he drafted in Wolfgang Campion from Detroit, a fellow scientist and a vitriolic and somewhat maverick campaigner for state and government funding for his various cryogenic projects. With detailed instructions from Skellern, Campion performed a painstaking operation during which the Professor's brain was removed from his ruined body and installed into what amounted to a ventriloquist's dummy.

From there, it was a relatively easy matter of perfecting a simple but effective motor system which allowed basic movements, and only a slightly more difficult (for Wolfgang) matter of creating a synapse-controlled mechanical voice box to enable Skellern to speak—after a fashion—plus an Optical Image Translator for him to see and a sensitizer pad developed specially by Warner Bros. Records so that he could hear.

This had taken place in 1996.

The intervening eleven years had seen considerable refinements—not least in the creation of an entire "wardrobe" of artificial bodies of varying shapes and sizes—though such refinements needed money, as did Skellern's band of "helpers."

And so it was that the Dummy was born, masterminding complex burglaries and heists around the country . . . for Skellern's brain could be housed in bodies which were perfectly capable of getting into seemingly impossible places.

He was here today to make the final preparations for a new scheme devised by his occasional colleague, Leonard Komerdie.

The plan was deceptively simple.

The theft of municipal and currency bonds from The Rock, one of the Government's floating airborne fortified warehouses tethered by mile-high tentacle rods to the site of the old Alcatraz Prison. The roll call, such as it was, would be Komerdie, Skellern, and Chester "The Bomb" Urquart, whose impressive exoskeleton membrane permitted a veritable arsenal of explosives and missiles.

Skellern walked awkwardly and seemingly nervously past the poolside to the special high chair situated well away from the water. One of his henchmen—Komerdie recognized the swarthy pallor of Rudolph Skellern, the Dummy's ever-dependable sibling—moved quickly across and attempted to lift his struggling boss into the chair, but Skellern waved him away, his left arm connecting with Rudie's cheek and knocking the man's Fedora to the floor. The loud crack echoed over the water.

"I can do it myself, I can do it," the Dummy's squawking voice trilled, with the complete lack of emotion necessitated by the voice-box circuitry.

The Dummy's brother stepped back and replaced his hat, rubbing his cheek with the other hand.

Skellern negotiated himself onto the chair and swiveled around.

"So, where is Urquart?"

Komerdie responded without looking up from his paper. "He'll be along."

"He is late."

"We said nine, and it isn't nine yet," Komerdie said as he turned the page.

Skellern lifted his left arm and looked at the watch set into his wooden wrist. Komerdie heard the faint whine of gears meshing. "It is almost five before," the Dummy said.

"So he's not late."

"Mmmm."

Komerdie rested the paper on his lap and clasped his hands behind his head. "Why are you doing this, Max?"

"Doing what? What is it that I am doing?"

Even after several years of knowing Skellern, during which time he had engaged in many conversations, Komerdie could still not get used to the complete absence of inflections in the Dummy's speech patterns. It often tended to make communication difficult—the monotone failed to impart emphasis or excitement, displeasure or reflection. Everything was simply delivered on the one level, the vocal equivalent of an EKG flat line.

The Comedian allowed his trademark smile to broaden and waved his hands in the air. "Everything!"

"I do not understand."

"I mean, why did you want to get involved in the bonds heist? Hell—" He sat forward on his lounger. "—why do I want to get involved?"

"I still do not understand."

Komerdie folded the newspaper and dropped it onto the floor beside his lounger. "It's a simple enough question. Why are you involved? You don't need the money."

The Dummy's head turned slowly to face Komerdie, and the Comedian noticed that something needed a little loosening oil in Skellern's neck joints. "My research," he said. "The money is for my research."

Komerdie leaned forward. "And what research is that, Max? You haven't done any research in years."

The Dummy's gelatin eyes stared unblinking. "It is what I do," the Dummy said at last, and the head turned away with a squeak.

"Have you ever wondered . . . have you ever thought that maybe you'd like to do something *else?*"

"Such as what? Or perhaps you have in mind to sit me on your lap and have the two of us do a long season ventriloquism act at one of the Vegas gambling hotels, fronting for Connick or one of the other headliners."

The Comedian did not respond.

A tall, good-looking young man with heavily gelled hair stepped onto the roof with Smolt. Komerdie's assistant waved him forward, and the man nodded with a big smile. He jogged across looking at his watch.

"You are late, Bomb," Skellern droned.

"And a big warm hello to you, too, Max," Chester Urquart said with a broad grin. He nodded to Komerdie. "Comedian."

"Coffee, Chester?"

The Bomb nodded gratefully. "Cool, man. Count me in for the java." He gave a mock salute. "Out last night. Late night," he said with a roll of his eyes. "I didn't have time for no breakfast."

"I didn't have time for any breakfast," Skellern corrected without emphasis.

The young man clapped his hands and nodded to Komerdie. "Looks like we're all ready to chow down," he said.

Komerdie shielded his smile.

As if on cue, Smolt appeared with a tray of coffee and two plates, one containing an assortment of Danish and the other bagels, slit carefully in half. A small, covered dish of cream cheese completed the picture. Urquart's mouth watered.

As he poured coffee into the cups—just two, for obvious reasons—Komerdie said, "I'm afraid I have a little bad news."

Urquart lifted his cup and, having first covered it as thickly as was humanly possible with cream cheese, transferred an entire bagel half straight into his mouth. He grunted questioningly as he chewed.

"Our project will have to be put on hold for a while," Komerdie said, having decided that the best plan was simply to come out with it.

"And why might that be?" Even without inflections, Max Skellern's voice was dripping with annoyance and menace.

The Comedian sat back in his lounger and sipped at his coffee while Urquart ate another bagel. "It's a personal matter. I have to leave the country for a few days."

Urquart nodded and made a grimace with his mouth. *Shit happens*, the grimace said. Nothing more sinister than that. Komerdie couldn't help but feel a genuine affection for the young man.

However, Professor Skellern was not going to be so accepting.

"That simply is not good enough, Comedian," he said. This time when he moved his head to stare at Komerdie, the wooden man's neck squealed like nails running down a chalkboard.

"It's my mother," the Comedian said. Somewhere below them, on the Manhattan streets, a siren *wah wah*ed into existence and Dopplered away again. "She's very ill."

"Aw, gee, I'm sorry to hear that," Chester Urquart blurted in a spray of crumbs.

"Is she going to die?"

Urquart winced.

Komerdie refrained from commenting on Skellern's lack of tact and simply nodded. "I'm afraid so, yes."

"She is going to die," Skellern said. "She can do it with you or without you. Either way it will not matter. Our project does mat—"

"I want to see her," Komerdie interrupted. "And I'm going to see her." He drank the remains of his coffee and wiped his mouth on a napkin. Resting the mug on the glass-topped table, he said, "Our project *does* matter, of course, but time is not crucial.

"Next week or even next month would pose no more or, indeed, no less problem than tomorrow or the day after. But—" He turned his head to face the Dummy. "—if you would rather draft in somebody else to handle the arrangements and the organization, then I'll understand."

"Aw, hey, your mom comes first," Urquart said. He looked across at Skellern and affected a big smile. "We can wait, can't we, Max?"

The Dummy sat for a few seconds without saying anything. Then he shuffled forward and clumped his wooden feet onto the deck. "I will speak with you, Komerdie. When I have given this some more thought."

Urquart made to say something and then saw Komerdie's single shake of the head.

As Skellern walked stiltedly away, the other two men noticed that even the Dummy's knee joints were squeaking. They looked at each other and hid their smiles. Urquart pushed the bagels away from him on the tray and reached for a Danish. "Great coffee," he said, nodding when Komerdie pointed to the covered pot. He held out his mug gratefully. "And, boy . . . do I ever need it this morning."

(3)

"Ask you what provocation I have had? . . .
The strong antipathy of good to bad."
    —Alexander Pope (1688–1744)

Two days later, Leonard Komerdie was walking through the arrivals gate at London's Heathrow airport, flanked by Sidney Smolt, Archie McIlveen, and Janette Skyzcky. Smolt—who looked for all the world a dead ringer for Bud Costello—McIlveen, and Skyzcky all carried plastic pistols, each one ready packed with five polished wooden balls fashioned from the darkest mahogany.

Each of them carried shoulder bags, various magazines, and newspapers—including a paperback by Ray Bradbury, its title a line from Shakespeare, which Komerdie had tried to read on the airship, but he had to give it up because he couldn't stop thinking about his mom—and, in Smolt's case, the travel blanket and set of earphones which passengers were supposed to use during the flight but leave behind on arrival.

Leonard was sporting a ponytail and a goatee beard, an excessively garish shirt and jogging pants outfit, thick-soled sneakers, wraparound Raybans and a Walkman playing *College Standards* by The Lettermen. The strains of "Graduation Day" hovered around the Comedian's head like the smell of cologne. "You know," a dewy-eyed Komerdie confided to Janette Skyzcky as they waited in line at immigration, "these guys were every bit as good as The Four Freshmen—and not as jazzy. I prefer close harmony without the jazz."

He had made pretty much the same observation just hours earlier on the plane, while Skyzcky had been trying to watch the new George Clooney movie about a man falsely accused of rape ("He could jump on my bones any day," she told Komerdie when she saw the movie advertised in the handout) *and* at a volume several levels higher than was really necessary.

Eventually their turn came and the passports were stamped without any questions. But then, why would there be questions? Archie and Janette acted their parts to the hilt—the wealthy playboy and his consort, plus the inevitable backup in the form of Komerdie and Smolt.

"What now?" Archie McIlveen muttered *sotto voce* as they moved into the main terminal building past rows of people holding up cardboard signs bearing scribbled names.

Komerdie removed is earpieces. "Now we split up," he said.

"Split up? That doesn't seem like—"

Komerdie took hold of McIlveen's arm. "Look, I appreciate your concern . . ." He turned to look at Smolt and Janette Skyzcky. "All of you. But I really must be left alone on this trip." He reached into his pocket and produced a letter of reservation for the Piccadilly Hotel which he handed to Sidney Smolt. "This will be all you'll need. I'll see you when I get back."

Smolt opened the letter and studied its contents.

"When will that be?" Archie McIlveen's frown said exactly what he thought about the arrangement.

Komerdie shrugged. "When I've done what I have to do."

He nodded, almost curtly, hefted his single travel bag over his shoulder and walked away toward the rank of taxicabs outside the terminal building.

(4)

"General good is the plea of the scoundrel, hypocrite and flatterer."
—William Blake,
from "Jerusalem" (1815)

The cab eventually made it into London and began threading its way through the labyrinthine network of streets toward the King's Cross railway station.

The English capital was changing.

Pollution control had reduced the number of vehicles on the streets to buses and cabs, with occasional delivery vans and, very rarely, private cars bearing permit stickers. And many of the streets were now being fitted with bumps to restrict speed. It gave the whole scenario the air of slow-mo film, with every now and then a bus or a cab or even an occasional bike slowing and bucking, once, and twice, before moving on at a temporarily quickened pace.

"What part o' the States you from, then, mate?" the driver inquired over his shoulder as they came to a halt at what looked like being a difficult junction to get out of.

"New York."

"Ah, New *York!*" came the response, as though

the very words answered every question about—or corroborated every belief in—America and, indeed, Americans. The driver edged forward, waving at a young man with facial tattoos driving a blue Ford Econoline with the legend

GRAFFITI INK. SAY IT WITH WORDZ

emblazoned on its side panel.

"Never been," he added as they pulled out into a line of cabs heading for Marble Arch.

"No?" Komerdie couldn't think what else to say.

"Never been *any*where in the States, mate," the cabbie explained. "Never had no desire. It's your home that's the most important, that's what I always say. I don't mind traveling around England, mind, don't get me wrong. There's a lot of nice places in England. But England is where I'm most comfortable, you know what I mean?"

Without waiting for a response, the driver continued. " 'Course, you probably feel the same way when you come over 'ere, you know what I mean? You probably think to yourself, 'I can't wait to get back 'home to them skyscrapers and stuff.' It's what you've been brought up with, that's what important."

Komerdie stared out at the hordes of pedestrians and the gaudy store window displays as they crossed Oxford Circus. "I'm from England originally."

"Go on!" the driver said, locking eyes with Komerdie in his mirror. "When d'you leave, then? You ain't got no English accent, mate. Not one as I can spot anyway."

"I left when I was nineteen. I arrived in New York with a few pounds in my pocket and nowhere to stay."

"You done all right for yourself, though, yeah?"

Komerdie nodded. "Yes, I've done okay. I suppose."

" 'Course you 'ave. Where'd you live when you was over 'ere, then?"

"Ilkley. Yorkshire."

"Ah, *Yorkshire!*" the cabbie intoned. It was like a mantra. "Beautiful part of the world. We love it up in Yorkshire, me and my missus. Went there for our honeymoon, back in '84. Yorkshire Dales. Beautiful! God's country, so they say . . . and you can believe it when you see it."

Komerdie nodded.

"Why'd you leave, then?"

The Comedian stared at the cabbie's face in the driving mirror and, just for a few seconds, he could see his father's eyes staring back at him, asking him that same question all that time ago. Coming up with an answer now, three decades later, was just as difficult as it had been then.

He shrugged. "Why does anyone make a break for the unknown?" He watched the London streets drift by outside the window. "I guess to make something of my life."

"And 'ave you? Made something of your life, I mean . . . not just making money?"

Komerdie couldn't keep back the smile. "There are some that might say that, yes."

The driver nodded, considering that. Then he said, " 'Ave you been back much, since you went over, I mean?"

Komerdie turned to the side and kept his eyes focused on the storefronts. "No, I haven't been back at all."

"Blimey! You must be noticing a few changes, then."

"A few," Komerdie agreed with a chuckle.

"So why've you come back now, then?"

"To see my mother."

"Mmm." The driver's eyes met Komerdie's in the rearview mirror, studied his face. "So you left . . . when? Twenty-five years ago? Something like that?"

"Thirty-two."

The cabbie whistled. "You really *must* be noticing the changes."

Komerdie nodded.

"She sick? Your mum, I mean."

Komerdie nodded again and turned away from the piercing eyes in the mirror. "Dying."

"Sorry to hear that, mate."

"Yeah, well . . . it happens to us all."

"So they say," the cabbie said with a smile.

The car jerked to a halt and Komerdie lurched forward in his seat.

"Jesus Christ, they're worse than bloody kids."

Komerdie leaned forward to find out the cause of the abrupt stop. Ahead of them, a young woman dressed in bright purple leotards, a purple eye-mask, and yellow boots and gloves was forming out of the wall adjoining a branch of HSBC Bank. A line of people at the ATM alongside were busy either running in one direction or another, or throwing themselves facedown onto the sidewalk. Emerging from the bank entrance, flanked by two burly men wearing bulky earphones and carrying large sacks, a tall man dressed completely in white—even down to the white bowler hat, gloves, and what appeared to be a blind man's stick—hefted the cloth bag *he* was carrying over his shoulder, lifted his foot in the air and brought it down with what should have been a dull thud. Instead, the resulting noise cut through everything like a pneumatic drill.

The cabbie grasped his ears and thrust his head forward against the steering wheel. His mouth was moving, Komerdie saw, though he, too, was intent on holding his own head to stop the high-pitched whine reverberating through the cab.

And the street.

Store windows burst outward in cascades of broken glass, and the cabbie's windshield erupted into a mosaic of veinlike scratches.

Almost as soon as it had started, the sound faded away and, in its place, the sounds of the city were now enhanced by chaos. Sirens shrilly howled, car horns and alarms beeped and whined, and everywhere people's voices called out.

The cabbie turned around and pointed to the tall man in white who, followed closely by the two men, was running down the sidewalk to where a white sedan had pulled against he curb. "That's White Noise," the cabbie said.

"Who's he?"

The cabbie shrugged. "Just another crook, mate . . . with the usual get-rich-quick schemes." He rubbed his hand over his windshield. "Bastard's buggered my windscreen."

Komerdie watched the man in white slide into the car and bark instructions to the driver. Even as the door was closing, the car lifted effortlessly from the road and moved vertically up the side of the building before maneuvering off to the right and disappearing over the rooftops.

They looked back at the young woman. She seemed dazed and was placating some of the pedestrians.

"Who's she?"

"She, mate," the cabbie said, his smile inflecting his words, "*was* Malleable Maid." He was leaning forward as they pulled away, staring intently through the pattern of cracks. "But one of them comics companies in the States—don't recall their name: comics ain't one of my things—anyway, they 'ad a bit character in one of their magazines called Malleable Man and they told her she couldn't use that name. Not Malleable *Man*," he added over his shoulder. "Malleable *Maid*."

"So what's she called now?"

As they moved slowly toward Russell Square, with the cabbie peering through his shattered windshield, Komerdie saw a bold PP emblazoned on the girl's ample bosom in a yellow circle whose sides fluctuated in and out like an amoeba's.

"Well, her name was Patricia—Patricia Leary—so she changed her surname to 'Pending' and now she's—"

"Pat Pending."

"Bang on, mate," the cabbie said. "And she says she's going to sue anyone she hears about using her name on a legal document."

"That's going to play hell with intellectual property rights."

The driver frowned and then nodded. He knew diddly about IP. "Bloody people! They're all barmy, you ask me."

"The heroes or the crooks?"

"All of 'em. The heroes aren't much better than the crooks, you ask me. They want to get a proper bloody job 'stead of flying around." He sniffed as he rolled down his window and waved nonchalantly to a bus driver who allowed him to pull around a stationary delivery van. "They want to try driving a bloody cab through London, mate . . . that'd sort 'em out.

"Yeah, heroes and villains," the driver continued. "They're all the bloody same if you ask me. Not much to choose between any of 'em."

Komerdie smiled as they pulled out onto Kings Cross Road.

"You want dropping at the front, mate . . . or should I take you 'round the back?"

"At the front is fine."

They pulled up and Komerdie paid the driver—with a generous tip ("God bless you, mate")—and sauntered into the station, buying an *Evening Standard* from a toothless old man at a kiosk festooned with magazines whose covers featured women displaying their anatomy in a variety of poses which must have been extraordinarily uncomfortable.

As luck would have it, his train was at the platform and within minutes he was heading out of London for the North.

He read the *Standard* from front to back page, drinking in the quaintness of the news—such as discovering that the Bank of England financial committee had increased interest rates for the third month running; that the Chelsea football team was threatened with relegation to the second division; and that The Troglodyte and Road Rage had filed a harassment lawsuit against Fastman after the faster-than-light hero had raided their secret (or not-so-secret, Komerdie thought) hideaway. The article was accompanied by a smiling—"smirking" might have been a more appropriate word—Troglodyte and Road Rage, resplendent in their costumes, respectively a dirty brown hooded one-piece and a garish red, orange, and yellow tight-fitting outfit topped with what appeared to be a sunburst effect springing from the sides of the man's head. In naming the pair, the caption went on to state that Fastman was unable to attend the preliminary hearing as, in the words of his attorney, he was "unavoidably delayed putting a little light back into a darkening world."

Komerdie looked up as they pulled into Peterborough Station and let his eyes play across the faces of the people waiting on the platform in the drizzle. They were as gray as the day itself.

In his sleep, brought on by the soothing motion of the train, Komerdie and many of his contemporaries, plus several heroes, all of their uniforms a blaze of color and outrageous righteousness or righteous outrage, stood as though under judgment before a massed throng of miserable-looking people in a featureless field beneath a persistent rain. One of the watchers—Komerdie recognized the cab driver immediately . . . though, in his dream, he wondered how that could be, for he hadn't actually seen the man's face full on—stepped forward and announced to the throng: *Yeah, heroes and villains . . . they're all the bloody same if you ask me. Not much to choose between any of 'em.*

When he woke up, the train was in Leeds.

Komerdie took a cab to Ilkley and drank in the passing scenery. And the changes.

When they hit Headingley, just a couple of miles out of Leeds' bustling center, the traffic slowed for no apparent reason. Then, minutes later, a blond man wearing silver shorts, silver ankle boots, and a matching sleeveless top appeared over the tops of the cars in front. He was carrying a petroleum truck, its hood covered by a silver cape fastened somehow to the wheel arches. Smoke was coming out from beneath the cape in straggling wisps.

"Who's he?" Komerdie asked the driver.

"Silverman," came the response.

"Silverman?" Komerdie turned in his seat as the traffic started to move again, watching the flying man disappear over the trees and toward Leeds. "He's a hero, right?"

"Yeah, a hero."

Komerdie turned back and settled in his seat. "So what does he do? I mean, Silverman? He turn things silver or something?"

The driver shrugged. "I think it's his name—Daniel Silverman. As to what he does . . . he flies."

"He flies? And that's it?"

"And he's strong. Those two'll do for starters." He leaned on his horn and persuaded a Volvo convertible to make the left turn he had been signaling for several minutes. "I lose track."

"He from Earth?"

The driver nodded. "Far as I know. He was a fuel science student here at the university. The story goes that he was experimenting with some chemicals and they exploded over him." He shrugged and glanced at Komerdie in the rearview mirror. "Do I need to say more?"

Komerdie shook his head. "It's a familiar story."

The driver grunted his agreement.

And they passed the rest of the journey in silence.

(5)

"What is our task? To make Britain a fit country
for heroes to live in."
—David Lloyd George (British Prime Minister, 1916–22)
from a speech delivered at Wolverhampton, 1918

As the woman in the blue uniform wheeled the
chair toward him, down the delicately paved path of
gray stones speckled here and there with tiny shoots
like diamonds in the rough, Komerdie's attention
was drawn to the tiny figure watching him, and he
wondered where time truly went.

"She's a little better today, aren't you, Mary?" the
woman announced as she drew up to Komerdie,
seemingly at a sufficiently high volume to interrupt
conversations in the neighboring villages of Add-
ingham and Burley-in-Wharfedale. But it was all an
act. She had told Komerdie that his mother was un-
likely to see out the week. The Comedian had not
known what to say then, and he did not know what
to say now.

"Hello, Leonard," Mary Komerdie said, her voice
soft and gentle . . . the way he had always remembered it.

"I'll leave you two to natter while I put the kettle
on," the woman said. Then, to Komerdie's mother,
"Now don't go tiring yourself out, Mary."

As the woman walked back up the path to the
main hospice building, he marveled at her stoicism
and her bravery. This was a job he could never contemplate being able to do . . . chatting animatedly
and making people comfortable as they neared their
final moments of life. He wondered if she cried at

night, when, in the silent solitude of her room, she reflected on her charges.

"Hello, Mom."

"Mom!" Mary Komerdie chuckled and shook her head, dislodging a wisp of wiry gray hair onto her forehead.

Komerdie knelt beside the chair and rested a hand on his mother's clasped hands. "Why do you laugh?"

"You called me 'Mom'—it's very American, isn't it?"

"What, 'Mom'?"

She nodded. "You used to call me 'Mum.' "

He rubbed her hands. "How you doing?"

She looked up into his eyes, and smiled with them. Taking his hand in hers, she let her eyes close slowly. "Oh, it's so good to see you, son."

"And it's good to see you, too. I'm sorry I haven't—"

"You're here now, son, that's all that matters," she said without opening her eyes. "Now is everything."

She let go of his hand and it flopped onto her skirt-covered legs. He felt their thinness and quickly drank in her appearance. There wasn't much of it, save for the ankles and the neck and the face, where the steroids had puffed out the skin.

She opened her eyes and looked at him, her expression a mask of regret, as though she wanted to apologize . . . to say she was sorry for being old, sorry for being so close to death.

"There's so much to say and to talk about," she began, "but I don't think I have the energy, son. You look well, though. Are you?"

"Well?"

She nodded.

"I think I'm okay," he said. "I go for my checkups every year." He patted his stomach. "Putting on a little too much here . . ." He took hold of the skin at either side of his chin. ". . . and here. And my hair's going . . . He pulled back his hair at the front to show the expanse of forehead.

"It looks fine to me."

He shrugged. "Well, you can't stop time."

She nodded. "More's the pity."

He wanted to be able to tell her she looked well, too, but he couldn't bring himself to lie to her. In the same way, he couldn't bring himself to tell her the truth. He figured she knew how she looked, and it wasn't "well."

"There are some things I want—"

"No, I don't want you to talk, Mom," Komerdie said. "I want you to listen. I've got something to tell you."

She lifted a wattled arm and, with a frail and shuddering hand of skeletal but beautifully tapered fingers, she shielded her eyes from the sun.

"I'm going to make it short and sweet," Komerdie said as he stood up. He lifted one of the chairs from a nearby table of ornate, filigreed white metal and placed it alongside her. "I've—I've made mistakes," he began.

Mary Komerdie's eyes opened wide and she started to speak, but the Comedian shook his head.

"No, let me finish." He reached for her hand and held it gently. "I've been wrong. That's the bottom line. I've been wrong, and I'm going to change. I just wanted you to know that."

Now an expression of abject horror washed over his mother's face. She pulled her hand free. "No, Leonard. It's me who's been wrong. Been wrong all my life, so it's good to feel that, here at the end—"

"Oh, don't talk like—"

"Now, hush a minute, Leonard," she said sternly. "We both know I don't have long. So does Kathy."

"Kathy?"

"The woman who wheeled me down here. Everyone knows I don't have long—none of us in here have long—so I don't have time to mess about with foolish talk. So listen to me now.

"The garden needs both the sun and the rain," she said.

Komerdie frowned.

"Oh, I knew I wouldn't be able to explain myself," she said. She closed her eyes, lifted a hand to her face, and scratched her chin. "It's only the bad days that make the good days seem good." She opened her eyes and looked at her son. "You see, it's me who's been wrong. All these years."

Komerdie started to understand. It was the faintest breath of understanding, but it was there, hovering in the back of his mind, getting bigger and growing stronger.

"If there were no *bad* folks," the old woman said, reaching across to lay a hand on Komerdie's shoulder, "then there wouldn't be any need for *good* folks. You *see*," she said emphatically, "what you do is every bit as important as what the heroes of the world do. You provide a balance."

"But what I do is wrong."

She nodded. "Of course it's wrong . . . but it's necessary.

"Human nature being what it is, we'd get tired if everything was always right. If there was nothing to fight for . . . nothing to protect against."

"You mean I'm performing some kind of service."

"That's exactly what I mean. The world needs you every bit as much as it needs the heroes."

Komerdie smiled. "The way the garden needs both the sun and the rain."

The old woman nodded.

"You must promise me," she said, squeezing his shoulder. "You must promise me that you'll carry on. Hold your head high and continue what it is that you do . . . and," she paused to allow a broad smile to wash over her face, "that you do so well, if what I hear about the infamous Comedian of New York City is correct." She removed her hand and squinted at him. "Do you promise?"

Komerdie frowned.

"Can't you just promise me this one thing?"

He thought for a few moments and then he nodded.

"Say it, then."

"I promise . . . *Mum.*"

"Good boy," she said.

The nurse *yoo-hoo*ed as she came out of the building carrying a tray.

"Tea's here," said Mary Komerdie.

"Great." He reached over and squeezed his mother's hand, not surprised in the least to feel it squeeze back.

(6)

"We can be heroes . . .
Just for one day . . ."
—*Heroes*, words and music by David Bowie
and Brian Eno

Mary Komerdie died in her sleep three days later. A nurse named Yvonne told Komerdie that his mother had been smiling when the nurse had gone into Mary Komerdie's room to wake her for break-fast. "She looked so happy," she told Komerdie. "And I'm sure it was all because you'd come to see her."

"Yeah, but I came a little late."

The woman shrugged. "But you came. Believe me, not many do."

In the two days that the Comedian had stayed at the small guest house in Ilkley, leaving for the hospice before nine o'clock and returning a little before seven p.m., he spent the time wisely, feverishly cramming a thirty-year relationship into almost as many hours.

The day on which he had been informed that his mother had "passed on," they had planned to go over by the small lake in the hospice grounds and have a picnic. But such was not to be.

There had not been much in the way of affairs to put in order.

Mary Komerdie hadn't had any surviving relatives and all her friends were in the hospice, waiting for their own time to be called. As a result, the funeral was a lonely affair attended only by Komerdie, Kathy the nurse, and a sprightly, red-cheeked woman with a voice like a foghorn—and who Komerdie later discovered was suffering from bowel cancer—plus the local vicar, who spoke of the dear departed with practiced regret.

And then, to the lilting refrain of Erik Satie's piano, the simple and surprisingly small coffin had slid through the doors and disappeared into the waiting flames beyond.

Komerdie had called Sidney Smolt at the Piccadilly and told him he was going to see them back in New York. He was going to hire a car, he told the faithful

Smolt, and drive around his old haunts . . . going to do some thinking.

That thinking continued for four full days and ended only when Komerdie was halfway across the Atlantic, equidistant from his past and his future.

The Comedian had arrived at Laguardia a new man . . . or at least, the old one reaffirmed.

And here he was, on the roof of the Komerdie building, greeting Maximillian Skellern and Chester Urquart who were already waiting for him.

Skellern was wearing one of his android bodies, a tall, hairless olive-skinned man with piercing gelatin eyes that watched Komerdie walk around the pool and flop into the lounge chair beside the table. Urquart was reading a comic book, oblivious to anything or anyone around him.

"Your mother died," Skellern intoned. "My condolences."

Komerdie nodded.

"Yeah," Urquart agreed, shaking his head as he dropped the comic book between his feet. "You okay?"

"I'm fine, thanks, Chester." He turned to the Dummy and nodded. "And thanks for your kind words, Max."

Before anyone could say anything more, Komerdie said, "So, we need to get things organized."

He produced a plastic wallet containing plans to The Rock.

"We gonna do it?"

"Of course we are, Max," Komerdie announced with a broad smile. "Why ever should we not?"

The Bomb's smile faded a little. "You're talking . . . funny," he said, pointing at Komerdie. He turned to Skellern. "He talking funny to you?"

"He is talking good sense," the android said, and, though Komerdie would have put it down to his imagination, the synthetic voice actually seemed to have some feeling in it.

Muted voices from the street below caused Komerdie to turn around, just in time to see a green-clad figure descend onto the roof, its cloak billowing out behind it.

Komerdie dropped the papers onto the table and thrust his hands into his trouser pockets. "Captain Chlorophyll," he said, effecting a small bow. "To what do my friends and I owe the pleasure of seeing you?"

"Cut the crap, Comedian," the hero rasped. "You've been away."

"I've been away."

"And now you're back."

Komerdie clapped his hands once. "Bravo, my dear Kapitan. Your powers of observation are quite impressive."

Chlorophyll jumped down from the small wall as Smolt and two others walked onto the roof. Komerdie waved them back.

"Why does that fact give me cause for concern?"

Komerdie shrugged and held out his hands. "Which particular fact: that I've been away or that I'm back?"

"You're underdressed, Bomb," the Captain said to Urquart. "And you're as flamboyant as ever, Dummy. A new outfit?"

Skellern nodded. "Just something I threw on."

Chlorophyll turned to Komerdie. "I know something's going on, Comedian, but, as you know, the Meredith Treaty prevents my using my powers to listen in on conversations or read any materials on

your property—" He turned to Skellern and Urquart.
"—or those of your accomplices."

"Friends," Komerdie corrected. "They're my friends."
Chlorophyll grunted.

"Why not get a search warrant?"

"I have no grounds save for a hunch . . . a big
hunch."

"It is not noticeable from this angle," Skellern said.

"Most amusing, Dummy." Captain Chlorophyll
stepped closer to Komerdie and the comedian took
a step forward. "Just be aware that I'll be watching
you," he said. "All of you."

"I'm sure we'll all sleep easier knowing that,"
Komerdie said dryly. "Now, if you'll excuse us, we
have business matters to discuss. Unless, of course,
you'd like to stay for coffee—my man Smolt makes
a wonderful blend of Samoan cappuccino."

The Captain turned around and thrust his hands
into the air, but before he could go, Komerdie called
after him. Chlorophyll turned around, frowning
suspiciously.

Komerdie walked up to him and extended his
hand.

"What's that?"

"My hand," Komerdie said. "What does it look
like?"

"What is it for?"

Komerdie shrugged and kept the hand extended.
"Let's call it a mark of respect."

"Respect? Since when did you respect anyone or
anything, Comedian?"

"I respect that you're doing your job," Komerdie
said softly. "I ask only that you respect that I'm
doing mine. Yin and yang," he said. "The balance
is maintained."

"The balance will only be maintained when you and your cohorts—"

"*Friends!*"

"—when you and they are behind bars. For good." Komerdie shook his head. "There'll always be others," he said.

"That's true, more's the pity."

"Ah, but have you ever stopped to think what you and *your* friends would do without us?"

Captain Chlorophyll looked away from Komerdie's eyes and down at the outstretched hand. Then he looked up. "Take care, Comedian," he said.

Komerdie dropped his hand. "And you, Captain."

Chlorophyll hopped onto the wall and leaped forward, dropping slightly toward the waiting street before the currents lifted him, and he twisted to the left and headed across the park.

"Everything okay, boss?" Smolt's voice asked from behind Komerdie.

"Everything is just fine, Sidney," Komerdie said without turning around. "Just fine." He watched the departing figure grow smaller and smaller, until it disappeared completely far out above the trees of Central Park.

For Kathleen Crowther (1921–2000), James Lovegrove, Malcolm Poynter, and Paul Stephenson . . . heroes all. See you in the funny pages, mum!

Science Fiction Anthologies

☐ **STAR COLONIES**
Martin H. Greenberg and John Helfers, editors 0-88677-894-1—$6.99
Let Jack Williamson, Alan Dean Foster, Mike Resnick, Pamela Sargent, Dana Stabenow and others take you to distant worlds where humans seek to make new homes—or to exotic places where aliens races thrive.

☐ **ALIEN ABDUCTIONS**
Martin H. Greenberg and Larry Segriff, editors 0-88677-856-5—$6.99
Prepare yourself for a close encounter with these eleven original tales of alien experiences and their aftermath. By authors such as Alan Dean Foster, Michelle West, Ed Gorman, Peter Crowther, and Lawrence Watt-Evans.

☐ **MOON SHOTS**
Peter Crowther, editor 0-88677-848-4—$6.99
July 20, 1969: a date that will live in history! In honor of the destiny-altering mission to the Moon, these original tales were created by some of today's finest SF writers, such as Ben Bova, Gene Wolfe, Brian Aldiss, Alan Dean Foster, and Stephen Baxter.

☐ **MY FAVORITE SCIENCE FICTION STORY**
Martin H. Greenberg, editor 0-88677-830-1—$6.99
Here is a truly unique volume, comprised of seminal science fiction stories specifically chosen by some of today's top science fiction names. With stories by Sturgeon, Kornbluth, Waldrop, and Zelazny, among others, chosen by such modern-day masters as Clarke, McCaffrey, Turtledove, Bujold, and Willis.

Prices slightly higher in Canada   **DAW: 104**

Payable in U.S. funds only. No cash/COD accepted. Postage & handling: U.S./CAN. $2.75 for one book, $1.00 for each additional, not to exceed $6.75; Int'l $5.00 for one book, $1.00 each additional. We accept Visa, Amex, MC ($10.00 min.), checks ($15.00 fee for returned checks) and money orders. Call 800-788-6262 or 201-933-9292, fax 201-896-8569; refer to ad #104.

Penguin Putnam Inc.	**Bill my:** ☐Visa ☐MasterCard ☐Amex_____(expires)
P.O. Box 12289, Dept. B	Card#_____
Newark, NJ 07101-5289	

Please allow 4-6 weeks for delivery.   Signature_____
Foreign and Canadian delivery 6-8 weeks.

Bill to:

Name_____

Address_____City_____

State/ZIP_____

Daytime Phone #_____

Ship to:

Name_____	Book Total	$_____
Address_____	Applicable Sales Tax	$_____
City_____	Postage & Handling	$_____
State/Zip_____	Total Amount Due	$_____

This offer subject to change without notice.

Don't Miss These Exciting DAW Anthologies

TANYA HUFF
VALOR'S CHOICE

"Readers who enjoy military SF will love Tanya Huff's VALOR'S CHOICE. Howlingly funny and very suspenseful. I enjoyed every word."
—*scifi.com*

Staff Sergeant Torin Kerr was a battle-hardened professional. So when she and those in her platoon who'd survived the last deadly encounter with the Others were yanked from a well-deserved leave for what was supposed to be "easy" duty as the honor guard for a diplomatic mission to the non-Confederation world of the Silsviss, she was ready for anything. Sure, there'd been rumors of the Others being spotted in this sector of space. But there were always rumors. Everything seemed to be going perfectly. Maybe too perfectly. . . .

0-88677-896-4 $6.99

Prices slightly higher in Canada   **DAW: 149**

Eluki bes Shahar

THE HELLFLOWER SERIES

☐ **HELLFLOWER (Book 1)** UE2475—$3.99

Butterfly St. Cyr had a well-deserved reputation as an honest and dependable smuggler. But when she and her partner, a highly illegal artificial intelligence, rescued Tiggy, the son and heir to one of the most powerful of the hellflower mercenary leaders, it looked like they'd finally taken on more than they could handle. For his father's enemies had sworn to see that Tiggy and Butterfly never reached his home planet alive. . . .

☐ **DARKTRADERS (Book 2)** UE2507—$4.50

With her former partner Paladin—the death-to-possess Old Federation artificial intelligence—gone off on a private mission, Butterfly didn't have anybody to back her up when Tiggy's enemies decided to give the word "ambush" a whole new and all-too-final meaning.

☐ **ARCHANGEL BLUES (Book 3)** UE2543—$4.50

Darktrader Butterfly St. Cyr and her partner Tiggy seek to complete the mission they started in DARKTRADERS, to find and destroy the real Archangel, Governor-General of the Empire, the being who is determined to wield A.I. powers to become the master of the entire universe.

KATE ELLIOTT

CROWN OF STARS

"An entirely captivating affair"—*Publishers Weekly*

In a world where bloody conflicts rage and sorcery holds sway both human and other-than-human forces vie for supremacy. In this land, Alain, a young man seeking the destiny promised him by the Lady of Battles, and Liath, a young woman gifted with a power that can alter history, are swept up in a world-shaking conflict for the survival of humanity.

☐ **KING'S DRAGON**　　　　　　0-88677-771-2—$6.99
☐ **PRINCE OF DOGS**　　　　　　0-88677-816-6—$6.99
☐ **THE BURNING STONE**　　　　0-88677-815-8—$6.99
☐ **CHILD OF FLAME**　　　　　　0-88677-892-1—$24.95